Through THE NIGHT

Lynette E. Theisen

THE P PRESS

Through the Night

Manufactured in the United States of America.

For information, please contact:

The P3 Press
16200 North Dallas Parkway, Suite 170
Dallas, Texas 75248

www.thep3press.com

972-248-9500

A New Era in Publishing™

ISBN-13: 978-1-933651-78-1
ISBN-10: 1-933651-78-4
LCCN: 2010902148

Author contact information:
www.lynettetheisen.com

For the purpose of poetic license, within this fiction book are various situations, including relationships between angels and humans, which are not interpreted from the Word of God, but are included for the sake of the storyline.

This book is dedicated to my beloved niece, Shanee Norrid
who was tragically taken from us on October 14, 2008.
You will forever be in our hearts.
RIP Pookie

I also want to dedicate this book to my
beautiful sister, Velora Norrid.
Your strength to continue living life to the fullest inspires me.
Your sweet love that you are so willing to give to
others is a blessing to all who cross your path.
I look at you, and want to be better.
I love you, sis!

He answered . . .

"The one who sowed the good seed is the Son of Man. The field
is the world, and the good seed stands for
the sons of the kingdom.

The weeds are the sons of the evil kingdom. The weeds are the
sons of the evil one and the enemy who sows them is the devil.

The harvest is the end of the age, and the harvesters are angels.

As the weeds are pulled up and burned in the fire, so it will be at
the end of the age.

The Son of Man will send out his angels, and they will weed out
of his kingdom everything that causes sin and all who do evil.

They will throw them in the fiery furnace, where there will be
weeping and gnashing of teeth.

Then the righteous will shine like the sun in the kingdom of their
Father. He who has ears, let him hear."

MATTHEW 13:37-43 NIV

ACKNOWLEDGMENTS

I first want to give thanks to my Lord and Savior, Jesus Christ. Without His love, mercy, and guidance, I would not be the person I am today. Thank you, Lord, for showing me my purpose and giving me this exciting journey to embark on.

I want to give thanks to my wonderful husband and great supporter of this endeavor. Thank you for your sacrifices and unwavering support. I love you, Steve!

To my four beautiful children: Bryley, Kylan, Alex, and Andi, who had to spend several nights "fending for themselves" or rummaging through laundry piled up in the hallway so that I could work on the book. Each one of you is such a blessing to me, and I love you with all of my heart.

To my parents, Elias Briones and Casey Rose, thank you for your constant love and believing in me. Dad, you really showed so much excitement and enthusiasm each step of the way! On days I was less confident, I knew I could count on you to lift me up. Mom, thanks for being there when I need you.

I want to give a special thanks to my Momma T, aka Ann Tyler. You helped me in so many different ways that I could never begin to fully thank you enough. You've loved me like your own daughter, and I will eternally be grateful for that. May the Lord continue to richly bless you with love, family, and friends.

This book could not have been possible without so many different people who helped along the way. It was surely a long, tedious process, but one worth working for.

To Cheryl Bowers, who took the chance of me thinking she was some "crazy woman" calling me on the phone to deliver the message God put on her heart. That message opened the door for me to walk through and begin my journey. By the way, I never thought you were crazy!

To everyone who was my "guinea pig" and read the original manuscripts, thank you for giving your honest feedback!

To my project manager at The P3 Press, Cynthia Stillar: thank you for seeing something in this book and helping to make it a reality.

The Lord has truly blessed me with so many amazing friends who have constantly encouraged me along the way. You know who you are, and each of you are so special and have been such a great source of strength for me. Thank you for all you do. Your friendship means the world to me.

ONE

The Dream

"We are ready to begin our next mission. You have been summoned for this significant assignment."

"I am at your service, master."

"Your task will far surpass being a mere temptation to the weak this time."

"I am up for the challenge, master."

"There is a family who is a pillar in this community. They are constantly helping others and spreading the gospel. Their faith appears untouchable. Fortunately for us, they have a young daughter. You must find her, for she holds the key to our mission. Strip away her innocence and break her unwavering righteousness! Once she has fallen, the rest will be putty in our hands. Now go quickly; time is precious."

It was the morning of my sixteenth birthday, and my mom was up early making my favorite breakfast. I could tell by the delicious smell, which played the part of an alarm clock and brought an end to my dream. I lingered in my bed a while longer, trying to capture the essence of this very unusual dream. Although to some, it wouldn't have seemed unusual at all.

I dreamt of driving around in a shiny, new red car with an incredibly gorgeous boy sitting next to me. He had amazing green eyes, jet-black hair, and spoke with a foreign accent. I remember feeling nervous around him and a bit flustered when I looked over at his perfect face, and he smiled at me.

I read once that dreams are our hidden desires or can carry certain meanings. I understood why I would dream of a new car; any normal sixteen-year-old who gets her driver's license would wish for such a thing. But what seemed odd was the good-looking foreigner on the passenger side. Don't get me wrong; I've noticed good-looking guys before, but this part of the dream intrigued me. Up until now, other than thinking some boys were cute, I never found myself overly attracted or excited about one. I had to wonder if dreams did signify a hidden desire, could it mean that now, with my "coming of age," my interest in them would change? Honestly, though, boys just always seemed like such a distraction to the girls who flirted with them. I've never really had time for any sort of dating relationship with school, church, dance classes, family, and time with my best friend Jamie.

On the other hand, maybe this dream signified that boys might finally find *me* attractive for a change. I've always been a simple kind of girl—like vanilla, I suppose—sweet, yet plain. My dad happens to think I'm the most beautiful honey-brown brunette he's ever seen, but then again, parents are supposed to think that.

Okay, Renee, enough of the analyzing. Better get out of bed before Mom has a conniption.

As I walked to my closet, an impulse to spice myself up a little more came over me. After all, it was a special day, and maybe for once I *wanted* to be noticed. Maybe it was time to expand this simple girl's uncomplicated interests. I mean, I am starting to become a grown-up now, so wouldn't I naturally begin to change?

As I browsed through my closet, realizing I had a turtleneck in every color imaginable, I knew trying to look more stylish was going to take some work. Though my options were limited, I did have a stash of clothes at the back of the closet that I never wore because they were more revealing than I was comfortable with. My mother had instilled in me at a very young age that clothes serve one purpose: to cover a person up. Every time she saw someone showing too much skin, she would remind me that, "You don't have to show everything that the good Lord gave you. It's best to leave *something* to the imagination!"

I had accumulated a few things from when Jamie and I would go to the mall and she would talk me into buying something that I really didn't want. "But you look so cute!" she would convince me. I added to the stash just yesterday a jean miniskirt with a sequin pattern at the bottom, an early birthday present from Jamie. She knew I never wore minis because of my "curse," long, lanky legs I inherited from my dad. Every mini I ever tried on seemed even shorter on me, but I knew this was her way of trying to make me a little more chic.

"Okay, found the bottom, now what to wear with it?"

There were several tops in my "TMS stash," short for *too much skin*, that I contemplated. Two of them were for summer, so they were an easy no. I decided on a vintage-style wrap sweater that had a cute satin ribbon that went around the waist. Jamie had given her approval on it once before, saying it brought out my blue eyes. My mother had brought it home from a resale shop in Pueblo, thinking it looked nice. I could tell it had to be very expensive at some point, with its extremely soft texture and dry clean only tag, but she only paid ten bucks for it and was proud of the bargain she found. It landed in the stash because the v-neck showed more cleavage than my comfort level allowed.

I paired them up and thought it was a good match, so I pulled out some thick leggings from my drawer and grabbed my brown leather boots to pull it all together. *"Yes . . . I like it! Mission accomplished."*

"Renee, come and eat, sweetie!" my mother yelled from the bottom of the stairs.

"I'll be right down, Mom."

I turned on some tunes and eagerly got dressed. Instantly feeling

3

a little more feisty, I began prancing around the room doing the whole model walk thing, pretending to pose for the paparazzi. I even blew a few kisses in the air to an imaginary crowd, all while laughing and having a good time.

When I finally stopped and peered into the full-length mirror to get a better look at myself, a wretched thought of narcissism crept in and gave me some doubts about my wardrobe choice. Seriously . . . just yesterday, I was fifteen years old. How would one day make that much of a difference?

Figuring my parents were anxiously waiting on me downstairs to wish me a happy birthday, I removed any doubt about my flashy look from my head and decided to go for the new me.

I quickly brushed my teeth, pulled back my hair in a brown headband, and ran downstairs. My mouth was already watering before I even made it to the last step.

"Happy birthday, sweetheart! I can't believe it. My baby is really growing up," my mother said as she pulled out my chair and gave me a kiss on the cheek. She's always been very affectionate. Her whole side of the family is, really. My dad, on the other hand, is more reserved, so I guess they balance each other out.

"You're not gonna start crying, are you, Mom?" I sighed. With every passing birthday, she would always get so emotional.

I saw a tear disappear into her right eye. "No, dear, I'll wait until you're gone before having my emotional fit! Now, eat your German pancakes before they get cold."

"Where's Dad? He's usually here before I am, reading his daily dose of *The New York Times*," I said as I took my first bite of the of the scrumptious blend of egg-battered pancakes dripping with butter, lemon juice, and a dash of powdered sugar, which only complemented the pure maple syrup poured on top.

With a hint of mystery in her voice, she replied, "Oh . . . he had to go to the office early today. He has a potential new client who wants to meet with him first thing this morning." Daddy was one of three lawyers in town. I personally thought he was a genius, graduating from Harvard in the top ten percent of his class and all. He never let it go to his head, though. He would help anyone, whether they had one dollar in the bank or a million.

"Do you want some OJ or milk to go with your breakfast?"

"Um . . . I'll take the OJ."

I watched her pour some juice in a small glass with a big smile on her face. Something has her keyed up. She's never this happy to wait on me hand-and-foot.

My mother is very smart, too, only in a different way. She's smart with people and has a gift of making others feel good. I love how she's always the first to volunteer at church or school functions, and that she's an amazing cook. As soon as she hears someone is sick, she's at his or her front door with a pot of hot, steamin' stew. For as long as I can remember, she has said, "God blesses everyone with one talent or another; it's up to us to bless others with it and use it for His will and glory." I'm still trying to figure out what mine is.

"Hurry up, sweetie, or you'll be late to school. How is your science project coming along?"

"I'm almost finished. I just have to add the finishing touches, and I'll get the extra ten points for turning it in early."

People have told my mom since I was little that I had an old soul. I remember overhearing Mrs. Livingood, our neighbor up the road, telling her in church one day, "That Renee . . . she is so mature and responsible." I was only six. I remember wishing someone would just say for once, "That Renee . . . she's such a pretty little girl." Maybe my early maturity was an only child syndrome; who knows?

"Don't you think it's a little cold to be wearing a miniskirt?" she questioned. I'm sure she was really more shocked with my choice of wardrobe than concerned about my getting cold.

"I thought I'd go a little spunkier today. Just the mood I'm in I guess," I said, trying to play it off like it was no big deal. Even so, I could tell she thought it was a bit much, or rather not enough, for school. She bit her tongue, though, on behalf of this day.

"What time do we need to pick up Jamie for dinner?" she asked.

"Around six o'clock. She has basketball practice until five, but she wants to go home and take a shower before going out."

Jamie was a very athletic girl and quite the opposite of me. We met in the third grade when a group of girls were making fun of me for wearing glasses. "Look at the four-eyed nerd," shouted Beth Middleton while the other girls just laughed . . . all but Jamie Baldwin.

She said, "Leave her alone! What did Renee ever do to you? She's one of the nicest girls I know, and I'd much rather hang around someone who's smart and wears glasses than someone who has to poke fun at others to make themselves feel better!"

I couldn't believe how tough she was. Beth was the most popular girl in our grade; and everybody wanted to be her friend—everyone but me, of course. I was everybody's friend and no one's at the same time.

"Do you like chocolate pudding?" Jamie asked as we began walking away from the scene. I thought it was an odd question, but this girl just stood up to Beth Middleton for me, so who was I to judge?

"Yeah . . . I guess."

"Good! Because it's my favorite snack, and if we're gonna be friends, we gotta know everything there is to know about each other." I looked at her a bit cautiously because I had really never had a best friend before, so I wasn't sure how this worked.

"That was awfully brave of you back there. Aren't you worried that she may start picking on you or even worse, start a fight or something?" I gasped.

"Nah! It's in my blood, you know," she replied.

"What's in your blood?" I questioned, rather confused.

"Bravery is, silly. I have a long line of brave people in my family.

Did you know that Baldwin means 'brave friend' in German? That's where my great-grandfather is from. You should hear the stories told about him!"

We have been like two peas in a pod ever since then. I now wear contacts.

"Renee, grab your things and let's go before you're late for school."

She was unusually anxious, and I couldn't help but feel annoyed by it. I've never been late to school, a habit she got me into since pre-K, and the roads had been cleared up from the snowstorm yesterday. So what was the rush?

"Okay, Mom. Let me just brush my teeth again so I can get all of the food stuck in my retainer out."

"I'll meet you outside, then. I'll be warming up the car."

I quickly ran back upstairs to my bathroom and did a quick wash and rinse. I was about to turn off the light and go when I caught a glimpse of myself in the mirror.

"This just won't do."

I rummaged through my drawers and took out the mascara, which I only wore on very special occasions. "You don't need that junk," my mom would say. "You were blessed with thick, long lashes. Don't go and ruin them." Her voice resonated in my head as if she were standing right behind me. And for the most part she was right, but the blackness of the "junk" made them really stand out. I carefully applied the mascara to each lash as today just so happened to qualify as special.

I quickly dabbed some pink blush on my pale skin to liven it up some before grabbing my mauve lip gloss to stick in my purse. I decided to just put it on after I got to school so my mom wouldn't go into complete shock at this new awareness I had of myself.

"Much better," I said before turning off the light. I ran back downstairs, grabbed my coat, scarf, and gloves, then out the front door, where I was bombarded with shouts of "Surprise!"

Shut up . . . *shut up*! Is that *really* Mom and Dad standing in front of a new red car with a giant white bow? Okay, so it was a 2007 Ford Explorer, but I didn't care; it still looked good to me! My mouth was stuck in the open-wide position for so long that my tongue began to get frostbite from the cold, wintry day. I could see the excitement in both of my parents' eyes. My dad, being the kindhearted gentleman that he is, quickly opened the driver's door and said, "My lady!" He bowed as if I were a princess. My mom couldn't hold back the tears any more, and they were now flowing like the Colorado River.

I was partially jumping, partially skipping, and running to the car all at the same time, saying, "Oh my gosh. I can't believe this! This is so great. Oh my gosh, oh my gosh! I can't believe it!" I couldn't help but repeat myself as a result of this unexpected surprise. I leaped into the driver's seat and began playing with every button, knob, and gadget before grabbing the steering wheel to turn it back and forth, just like I used to when I was a kid and would pretend to be driving down the road.

I sat still for a minute to take everything in, to engrave this great moment permanently in my head. I glanced over to the passenger seat to see if this was really real, or if I was still having my incredible dream. In the handsome boy's place was . . . was . . . my mom.

"Buckle up for safety," she quickly said.

Okay, so the shiny, new red car part of the dream came true, and that was definitely good enough for me. Besides, what would I have in common with an overly good-looking foreigner who I could barely understand anyway?

"What are you waiting for? Put her in gear, and let's get you to school," my mom said.

"Uh . . . Mom? Are you planning to stay in the car all day while I'm in class?"

"No, silly. Your dad is going to follow behind us, and then he'll bring me back home. We just want to make sure you get to school safely since this is a new vehicle you're not used to."

This was so typical of them. They have been overly protective since the day I almost wasn't born. I am frequently reminded that I am their miracle child, and my soul had to fight to come into this world. They had tried for eight years to have a baby. There was one pregnancy before me, a baby boy, but my mother miscarried in her second trimester. She said after she lost the baby, she prayed every night that God would bless her just one more time. If she could just get a second chance, she would promise to make sure His "gift" would lead a godly life and would do His good works here on earth.

A little over a year later, her prayers were answered. My mom did everything by the book. She ate all the right foods, she never took any hot baths or showers, she stopped polishing her nails and getting her hair highlighted, took her vitamins daily, and she prayed every single night for God's angels to keep me safe. I wasn't due until April 4th, but my mother's body began to reject me, just as it had done to my unborn sibling. She went into labor on February 17th and began bleeding profusely while trying to push me out. I wasn't cooperating, though, because my umbilical cord had wrapped around my neck. Dr. Lazaro gave instructions to all of the medical staff for an emergency C-section. Thirty minutes later, the announcement was made.

"It's a girl."

The nurses quickly took me to the other side of the room so they could thoroughly check me over and know exactly what they were dealing with. I only weighed 3.9 pounds, but to everyone's surprise and relief, I was miraculously healthy. I was a little blue at first from the cord choking me, but the odd color quickly went away after I took my first solo breath and began to scream at the top of my lungs. The doctors and nurses couldn't believe it. My mom said I only screamed and cried for about a minute or so and then quieted down as if I were being comforted by someone. She has always told me that God must have sent a very special angel to watch over me.

And here I am, sixteen years later, on my way to Custer County

High in my new Explorer with my mom in the passenger seat, having her little emotional breakdown because her baby is growing up. And I'm okay with that.

"Thanks, Mom! I love you so much."

She looked at me with her hand to her chest and whispered, "I love you too, sweetheart."

I was at my locker getting organized for the day. School would be in session in fifteen minutes, and I had a paper due for honors English that I needed to go over one last time. I tried to concentrate on it, but I was still pumped from this morning's surprise. I was anxious for Jamie to get here so I could tell her all about it, knowing she would be equally as excited. She usually didn't show up until just before the bell rang.

I looked at my watch, and there was still time to kill. *I know. I'll go wait out on the front steps for her,* I thought, finding myself extremely eager. Jamie kept a magnetic mirror on her locker, which was right next to mine, so I dabbed my lip gloss on, then headed outside.

As I was waiting, freezing half to death, wishing for once she would just get here early, the wind suddenly picked up. It shook all the snow off the seemingly lifeless trees, sprinkling a million flakes onto the ground like powdered sugar. It was quite beautiful, actually, reminding me of the snow globe Grandma J gave me for Christmas when I was three. My mother said it kept me entertained for hours; I would shake it up over and over then watch the snow gently settle onto the tiny village while it played "O Holy Night."

I remember there was a beautiful angel watching over the village, somehow suspended in the air, and engraved on the bottom an inscription read, *There is no fear in love.* It became a little tradition for me every Christmas to take it off the shelf it sat upon, wind up the music, and shake it over and over. When I was older, Grams told me that she had that snow globe since she was sixteen. Someone very special gave it to her, and that's why she wanted to pass it down to me. When I accidentally dropped it on the tiled floor two years ago, it shattered all over the place. I cried for hours.

The whistling wind grabbed ahold of my red scarf, which wasn't properly wrapped around my neck, taking me out of my reminiscence. It swiftly tumbled toward the parking lot, but I wasn't about to go chasing after it; that's for sure. That's when all of the commotion started.

What's going on? I thought as I saw everyone looking over to the south side of the parking lot. There was an unfamiliar vehicle pulling up into the student parking lot, one that apparently seemed to impress every single guy in school who hadn't gone inside yet. It was a black BMW "crotch rocket" . . . whatever that means. The only reason I knew that much was because I heard Brandon Grinn say, "Hey guys, check out that dude on the crotch rocket!" As he studied the bike closer, he was even more impressed. "Dude, I've never seen the BMW K1300 in person before. He must be crazy taking that beauty out in this freezing weather."

Yup, *crazy* . . . that was my sentiment exactly. But who was I to judge? I was more excited to see Jamie pull up right behind him. She quickly told her mom bye and ran up to see me with a "what are you doing outside" look on her face. I was about to explode with excitement and blurt out the good news when the commotion started all over again, this time by the female species.

Jamie's attention quickly shifted from me to the strikingly handsome "motorcycle dude" who just took off his black, shiny helmet. It was like he was in some shampoo commercial or something. He shook his head back and forth to get his dark brown hair out of his eyes, and it miraculously fell back into place. He then took off his mysterious, dark glasses and looked around, as if he were looking for someone he knew. His long muscular legs lifted off the black and charcoal gray cycle. He pulled his right leg all the way over so smoothly, almost in slow motion. With helmet tucked neatly under his arm, he began to walk our way before suddenly stopping a few steps from his bike to pick up my scarf. I gasped for a moment, but realized he would have no idea that it belonged to me. *Darn . . . I really liked that scarf, too.*

As he continued to saunter our way, I couldn't help but notice his sultry green eyes, which were complemented by his dark skin tone and chiseled cheekbones. He walked with such grace, a coolness that was far beyond Custer County High. His black leather jacket was unzipped, showing his plain white t-shirt. He didn't need anything fancy to make a better impression among 403 high school students that were in complete awe of his very presence. Note: there are 404 students at CCHS. I was more annoyed than impressed at this inhuman, godlike creature that took the attention away of my best friend just as I was about to tell her the most exciting thing that has happened to me in my sixteen years of living.

"Uh, hello! Earth to Jamie. Come in, Jamie!" I uttered while snapping my fingers in front of her eyes to help her out of her stupor.

"Oh, sorry Ren. Hey . . . cool outfit!" she said when she recognized the skirt she gave me. "So, what's up?" She continued halfheartedly, as she was trying to take her concentration off of model boy over there. Ren was a nickname Jamie gave me after becoming my best friend. She's the only one who has ever called me that.

"Did you forget what day it is?" I asked, somewhat agitated. I'm not really the attention-seeker type, but we've both always made a big deal out of our birthdays, so her lack of interest kinda hurt my feelings. Surely the excitement of turning another year older doesn't start to go away when you're sixteen, does it? I thought that wouldn't happen until the big 3-0.

"Of course not, Ren-Ren! It's Tuesday, and we're gonna be late for class," she said with a huge grin, knowing good and well that wasn't the answer I was looking for, and tugged my arm to walk with her into the building.

"Well, I guess I won't be giving you a ride to school in the mornings in my new car, then!" I growled with a similar grin back at her.

"No way! Seriously? Your parents got you a new car?"

"Well, it's not exactly new, but I love it! It's a 2007 Explorer. My dad made it a point to tell me that it's a 4X4 so that I never get stuck in the snow, or at least have less of a chance of that happening! It's got leather seats, tinted windows, and an awesome six-disc CD player," I went on and on excitedly.

"That's so cool! Let's take it for a spin around the parking lot at lunch," she suggested.

We really weren't supposed to leave the building during school hours, but my excitement got the best of me, and I thought, *What harm could it be to take it for one spin? We'll still be on school grounds, right?* I hesitated as a second thought of rule-breaking crossed my mind. *What if we get caught? My parents would be so disappointed.*

I must have shown my doubt on my face because the next thing I heard was, "Come on, Ren. It's a special day. It'll be okay. We're not doing anything bad." She convincingly said, eyes half rolled.

"Okay . . . I'll meet you at the lockers at a quarter to twelve then," I replied, eager for the adventure.

It was third period, and Mrs. Moran was finishing up her lecture on the Roman Empire.

"Your next assignment is a three thousand word essay on a famous Roman Emperor of your choosing. It will be due one week from today. See you tomorrow, and be ready for a quiz on today's lecture," she announced.

The whole class sighed simultaneously at the news. I grabbed my books and was the first one out the door. I rushed down the stairs, accidentally bumping into people along the way and having to give several apologies. Finally, I made it to the locker corridor. Jamie wasn't there, yet, so I put my books in the locker, grabbed my lunch, grabbed her lunch, and waited. *Where is she?* I wondered after a few minutes passed.

My excitement made me an impatient person today. I looked at my watch and it was almost noon. Hmmm . . . maybe she thought we were going to meet by the doors leading to the parking lot. I started to walk around the corner when I saw them.

Jamie had apparently gotten sidetracked once again by the crazy model dude. I saw her smiling and twisting her hair around her finger over and over. Ugh! An obvious sign she was very impressed with him. She was naturally more of a flirt than me and usually instigated all of the conversations with the guys when we would go see a movie or go to Pizza Madness. She was undoubtedly a pretty girl, with a tiny waist and muscular legs from cheering and sports, but her self-confidence is what I think was her best feature. She could walk into any room and smile from ear to ear, showing off her overly white teeth, and capture the interest of everyone in there. She's only ever had one serious boyfriend, though, which ended with heartbreak—his, not hers.

I walked up and cleared my throat to interrupt her conversation with the new student.

"Hey, Jamie. Whatcha doin'?" I casually asked.

"Ren! Sorry I'm a little late, but Mr. Lender asked me to show Kyran around. It's his first day, and we happen to have first period together."

She looked at him and gave another flirtatious smile. *Gag.* I just looked at her, silent, not really sure what to say or think at this point. My lack of response kept her talking.

"And I had to take him to his other classes, too. It would be rude of me to let him get lost on his first day, wouldn't it?" she said in her nicest possible voice, trying to convince me of her good stewardship.

Of course, she didn't think of how rude it would be to diss her best friend when they had plans together. Even so, I could see exactly why she had an interest in Kyran. There was an aura about him that was very magnetic; it was more than just his handsomely, devilish good looks and the fact that he was a junior.

As I tried to nonchalantly glance over at him, our eyes locked for a second. I quickly turned to Jamie and said, "How good of you to help out the new guy. Now can we go? We only have thirty minutes left for lunch."

"I hope you don't mind . . ." she started to say.

No, don't say it . . . please don't say what I think you're going to say.

". . . but I invited Kyran to come along with us. I would hate for him to eat all alone in the cafeteria," she said so deviously.

Oh, mercy. I couldn't look like the bad guy here, so, of course, I said, "Sure, if he really wants to."

I looked right over at him, with more confidence this time, and said, "We're just taking a quick spin in the parking lot. It really would be kind of boring for you, but if you really want to come, that's fine with me."

I tried my best to make it unappealing to him. Surely this macho guy wouldn't want to be seen taking a spin in the parking lot with a couple of sophomores, would he?

"I would love to come," he said in a thick, pacifying accent.

That was the first time I had heard him speak. I should have known he wasn't from around here. Who else in their right mind would drive a motorcycle in this kind of weather? He held out his hand to me and properly introduced himself.

"I'm Kyran. *Bello fare la tua conoscenza*," he said as he gave a slight bow.

Completely caught off guard by his other language that sounded so beautiful with each unfamiliar word spoken, all I could do was stand there with a dazed look, unsure of what I should say back.

"That means 'It's my pleasure to make your acquaintance' in Italian," he said, perhaps hoping to actually get a response from me this time.

Still stunned by his exceptional manners and mature appearance, I held out my now sweaty palm to shake his, and said, "Oh, I'm Renee, it's nice to meet you, too." I released his hand as quickly as possible.

We walked out to my car, and the original excitement that had consumed me earlier came back as we approached *my* new SUV.

"Well, here she is," I announced.

"Sick!" Jamie cried out excitedly. "Can I drive?"

"No way! I've only gotten to drive her once. Let me break her in some more before you start trying to take the wheel. Besides, you still have two more months before you get your license."

She couldn't help but roll her eyes at me. I tend to be a little motherly sometimes. As I hopped into the driver's seat, she climbed into the middle of the back.

"What are you doing?" I asked, surprised at her latest move.

"I'm being a 'gentlewoman' and letting Kyran take the front seat," she said with a playful grin.

"Certainly no gentleman would allow you to do such a thing. Please, Jamie, take your place up front," he said indulgently in his soft, comforting voice.

"Yes . . . *please* take your place up front," I concurred, with my eyes widened and head cocked. I was giving her "the look."

"Absolutely not. I'm already back here; so let's fire this puppy up and go!" she insisted.

Too much time had already passed, so I gave up trying to argue with her and put the keys in the ignition, revving up the engine as if I were going to race someone. Intuitively, I looked over to the passenger side where Kyran was sitting, smiling right at me.

Odd, I thought, *it is just as I had dreamed.*

TWO

The Pursuit

As I drove home from school, I began thinking of what an almost perfect day it had been with my almost brand new car. The only thing that went wrong was Kyran showing up and stealing my thunder. I was lost in that thought when suddenly a red ball came flying across the street. I instinctively slammed on my brakes, thankful the roads had cleared up yesterday.

My heart was beating so fast; it was the only part of my body that didn't feel paralyzed. I looked straight ahead and saw a young boy with remarkably noticeable sky-blue eyes. He couldn't have been more than seven or eight years old, and he was looking right at me. I looked at him intensely, trying to remember if I knew this kid from somewhere. He looked oddly familiar. *I'm sure I must have met him at some church function or when I volunteered to be a camp counselor for the younger kids.* He continued to stand in front of my car, looking at me, and finally gave a slight wave with an expression of eagerness upon his face. I peeled my right hand off the steering wheel and gave a quick wave back. On that signal, he proceeded to cross the road. I waited for him to grab his ball and cross back over before I slowly began to accelerate, still a little shaken at the thought of wrecking my car the first day I had it—or worse, hurting this kid. The thought gave me goose bumps all over my arms. I looked back in my rearview mirror, but the boy was gone.

When I finally got home, I told my mom about the day's events, with the exception of the new guy and the spin around the parking lot. I always shared everything with her, but I knew she wouldn't be too pleased that I broke the rules and had some stranger in my car while doing it. We picked up Jamie at six o'clock as planned and went to my favorite restaurant, Celdor Asado, which is known for its amazing, fall-off-the-bone ribs. It had become a tradition over the last five years; one I looked forward to every time with the same enthusiasm. Jamie and I shared a whole rack, then followed it up with their freshly made cheesecake with raspberry sauce drizzled all over. It was the perfect conclusion to my birthday: being surrounded by the ones I loved the most in my life. Nothing would ever change that.

The next day at school, I was at my locker with my head buried inside it, listening to my iPod. When I closed the door, I was startled to see that there was a person standing on the other side. My heart raced, astonished by the unexpected guest. Kyran smiled as big as he possibly could, showing his stunning, pearly whites.

As I took the earphones out, I said, "Oh my gosh, Kyran! You scared me. What are you doing?"

"I'm sorry," he said so convincingly. "I noticed you here when I was walking by. I thought I would come and say hello. I didn't mean to scare you."

"That's okay. Why are you here so early, anyway? Everyone else usually waits until the bell is about to ring," I said incredulously.

"Yes, well, I thought I'd get a head start on the day," he admitted.

Wow, that really impressed me. It was the last thing I would have expected from a guy like him. It sort of made me, well, intrigued.

"Where are you going?" he said with his still freshly delectable accent.

"Ummm . . . I have chemistry first period which is right up . . . "

He stopped me in my tracks and said, "No, *bellissima,* where are you going today after school?"

Uhhhh was all that came to my mind. I didn't know what to say to this unexpected question.

He was keenly aware of my cautious silence and said, "Sorry if I am so bold. I hope I didn't offend you."

"No, of course not, I guess that was twice today that you caught me off guard. I actually have plans, though. On Wednesdays I go to youth group at my church," I explained, glad that I had somewhere to be. He made me nervous just being around him.

"What about tomorrow night then? I would love to take you to the coffee shop and learn more about what there is to do in Westcliffe," he said so melodically.

The opportunity to tell him about the town I loved and grew up in was tempting. Westcliffe was small but full of charm. Part of its attraction was the fact that we are surrounded by the Sangre de Cristo and Wet Mountains, tucked neatly away from the rest of the world, allowing Westcliffe's natural beauty to remain preserved. On Saturday nights we would either go to the historic Jones Theater, which played one movie each week and doubled as the performing arts theatre, or to Pizza Madness, which served up the best pizza around and would usually host live bands or have karaoke. I could let him know that after football games everyone would meet up at Cliff Lanes for bowling and burgers. And I could also tell him about the incredible hiking and ski trails or how each summer we would go river rafting on the Arkansas River, which was only a thirty minute drive away. But I won't.

"Sorry, on Mondays and Thursdays I have dance class. Why don't you ask Jamie? I'm sure she would love to tell you all there is to know about this place. Anyway, I gotta go. I don't want to be late for class." And with that, I quickly walked away, leaving him standing alone.

"Yes, I'll do that then," he said a little louder to make sure I could hear him from behind.

Relieved to get into Miss Adamma's chemistry lab, I let out a sigh as I sat in my chair on the front row, almost out of breath.

"What are you doing, child?" she asked curiously with her African accent.

The bell had not yet rung, and she probably noticed a bit of sweat running down the side of my face.

Miss Adamma came to the US to study at the University of Colorado, ultimately getting her masters in education. She decided to get a green card so she could teach here full time, hoping to one day acquire her citizenship. She was so sweet and naturally beautiful. It was obvious in her voice and body language that she loved to teach and loved her students. This was a dream come true for her.

She told us a story of her childhood on our first day of class. She had once lived in a small, extremely poor village outside of Tanzania. It wasn't uncommon for children to be sold off as slaves for very little money. She said her parents were so desperate themselves that they were about to sell her into slavery in order to provide food for her younger siblings. That is, until the great messenger showed up. She spoke of the missionary man as a savior. She explained that had it not been for him, her life would have been a living hell, if she would have even survived it at all. "He taught me about Jesus Christ, and through Him, I can be saved," she said with gratitude on her face. "For once I saw there was hope, and that I, too, was allowed to dream beyond the borders of my village. For that, I am forever grateful."

"Who, me?" I asked as if she had called me out in front of the whole class.

"Of course, child, who else do you think I would be talking to?"

"I just, uh . . . uh . . . wanted to make sure I was on time so that I could give you my science project before anyone else got here.

You know, in case you had any questions for me or something," I stammered frantically.

She looked at me with one eye, you know like your mother gives when she's not sure if she should believe you or not. I walked up to her and handed her my project and watched as she reviewed it halfheartedly. Other students began to trickle in, yet she was too involved in what she needed to tell me to greet them.

"Renee, if you ever need to talk, I am here. Okay?" On that note, the bell rang, so I gladly took my seat.

I was able to avoid any contact with Kyran for the rest of the day, and the rest of the week for that matter. With it, though, I also had to somewhat avoid my best friend, which really stunk. She was obviously interested in Kyran, along with every other girl in school. So, on a good note it kept him preoccupied, and she certainly didn't seem to mind either. I kept myself busy with schoolwork, church, and dance to help the time go by until Jamie was either over her little crush or made the announcement that they were now an item. And even though Kyran spent most of his free time with Jamie and a few other hopefuls, I noticed that the few times I happened to pass by him, he would always look up and over to me as if some radar alerted him of my presence. I would just keep walking, head down and eyes glued to the ground, as if I didn't notice him.

I don't know why, but he made my stomach feel all tied in knots. It wasn't like I had never spoken to a boy before; there was just something about him that made me so timid. No doubt he was the most gorgeous guy I had ever laid my eyes on in person, but it was more than that. It was as if I were afraid I wouldn't be able to control myself with him, as if he made me vulnerable somehow. Whatever the case, it really didn't matter because Jamie seemed to like him a lot, and so there was really nothing to worry about. I was sure she would have him wrapped around her finger in no time.

It was eight thirty in the evening and dance class had just ended. I started taking ballet when I was five and jazz a few years later. My mother entered me into ballet first to help cure my clumsiness, the result of my lanky legs, and to give me a little grace. It certainly cured me, but dancing gave me so much more than that. It was so liberating and a beautiful way to express myself, both creatively and physically. It was the only time my shyness had no power over my thoughts and movement, which gave me the freedom to be as delicate as a butterfly or as vigorous as a tiger. I usually opted for the butterfly.

I asked Mo, short for Maureen, if I could stay a little longer and practice my routine for the upcoming performance next month. This recital was particularly important to me because it was the day before my father's birthday, and this dance was a tribute to him. I must have listened to a hundred songs that would let him know how much I loved him. I knew when I heard the words to "In My Arms" by Plumb that this would be the song to bring him to tears first, then to his feet. The amazing lyrics would let him know that even though I'm not such a little girl anymore, I still feel safe in his arms.

I needed to keep practicing to make sure my grand *jeté* and *fouettés* were absolutely perfect. Mo had been my instructor for the past seven years, so we were very close, and I knew I could persuade her into extending our practice.

"Sorry, Renee, but I have plans tonight with my husband. He's taking me out on a date!" she said excitedly. It was so cute how she still adored him after all these years together.

"Ah, come on, Mo. Please, please!" I begged. "I know where the extra keys to the studio are. I promise to lock up for you, so it's not like you'll have to stay and wait. Please!" The perfectionist in me wouldn't give up trying.

"Okay, Renee." She quickly gave in, knowing she was about to embark on a battle she didn't have time for. "But don't overdo it. You don't want to get worn down or strain a muscle," she said with genuine concern.

"Thank you. I promise; I'll be careful."

And with that, she was off to her date.

I turned the music back on and began my routine. Halfway through it, dissatisfied with my performance, I started over. This seemed to be a continuous pattern for the next thirty minutes, and I began to get frustrated. I just couldn't seem to jump high enough or turn fast enough. *I must be getting too tired,* I convinced myself. *Try one last time, and then call it a night.*

I started the music over, and on my second turn I spotted something red in the mirror. I stopped immediately to see what it was.

"I didn't mean to interrupt. Please continue. You're quite good," the unexpected visitor implored.

"Kyran, you've got to quit doing this," I exclaimed, noticing he was wearing my red scarf around the top of his black leather jacket. I intentionally failed to mention I was the one who lost it the day he found it.

"Doing what?" he asked innocently.

"Scaring me, that's what. So, what are you doing here anyway? Are you following me?" I accused.

"Don't be ridiculous, *amore.* I was driving through town and saw your car out in front of the studio, so I thought I would stop by for a minute. Please, continue. You have a captive audience!" he admitted. I noticed two small dimples on each side of his stretched lips. My heart beat a little faster.

"Actually, I was just about done. I'm a little worn-out and can't seem to get any of the moves right. Besides, I really need to get going," I said. I began packing my gym bag with my back to him, careful not to look into his eyes.

A childhood memory flashed into my head of our ranch cat, Oscar, when I saw him hypnotize a nice plump bird that was happily perched on the fence. He had watched it so carefully . . . so patiently. He knew eventually, the bird would look into his hypnotic eyes and once it did, it was a goner. Oscar was a very fat cat.

"Please, just one more time. Perhaps I can help you somehow." I could hear his spellbinding voice getting louder; he was growing closer to me with each word spoken.

"Really, that's very nice of you, but I have to go. I don't want my parents getting worried and putting out a search party for me."

I grabbed the remote to the CD player to turn the music off when he loosely wrapped my red scarf around my neck from behind me. Instinctively, I crossed my arms as if to shield myself from this alluring outsider, and then he tenderly placed his arms atop mine, capturing me into his human cocoon. I found myself completely stunned while melting into his embrace. I could feel each beat of his pounding heart through his muscular chest on my back. He spoke softly into my right ear, "Please, try your routine one last time. Don't think about the dance itself, but what it means to you."

He then took the remote from my hand to start the song over. As he let go of our embrace, I began my routine, only this time picturing my father watching me with proud eyes. I unwrapped the scarf from my neck and used it as a prop, adding to the routine that little something that had been missing. As I executed each jump or turn, I didn't really think about them; I just moved my body to the flow of the music. I became one with it.

Suddenly, I realized I was no longer performing for my father in my mind. I could see Kyran in the mirror, watching me as I continued to dance. I could feel the power of his stare rushing through my blood, giving me a surge of energy. When I came to the part where I complete a triple *fouetté* turn, I was positioned directly in front of him and couldn't help but look deep into his seductive green eyes with each rotation. I liked having his absolute attention as I continued to sway my body for him, and it scared me. He was able to bring something out in me that I never knew existed. A passion that filled my very essence, unleashing the tiger from deep within. It showed in my fluid rhythm as I was finally able to complete the dance with total satisfaction.

When the song ended, I heard clapping as Kyran said, "*Brava, bellissima, brava!*"

Ending my routine on the floor, Kyran came over to me and held out his hand to help me up. My breathing was still heavy. His eyes were merely inches from mine. I had never been so close to any other male besides my dad. I stood motionless as if I were a butterfly that had been stunned by the venom of a spider.

Kyran rubbed the side of my face gently with the back of his hand and said, "You see, *amore;* you are a fantastic dancer."

I looked down, feeling embarrassed by the situation, and then he grabbed my chin to lift my face up to meet his. I could see his eyes getting closer to me when the next song began to play. I immediately came out of the trance I seemed to be in and quickly turned around to grab my bag.

"Kyran, I really have to go now. It was good to see you. And thanks for the scarf," I said as I stuffed it into my bag. "See you in school tomorrow. Okay?"

"Yes, of course." I could hear footsteps striding across the wooden floor. And then an unfamiliar word came to me as he walked out the door. *"Domani!"*

I quickly turned off the lights, locked up, and drove home. *Domani.* I repeated the word several times with curiosity. As soon as I walked in the door; I went straight to the computer to look up this last mysterious word that came from his mouth. I quickly typed the word into the Google search engine and up came the word: *tomorrow.*

THREE

Failed Resistance

I was restless in my sleep that night. I kept dreaming of a dark mist that seemed to follow me everywhere I went. I would try to run from this shadow of darkness, which would only reveal its cat-like, sharp eyes to me, but no matter how fast I ran, there the eyes remained. I felt confused and lost. I wasn't even sure where I was trying to run to; I just knew I needed to get away. I was sprinting as fast as I could until my legs began to feel like they were going to give out. My feet felt like they were glued to the ground and with each step I tried to take, I was being pulled back. The darkness was getting closer and closer, and I was getting wearier, no longer having the stamina to keep trudging forward. I shouted, "Go away! Leave me alone!" And with that, I woke up drenched in sweat. I looked over at the clock that sat next to my bed and saw it was almost midnight. I was afraid to fall back asleep, afraid of the dark ghost that haunted my dream, and all I could think to do was pray.

"God, forgive me for my sins. Thank you for your mercy and grace upon my soul. I give this night over to you. Please give me peaceful rest. In your name I pray. Amen."

I rolled over and briefly thought of Kyran. He was such a perfect guy. He was the guy of my dreams, obviously, but why would he have any interest in someone like me? The next thing I knew, I was waking up to the beeping sound of my alarm clock. I was thankful to have made it through the night.

That morning, when I arrived at the sophomore corridor, I noticed Kyran leaning against my locker. I looked down and tucked my hair behind my ear, having decided against a hair band, and casually said, "Hey!" I was careful not to look right at him.

"Good morning, *amore*. How was your night?" he asked.

"Fine, thanks," I said, trying to keep the conversation light and casual. "How was yours?"

"Restless." He paused and then said, "Renee, may I take you out for some coffee after school today? I would love to get to know you better."

"Look, Kyran. I don't think that's such a good idea on so many levels. Not that I don't find you, well, you know, attractive," I stammered. "Every girl here would love to jump at the chance to have coffee with you. But to be honest, I would never do anything to hurt Jamie. She's my closest and dearest friend, and I would never dream of hurting her. I am flattered by your invitation, but will have to pass." And with that, I walked away before Jamie showed up and got the wrong impression.

As the day progressed, I couldn't help but think of Kyran every hour of the day. I had to ask myself: if it weren't for Jamie, would I have taken him up on his offer? *Yes! Why wouldn't I? He's incredibly gorgeous and I can't seem to get enough of that accent!* I admitted to myself. But something still didn't feel right about it; I just didn't know what. I mean there's no harm in having coffee with someone, right? Isn't that what friends do? *Maybe I should just talk with Jamie about all of this. No . . . I can't. That would just put some sort of awkward competition between us, and it's not worth it.*

The last bell of the day broke my arguing thoughts, so I grabbed my books and walked out of class, still in a daze. I wasn't used to getting this kind of attention. My name wasn't Beth Middleton or even Jamie for that matter. Beth would probably hyperventilate and go into convulsions if she knew about the attention I was receiving from Kyran. Rumor had it she was going to break up with Brad to make herself available. She had no qualms about letting others know she was interested in Kyran, especially Jamie. She would love to finally get her revenge from all those years ago when Jamie so easily put her in her place. A smirk seemed to sneak upon my face at the very thought of the whole thing when suddenly Jamie came running up behind me, yelling, "Ren . . . we've been invited to go out after school today. You'll never guess who wants to take us out for an espresso!"

"Let me take a stab at it. Would it happen to be Kyran?" I casually answered, acting like I didn't have any excitement about the prospect of it all.

"How'd you guess? Isn't it so exciting? And it gets even better," she continued.

"More exciting than coffee with Kyran! What could it ever be?" I asked with a hint of mockery.

"He wants us to ride there with him!"

"And how do you suppose the three of us are going to fit on that motorcycle he likes to zip around on?" Ick . . . I sounded like my mother just then.

"Well, my friend, he didn't drive his little crotch rocket to school today. He brought . . . are you ready for this? His Porsche!" I could see the immense pleasure on her face at giving me the news.

"Jamie, aren't Porsches two-seaters?" I asked, holding back any inclination of being impressed by his foreign, way-too-expensive sports car.

"That's okay. I'll just sit on your lap. Come on. It'll be fun. Live a little, why don't you?"

"I'll pass. You go have fun, and I'll see you tomorrow." Although it killed me to say that, I knew I was doing the right thing.

"No, Ren. I want you to come too. Please! Please! How about if I ride with you, and we'll just meet him there. Will you go for that?" she begged and gave me the puffed-out lips and sad puppy dog eyes. That's a stunt she usually pulls when she wants me to do something.

"Okay, Jai. I'll go," I sighed. I called her Jai on occasion, usually when she was getting me to take part in some scheme she had worked up.

"Awesome! I'll go tell him we'll meet at Candy's in ten minutes, and I'll meet you at your car."

"Great, should be interesting!"

A few minutes later she came running over and hopped in my car.

"Did coach cancel basketball practice today?" I asked.

"Oh, crap!" she exclaimed. "I got so caught up with Kyran, I completely forgot."

She looked at her watch. "I've got five minutes to change and be out on the court, or coach will make me run ten suicides. Hurry, Ren, drop me off at the gym."

I got her there as fast as I could. I hated the thought of her having to run any suicides, even though I really didn't know what they were. I just knew they didn't sound good.

She quickly got out of the car and yelled back, "Tell Kyran I'm sorry. Thanks, Ren," and she was off like lightning.

It wasn't until I started driving off campus that I realized something. Panic struck my heart and it began to throb a little faster. I could see the sweat from my hands on the steering wheel. I was now left alone to have coffee with the mystery boy wonder. I thought, *Oh, Lord, what should I do? I don't know if I want to be alone with this guy.*

My gut was telling me to just call up to Candy's Coffee Shop and ask them to give him a message since I didn't have his cell number. But surprisingly, the other part of me—the curious side—couldn't seem to resist the temptation of spending the afternoon with this amazing guy. He should have been making movies in Hollywood, but instead came to our quiet town and is sitting at the coffee shop waiting for Jamie and me to show up.

While my every thought sided with my initial gut reaction, I somehow found myself robotically driving in the direction of Candy's. Ten minutes later, I arrived and parked my car outside. I sat there, motor still running, debating on what to do. I had been listening to my favorite CD, *Comatose* by Skillet, while driving; but hadn't paid much attention to it until I heard "Whispers in the Dark" come on.

I was introduced to and immediately mesmerized by this hard rock band at a summer youth camp two years ago. I was in awe of this young, hip group that would rock your face off all in the name of Jesus. The drummer and guitar player were both beautiful, young women who had the talent and stamina to bang their heads while playing their instruments. They left a lasting impression on me, a reserved, somewhat shy girl. I became one of their biggest fans, officially calling myself a "Panhead." Their music had a way of making me, usually a calm-spirited girl, turn into this excited, energetic, head-banging fool! They brought out a different side of me that I didn't know I had until that memorable summer.

As I sat there, still contemplating going in, I began to sing along with the song. I figured this would be a good time to test the speakers in my new car and turned the volume up until I could feel the base pounding in my chest. I began wildly belting out the chorus at the top of my lungs, while bobbing my head up and down, and thumping my hands on the steering wheel.

I was right in the middle of this self-gratifying craziness when I heard a "knock, knock, knock" on my window. The thought of looking like a complete idiot didn't even cross my mind until that knock. Embarrassment struck me as I looked out, and to my dismay, there was Kyran, smiling with a slight chuckle coming from beneath his breath. I rolled down the window only a quarter of the way.

"Kyran! I didn't see you coming," I said, a bit winded.

"Sorry, *amore*. I noticed you sitting out here for a few minutes and thought I would come and check on you. I must say, I liked seeing you go a little wild in here," he said with shock in his voice.

"Well, don't act so surprised. There's a lot you don't know about me," I snickered.

"Don't be so defensive, my little head-banging darling. I found it so amusing. Now, please, let's go inside so you can tell me more about the things I don't know of you yet," he said so persuasively with his amorous accent. He opened my door and held out his hand like the perfect gentleman. I just stared at him as he grinned at me, not moving.

"Come," he said, "it's just coffee. I will be a complete gentleman. I promise."

I rolled my window back up, turned off the car, and cautiously placed my hand into his. He gently pulled me closer to him and escorted me in. We ordered our coffee along with a crumb cake to share and began talking.

My nerves eventually subsided, and I was able to open up to him about me, Jamie, and my family. I even confessed how big of a nerd I am, and how he's taking a risk on his reputation just being here with me. He just seemed to shrug it off as if he didn't care. He sat patiently and listened so intently, surrendering his own words, so that I could continue with my blabbering. I had never been able to talk to another guy so freely, giving so many details about myself. There was even a moment when he gently wiped a crumb from the corner of my lips without saying a word, as if it were so normal for us.

"I'm sorry, Kyran. I've been so rude in talking about me this whole time and haven't even given you a chance."

"Don't apologize; I've loved every moment of our time together. Perhaps we can go out again on Friday so I can get to know you a little better?" he asked.

"I want to know more about you, too, like where you came from and what would possess you to drive a motorcycle in the freezing cold," I said, never giving an answer to his proposal.

Amused at the second question, he laughed and answered sincerely, "I didn't want to make a big scene my first day at a new school."

I looked at him, a bit confused. "Oh, because driving up on a BMW motorcycle in this weather isn't making any sort of scene or statement?" I giggled. "Help me understand that one."

"I guess in your eyes, that's how you would see things. You must know that my family moves around a lot. We have a long history of being extremely wealthy with a strong taste for buying the finer things in life. My choices were the motorcycle, a Porsche, a Lamborghini, or the family limo. So, I chose the least noticeable of them all and went with the cycle."

Funny, it seemed to make perfect sense to me.

The ringing sound of my cell phone interrupted our engrossing conversation. I noticed it was my mom calling. "Oh, my gosh, Kyran. Look at the time. My mother is gonna be so upset with me."

"Hello!" I answered the phone.

My mom was not too pleased on the other end.

"I'm so sorry, Mom. I've been at Candy's, just hanging out with a friend. I'm on my way now. I know, Mom, I'm so sorry. I just lost track of time, but I'll be there in a few minutes. Okay, I love you, too," I said, feeling terrible as I hung up. I hated the fact that I made her worry about me.

"I'm sorry, but I have to go. Thanks for the coffee and cake. I had a really good time. See you tomorrow?" I asked, surprised at the question because I knew I would see him; we went to the same school. But it let him know that this time, I wanted to see him. My wall was starting to break.

"*Sì, la mia bellissima,*" he said with a subtle wink.

I slightly blushed, unsure of exactly what he said, but feeling he gave me a sweet compliment.

"See ya," I softly replied, before leaving him sitting at the table. I sensed that he was watching me as I walked to my car, probably just making sure I got there safely. He was everything a girl could possibly want in a guy, and far from what I had expected from him. There was only one problem . . . Jamie.

FOUR

Just Friends...Right?

Before I had the front door completely opened, I heard, "Renee? Is that you, sweetheart?"

"Yes, Mom," I yelled back as I hung up my coat.

"Can you come here, please?" she asked in her "I'm trying to remain calm to assess the situation before I get angry" voice.

I entered the kitchen where she was finishing up dishes, and my dad was at the table eating the last of his cherry pie my mom baked for him. I casually said, "Hey, Daddy," and gave him a kiss on his cheek.

"Hi, Princess!" he replied, chewing his last bite. He was always the pushover, so I knew I had more to worry about with Mom.

She cleared her throat, wanting my attention. I was sure she knew I was stalling.

"What's up, Mom?"

"Care to explain why it's two and a half hours since school let out, and you are just now getting home?"

Daddy gave my mom his plate, along with a peck on her cheek, then whispered something in her ear before announcing he was going to his recliner to read. As he walked away, he gave me a quick wink, so I'm sure he must have told her to go easy on me.

"Sorry, Mom, but I got caught up in a deep conversation with .

. . with . . . a new kid in school. Jamie had set the whole thing up for all of us to get to know each other a little better and then bailed on me when she realized she had basketball practice. I couldn't be rude and not have anyone show up at all, could I?"

"That's all fine and dandy, but where is the common courtesy of a phone call so that your father and I don't worry ourselves sick about you? I called you three times before you finally answered. The only reason I didn't completely panic and go out looking for you was because Jamie called and told me where you were. She mentioned she had tried calling you as well and couldn't reach you."

"Really? I never heard my phone ring until I answered it when you called. It was a little loud in there; and like I said, I got caught up in a great conversation." With the most beautiful guy in all of Westcliffe, but she didn't need to know that.

"So who is this new kid, anyway?"

I didn't want to go into much detail because then she would start asking a million questions, so I casually said, "His name is Kyran, and his family moved here a couple of weeks ago. I was just trying to be nice to him, Mom, that's all. It's tough being the new kid, you know?" I had to throw that in to get her sympathy vote.

"I suppose that was very nice of you, but just make sure you remain my responsible little gi . . . I mean, daughter." She caught herself midpoint, recognizing my newfound maturity with the turning of age sixteen. "So, did you invite this Kyran to church? I'm sure his parents are looking for a good church to attend."

"No, we really didn't talk much about church. I'll see if he might want to go to our youth group some time. Anyway, I've got some homework to do, so can I just make myself a sandwich and hibernate in my room for the rest of the night?"

"Okay, sweetie, but give Jamie a call. She sounded a little worried, too."

I made myself a ham and cheese, grabbed a bottle of water, and ran upstairs. I immediately picked up the phone to start dialing

Jamie's number and then hung it up. What was I gonna say to her? "Kyran and I had such a great time together that he asked me out again?" I couldn't tell her the truth because that would really hurt her feelings. And I couldn't lie to her either; that would be so wrong. Now that I thought of it, Kyran didn't even ask where she was when I arrived solo. Hmmm? That was strange, since he asked her to Candy's in the first place. Even so, I still felt terrible about having such a good time with him today. Maybe by the morning she would have forgotten all about everything, and all this worrying would be for nothing. With that thought, I worked on my homework and called it a night.

The nightmare came back to me once again. I was walking to my car late in the evening and it seemed unusually quiet, like something had spooked every bug and animal, making them silent in the night. I looked around as a strange feeling came over me, and that's when I saw some piercing green and yellow eyes in the midst of a black vapor. It started to pursue me. I tried to get in my car, but it was locked. Panicked, my hands unsteady, I searched my purse for the keys. I couldn't find them. Frustrated, I threw my purse to the ground and began to run. I noticed the dark shadow was chasing after me once again. I could never see any part of this thing other than its wicked eyes, as it hovered behind me like a cloud of gloom filled with evilness and despair.

"Go away!" I shouted, but there it remained, following my every move and getting closer. I ran all the way to the dance studio, but the doors were locked. I banged on them as hard as I could. "Someone, please let me in," I pleaded, but no one answered. I started to run again as fast as I could in no particular direction, not really sure where I was going. I stopped to look around, trying to figure out which way to go. I felt desperate, cold, and confused. I began to shiver. *Run!* I thought. I knew I needed to just keep running before it caught up with me. I could feel it creeping up on me, making my feet feel heavy as if running through sand on the beach. It was getting harder to keep up the pace, but then I saw something bright up ahead. Yes . . . it was becoming clearer. There were lights on at the coffee shop, and it gave me a sense of hope.

I continued running as fast as I could, barely able to catch my breath anymore. I could feel it beginning to engulf me into its thick blackness, smothering me with its horrific fumes, which smelled like that of a rotting, dead animal. I was able to force myself out of the holding cell this intangible monster had me in and swiftly opened the door to dart inside. I was horrified when I didn't see anyone there who I could rush to. "Hello," I yelled out. "Is anyone here? Can anyone help me? Please, I need help!"

I looked around the empty room. Coffee pots were steaming as if ready to serve the warm drink to a paying customer, but no reply was given, just complete silence. I glanced at the front door just as it began shaking immensely, bringing with it a loud thunderous noise, when it suddenly and abruptly opened. I was nearly blinded by the extremely bright light bursting through it. It was not what I was expecting.

"Hello? Who's there? What do you want?" I boldly asked, though I stood there feeling helpless, crying and shaking.

"I am here," was all I heard before waking up completely soaked with sweat.

I looked over at the clock, and it was almost five in the morning. I sat up on my bed a minute to catch my breath. "Thank you, Lord," I said. The prayer seemed to methodically come from my mouth when I realized it was all just a terrible dream, and that I was safe in my own bed in my own house. The muffled sound of horses neighing in the background also brought a sense of reassurance to me. I looked out of my window and could see them, dimly lit by the full moonlight, which was casting a shadow on them. The horses were stirred up and playing with each other. I had a hard time going back to sleep, still a bit shaken by the nightmare, so I opened up my

Bible, which I always kept at my bedside. I began to read Joshua 1:9. *"Have I not commanded you? Be strong and courageous. Do not be terrified; do not be discouraged, for the LORD your God will be with you wherever you go."*
I found great comfort in this verse, and after reading a few more minutes, I found myself dozing off.

I walked up to my locker to put my things away and get ready for the day. I had just finished organizing all of my books and papers when I began to wonder if Kyran would be on the other side of my locker door when I closed it. I paused for a slight moment with my eyes closed, as if making a wish before blowing out birthday candles, and then closed the door. A feeling of disappointment came over me when he wasn't there. I leaned back against the lockers to wait for Jamie. The bell rang, and the halls were crowded as everyone scattered about, trying to get to their classes. I looked at my watch and decided to head to first period before I was late. It was odd that Jamie hadn't shown up yet. *I'll just catch up with her during lunch.* I couldn't help but feel a slight sense of relief at not having to talk with her this morning. I was saddened at the thought that this was the first time in seven years that I didn't want to have to speak to my best friend in the whole world. What had gotten into me? Jamie was like my sister, and I felt ashamed of my feelings. I knew right then what I needed to do. I had to tell Kyran that I could not go out with him Friday or ever, and at best, we could be friends.

There, I thought, halfheartedly convincing myself. *Now there's nothing to feel guilty about. We're just friends and there's nothing wrong with that.*
I walked into chemistry and saw Kyran talking with Miss Adamma. *What is he doing here?* I wondered.

"Listen up, students. We have a new student that will be joining our class. In case you haven't met him, this is Kyran. Please make him feel welcome."

My heart fell to the pit of my stomach as he grinned at me and started walking to the seat directly behind me. *Oh . . . this is not good, not good at all!* I turned around to him and whispered with a hint of panic, "What are you doing in here?"

"Taking chemistry, *amore.* What do you think I am doing?"

"Don't get witty with me. I'm serious. Why are you *now* in this particular chemistry class after being here a week already?" I said incredulously.

"I must say, this was not the response I was expecting. I thought you would be as pleased as I was to be in class together," he replied.

Feeling a bit guilty, I responded, "Well, of course I'm pleased . . . kind of. It just makes things more difficult, that's all."

Just as Kyran was about to speak, Miss Adamma cleared her throat to get my attention and said, "Renee, is everything okay?" I noticed her eyeing Kyran somewhat suspiciously.

"Yes, ma'am, just welcoming the new guy."

"Fine then. Open your books to page 245, and let's begin."

As soon as the bell rang, I headed out of class, leaving Kyran behind.

"Renee . . . Renee," I could hear him calling me just a few steps behind. "What's your hurry, *amore?*"

He quickly caught up and stopped me in the hallway as I said abruptly, "Look, Kyran. I would be completely lying to you and to myself if I said that I wasn't interested in you and flattered by all of the attention you've been giving me. But this can never happen between us because Jamie is my very best friend, and I can tell she likes you. Okay? It's best that we get this out of the way now before either one of us gets too emotionally attached and one of our hearts, mine in particular, gets broken." With that I began to walk off, hoping to get through the rest of the day without having a meltdown.

Why am I so worked up over this guy? I thought, almost mad at myself for allowing him to have such control over my emotions.

I looked down at my watch. *Three more hours before lunch, and then I'll see Jamie's reassuring face. We'll talk, have a few laughs, and all will be back to normal, just like it's always been.*

"Where is she?" I mumbled aloud. I had already been standing at my locker almost ten minutes after the lunch bell rang, and still no sign of Jamie. It was so unlike her not to tell me if she wasn't going to be in school. Then the thought crossed my mind. I remembered my mom saying Jamie had tried calling me last night. I got my cell phone out of my purse and listened to my messages.

"You have four messages," the phone voice said.

I couldn't believe I didn't hear the phone ringing the whole time I was with Kyran, and then I remembered how mesmerized I was by him.

First message: "Renee, it's four thirty, sweetheart. Did I forget about you telling me that you'd be staying after school today? Call me and let me know when you'll be home."

Next message: "Renee, it's Mom again. It's five thirty. Now I'm starting to get a little worried, sweetie. Call me, or I'm coming out to look for you!"

Next message: "Renee, it's Mo. Just calling to see if you wanted to schedule an extra practice this week. Let me know."

Next message: A puny voice mumbled some soft words. "Ren . . . what's going on? I've tried calling twice and haven't reached you. How's Kyran? Was he disappointed I couldn't make it? Anyway, I seem to be coming down with the stomach flu or something. I puked all over the gym floor during practice. I probably won't be at school tomorrow. Don't worry about calling me back tonight. I think I'm gonna hit the sack early and try to get some rest."

I had to admit that there was a sense of relief that Jamie wasn't here today. *I know,* I thought to myself, *I'll be the best friend ever and take her some chicken soup from The Rancher's Roost Cafe after school.*

I hated that she was sick, but it gave me some extra time to get over everything that had happened. I walked into the lunch room and sat down in my and Jamie's usual spot with my sack lunch in hand. I was just about to take the first bite of my sandwich when I heard a familiar voice from behind me.

"May I join you?" Kyran asked.

I looked back, only to see this sweet, inviting grin coming from "shampoo model boy," who was holding his lunch tray. This was my perfect opportunity to make my earlier point to him very clear and say, "No, thank you," and eat lunch all alone with no one to talk to. Or, I could let him eat with me this one last time and savor this last bit of time we would have alone before Jamie came back.

"You know, *amore*, I don't take rejection very well. Please, may I sit before the whole cafeteria sees you completely blow me off, and I lose every ounce of my pride?"

"Sit," was all I could say with a huge smile on my face and a giggle in my voice as I finally took a bite of my sandwich. I had a hard time resisting those dimples. *Dang it . . . he's just so cute!*

"I thought you'd never ask!" he said jokingly, showing his humorous side. "Thank you for sparing me the humiliation of having to walk to another table with my tail between my legs."

I chuckled again and said, "No problem. That's what friends are for." I emphasized the word *friends*.

"Well listen, friend," he mocked. "I have to go look for something to wear for my parents' dinner party on Friday night. I thought since you will be my special guest, you could help me buy something to wear for the occasion after school today. I made sure not to drive the, what do you call it? The 'crotch rocket?'" He said this as if we had already discussed these plans before.

"Excuse me? I don't recall saying I would go to any dinner party with you," I said, a bit caught off guard.

"*Sì, amore*. I told you I wanted to take you out Friday night; I just didn't mention where. You didn't say no, so I had to assume it was a yes. Please, don't leave me alone with a house full of adults where I must pretend to be the least bit interested in what they are saying. It will only be bearable if you're there with me. What do you say?" he pleaded.

"I say that I have plans to go to Jamie's basketball game Friday

41

night," I said, happy to have a good reason to turn down this very enticing invite.

"Well, then, as a good friend, can you please escort me to find proper attire for the dinner party? I'm terrible at picking out my own clothes, especially when I have to dress up."

"Sorry, Kyran. I told you that I have youth group on Wednesday nights at seven o'clock. Want to come?"

"Let's make a deal, shall we? If you help me find something to wear right after school, I'll have you back in time for youth group and may even consider going to the service," he offered.

I thought about it for a minute. An impromptu shopping trip did sound like fun. Although, I had told myself I would take Jamie some soup today after school. I looked at him just as I was going to force myself to decline when he gave me the same puppy dog eyes and lips that Jamie seems to use on me . . . and it always works too! I was such a sucker sometimes. Besides, Jamie had no idea I even thought about dropping by today. She probably wanted to be left alone anyway, with the way she was feeling and all.

"Okay, Fabio . . . I'll help you out. Let me just call my mom and ask her if it's okay."

He gave one of those manly chuckles when I gave him the nickname and commented, "I love your sense of humor and audacity. Not many people would consider calling me such a name and get away with it, you know." Then he poked my ribs with his fingers as I was trying to dial home.

"Stop!" I said with a laugh, slapping his hand. "My mom's about to answer."

"Hello."

"Hey, Mom, what'cha doin'?" I casually asked.

"Is everything okay? Why are you calling me at this time of day?" she asked, a bit worried.

"Everything's fine. I just wanted to see if it would be okay for me to go shopping after school. I need to help Kyran pick something out to wear for a special occasion on Friday, and I seem to be his only friend at this time," I said while looking at him, once again emphasizing the word *friend*.

"Is Jamie going too?"

"Nope . . . she's home sick with the stomach flu or something. So can I? Kyran said he'll have me back before youth group starts tonight," I added before she asked.

"Well, I guess so. Be careful, though, and call me if you need anything . . . anything at all. Okay?" She was unsure of how to handle the fact that I was to be alone with a boy. This was something she'd never had to deal with before.

"I will, Mom, thanks. Love you!"

"Love you, too," she said. And with that, we hung up.

I looked at Kyran. "Okay, Ricardo, it's all set. Although, honestly, I don't know how much help I'm going to be. Fashion's not really my thing," I admitted. I was beginning to feel a sense of excitement at the thought of hanging out with him, though, even if it meant having to dig deep down inside to bring out any sense of style I had.

"I don't think that will be an issue," he said confidently.

"You do realize your options are quite limited here in the big town of Westcliffe? We usually have to drive to Pueblo or Canon City to find anything nice to wear."

"I'm sure we can come up with something," he said with a devilish grin.

"I guess I'll meet you in the parking lot after school then," I said as I stood up to throw away my half eaten lunch, too distracted to eat. Kyran walked me to my next class. I couldn't help but feel a sense of triumph as we walked past Beth Middleton and her little entourage, consisting of Harmony, Tori, and Heather, or the "Trio of Bethannies" as Jamie liked to call them. I could see the shock in their faces, and I admittedly enjoyed the bit of jealousy Beth so obviously displayed.

FIVE

The Unexpected

I met Kyran in the parking lot as planned, and we drove off in his Porsche. We went down Main Street toward the shops, but then we turned left onto 69.

"Hey, you took the wrong turn," I said.

"I know exactly where I'm going," he replied, completely focused on the road ahead.

"What are you up to?" I asked with a bit of excitement, nervousness, and curiosity all rolled into one ball.

"I told you, we're going shopping."

"But this is not . . . " was all I could get out before he hushed me.

"Just relax and enjoy the ride!"

We continued to drive out of town and in a direction I had never taken to go shopping. Suddenly, he turned right onto a small dirt path where a gate that had once been closed and secured was now opened, as if expecting our arrival. I gazed over at Kyran, completely mystified by his secrecy. He looked over at me and gave me a sultry grin and stopped the car in the middle of an empty field. As if right on cue, a helicopter came from behind the mountaintop just on the other side of the range and landed about a hundred feet from where we were parked.

"What is going on?" I asked with an alarmed voice.

"You don't expect to find something for me to wear at the local stores, do you?" he grinned as he got out of the car and quickly ran around to open my door. He held out his hand, and I warily placed mine into his as he pulled me out of the car.

"Come, love, there is no time to waste."

We quickly ran underneath the heavy wind caused by the loud, whirling blades of the helicopter and dashed into the cab. As soon as the pilot closed the door, he took his place up front and began the procedures for takeoff. Kyran had me put some headphones with a mouth-piece on so we could talk. Stunned by this unexpected escapade, I found myself completely speechless.

Am I dreaming again? I had to ask myself.

Something like this just doesn't happen in Westcliffe and, more markedly, to me! We were lifted off the ground and flew high into the bright, sunny sky. As I looked down, I could see our ranch with the green metal rooftop on our house. The horses were running around wildly with the concept of being free as they roamed on our twenty-seven acres. We then swooshed over the Sangre de Cristo mountaintops and began making our way to who-knew-where! I was in complete awe from the pure beauty these mountains signified. They were named by a Spanish explorer in the 1700s, who cried out "Blood of Christ" as the sun rose and gave a red tint to the snowy peaks, bringing them alive. Their magnificence and boldness always gave me such a sense of peace, as if they protected us from the rest of the world. And now, I got to see them in a whole new light, as I flew high above these wondrous beauties. I kept my eyes steadfast, looking out the window until we were finally past the splendor that had lain before me.

Then, realizing we were traveling far from home, I came to my senses and said in sheer panic, "Kyran, you have to tell me where we're going. I can't just take off in a helicopter and not know where I'm going or not tell my parents. They would *freak!*"

"I suppose I can tell you now, since there is no way for you to escape! We are going to Denver to visit a favorite store of mine. Since time was of the essence, I had to take our family helicopter so that we would make it back in time. Do you hate me for deceiving you?" he asked so harmlessly, showing off his dimples.

"Well, I guess I could forgive you, *this* time!" I said a bit snobbishly. "But please, no more surprises like this. Okay?"

"Whatever you say, my lady."

An odd feeling came over me when he said that. My dad is the only person who has ever called me that or treated me like a princess. Just then, he reached for my hand and held it tightly between both of his. They were extremely warm to the touch, and I felt a tingling sensation move through every cell of my body. I had to look out the window and pretend to be more interested in the sky so that he wouldn't see me blush. The usually three hour trip to Denver only took us about thirty minutes.

We landed at what seemed to be a private airport, where I noticed a black Mercedes parked nearby. The pilot quickly rushed us from the helicopter and escorted us to the posh vehicle that awaited our arrival. Kyran, being the perfect gentleman that he was, opened the passenger door for me and closed it after seeing I was comfortably settled in. He dashed around to the driver's seat and placed the already running engine into the drive position. Off we went, speeding down the runway as if we were to lift off. I could see that Kyran had an acquired taste for speed, and I instinctively and quickly put my seatbelt on. He only looked over at me and smiled, probably sensing I was a bit timid with this little adventure and the fact that he was going ninety miles per hour. He took my hand and held it up to his lips. He gave it a gentle kiss with his smooth, soft lips and said, "Don't worry, *amore.*"

I should have believed him. I had every reason to, so far. But something inside my head was saying, "Don't."

Don't what? I started to question myself.

Don't trust him, don't do this, don't fall for this amazingly perfect guy, or perhaps don't miss out on this mind-blowing, once-in-a-lifetime opportunity? Don't? I didn't quite understand myself, so I ignored the little voice, picked option "D," and allowed myself to fall deeply into this fantasy that I found myself in. I relaxed my head on the headrest of the fine leather seat that I was quite comfortable in and looked over at Kyran with a contented smile.

We had now entered the city limits, and I read a sign that said, "Downtown 10 miles." Our pace was now a little more in my comfort zone, and I patiently waited to see where we were going.

We pulled up to an attractive store that seemed to model all the latest and greatest in fashion in the front windows. Naturally we pulled up to the valet, and the young, blonde boy in a red coat quickly opened my door. He reached out for my hand, and as I placed it into his white glove, I looked into his strangely familiar blue eyes. "Don't," was what I thought I heard his cautionary voice say.

"Pardon me?" I asked to be sure.

"Yes," the young boy replied, looking into my eyes as if to say the answer was "yes."

"Nothing, never mind, I thought I heard you say something to me." I answered back shyly.

He shut the door and met up with Kyran at the front of the car. I noticed a harsh glance between the two, both with squinty eyes, completely focused on each other for just an instant, and then the valet attendant swiftly took the keys from him and ran around to the driver's seat to park the car.

"What was that about?" I asked.

"What?" he asked as if nothing had happened, and it was all my imagination. He placed his arm behind my lower back to help direct me into this stimulating in-vogue store that I had never seen before. We were quickly greeted by a dark-haired woman with perfectly applied makeup and snug clothes that outlined her perfectly proportioned body.

"This way, Mr. Dellamorte," she said as if this were some routine with him.

I looked over at him, and he simply said, "I told you this was my favorite store!"

We were escorted to the very back and up some stairs where we approached a closed door that said "Private" on it. We entered into a magnificent room with purple velvet drapes lining the walls from floor to ceiling. The lighting was dim, which brought out the flames from several candles that were scattered about, giving off a very pleasing scent. I noticed a podium, much like the preacher's at our church, resting at one end of the room. We were promptly seated at the other end of the room where several white, cozy chairs were purposely placed.

"Uh, Kyran," I said, and looked at him, feeling confused and out of place. "What are we doing? I thought I was here to help you find an outfit for your fancy dinner party."

"You are," he said softly, as if we were in a library. "You had better pay attention so that you can help me decide what we are going to wear."

And just then, just as I was about to argue the "we" point, music filled the air, and a bright light shone upon two models that came out of each side of the room. Apparently there were several doors hidden behind the draped walls, which was the perfect setting for a private fashion show. They walked from the front of the room to the back and did their little model turns right in front of us before disappearing once again behind the magical curtains. *Huh . . . so this is how rich people shop.*

Two more models came out and followed the same routine as their predecessors.

"Mark and Jean are wearing the perfect evening attire from D&G . . ." the consultant announced.

I tuned her out and had to ask Kyran what D&G was. He smiled and whispered, "That's the designer, *amore.* Haven't you ever heard of Dolce & Gabbana?"

"Yes . . . of course," I whispered back. I was pretty sure I had.

"Next you will be quite pleased with Prada's latest line in evening wear made for the modern man and woman."

"Kyran, they all seem to look very nice. I'm sure you could go with any of these and look completely amazing," I whispered. I honestly didn't know how much help I could be. After all, my big shopping sprees were usually at the local department stores.

"Surely there was something that sparked your interest," he replied.

"They are all very nice, really. But . . . "

Just then two models came out as the commentator said, "Amber and Jade are wearing a more classic look from Chanel . . . "

Yes, that was it. I loved them both. The outfits completely complemented each other. The female model was wearing a beautiful, elegant, classic black dress. As she turned around, I noticed a nice V-line on the back, complemented with a thin, shiny black belt. It looked so elegant.

Kyran must have seen my eyes widen with delight and said, "You love this. I can see it written all over your face." He gestured to the lady. "Madam, we'll take the Chanel."

"Kyran . . . no, I can't let you buy this for me. We're here to get *you* an outfit. Remember? This is way too much for me, and I probably would never have anywhere to wear it," I argued.

Before I knew it, the very helpful associate pulled me up from my seat with a tape measure in hand and began taking all of my measurements.

"Think of it as a late birthday present," Kyran said with a devilish grin across his face.

I looked at him and only sighed. How could I argue with such a beautiful face? He stared at me with an adoring smile as the lady instructed me to turn this way and that way, arms out, back straight, look forward, etc . . .

"Okay, Mr. Dellamorte, I am finished," the lady said to Kyran.

"Excuse me, love, as I take care of this," he said, and with that, he walked away with the sales associate.

While I was waiting, I walked back downstairs and browsed around the store. A beautiful black leather jacket caught my eye, so I sauntered over to the mannequin that seemed to proudly display this beauty. Oh, it felt so soft and smooth. I had never felt leather like that before. Out of curiosity I looked at the price tag.

"Oh my gosh!" I blurted out loud, caught off guard by the outrageous price.

I looked around, embarrassed by the spontaneous outburst. Thankfully no one else seemed to be in the store. *$950 for a jacket? They must be crazy,* I thought to myself.

I continued to look around some more and continued to be shocked by the overpriced items throughout the very proud store. I couldn't help but think how many hungry mouths could be fed with all the money that would be spent on these clothes. I guess the humanitarian came out in me, and feeling a bit perturbed, I walked to the front door to wait for Kyran. I noticed the valet attendant standing, waiting for a potential customer to arrive or depart. I watched him with curiosity, trying to figure out if I had possibly met him before. He really didn't look familiar, other than his noticeable eyes. Maybe I was just going crazy or something. How can someone's eyes look familiar? He turned toward me and saw that I was staring at him. Mortified at being caught, I quickly hid behind a mannequin, which probably only added to the humiliation. Just then, Kyran walked up.

"Ready, *amore?*" he asked.

I noticed he didn't have any bags in his hand.

"Yes, but where are the bags?" I asked, confused.

"They will arrive tomorrow. I'm hungry; how about you?"

Now that he mentioned it, I felt pretty hungry, too. We hadn't eaten anything since lunch, and I only ate half my lunch at that.

I looked at my watch and saw it was almost six o'clock. "Yes," I answered, "but we only have an hour before youth group starts. Can we just pick something up on the way back to the helicopter?"

He hesitated and appeared to be in deep thought as he escorted me out of the store and noticed the young attendant waiting for us. Kyran flicked the valet ticket at him to get our car. Upon picking the ticket up off the ground, the attendant quickly ran to the parking garage. I thought that was kinda rude of Kyran and considered saying something to him, but bit my tongue.

"Let's forget about the youth group and continue this wonderful evening we are having," he implored.

"No, Kyran, I promised my mother I would make it back in time."

"Do you always do what is expected of you? Don't you ever do what you want to do and what feels good or fun?"

I wasn't sure where this was coming from and replied, "Yes and yes. I do what is expected of me because that is what I choose to do. And, of course, I do things that are fun. I came here with you today, didn't I?"

"Yes, but don't you want this to continue? You go to youth group every Wednesday. What harm would it be to miss just this once? There is a wonderful, charming restaurant I want to take you to. I know you would love it."

The Mercedes pulled up in front of us, and before the valet attendant could come around to open my door, Kyran had it open and helped me in. He quickly closed the door as the attendant walked around to my side. They began exchanging words, and I could see anger on Kyran's face. He seemed to have his chest puffed out and arms cocked back as if he were showing this guy how tough he was. I was about to roll down my window to see what was going on when Kyran walked away and got into the car. We sped off. Kyran was furious at what just occurred, and I wasn't quite sure what to say.

A couple of minutes passed and he hadn't spoken either.

"Kyran, what was that all about?"

"Nothing that you should worry about, love. Let's just say there is a history of bad blood between us. Okay?"

"Oh, okay, sure."

With each passing minute that ticked away on the lit clock displayed on the dashboard, I began to worry about being late for church. I had to say something, though, so that he would know we needed to get back.

"I hate to be a party pooper here, but I really have to get back home. I can't . . . "

"Of course you can't, Renee. You can't just go out with me and have a good time and not worry about anything else, can you?" he snapped.

This was not a side of him that I had seen before, and I was taken aback by his response. I crossed my arms and sat silently as he continued to drive way too fast.

"Slow down, Kyran. You're scaring me."

I could see a tense anger in his face, and his usually magical green eyes seemed to have a fiery tint to them that almost glowed in the dusk of evening. My imagination must have somehow been deceiving my eyes since it was humanly impossible to have glowing eyes. He continued to race down the road, weaving in and out of the cars, passing them by as if they were at a standstill.

"Kyran, slow down!" I yelled again, frightened.

I could feel tears uncontrollably dripping down my face. He glanced over at me with a glare in his eyes as if he were in some other world or something.

"Please, Kyran," I said softly, almost in a whisper, "you're gonna hurt someone."

I then reached over with a shaking hand to touch his shoulder in an effort to grab his attention, not knowing how he might react to my attempt. His face quickly jerked to the right, and his narrow, gleaming eyes looked into mine. His trance-like state seemed to instantaneously shatter, and he began to slow down. The relentless apologizing quickly followed.

"Renee, I am so sorry. Really, I am. I didn't mean to frighten you. Forgive me, please," he begged.

"Just get me home," I stated firmly.

"Renee, plea . . . " he began to beg again.

"Just get me home," I demanded.

The helicopter ride back home wasn't quite as exhilarating as the ride up there had been. As Kyran drove me back to school where my car was still parked, not a single word between us was spoken. What started out as the most exciting adventure of my life ended with doubt and confusion. The joy had been stripped away by his dreadful actions caused by the anger he harbored. All I could think about as he was speeding down the road like a madman was that we were going to either kill someone or be killed. The thought of it all made me sick.

When we finally pulled up to my car, I got out and ran toward it, anxious to get away from the guy I thought was everything I had been wanting in a boyfriend. I nervously dug for my keys in my purse, but couldn't find them. Kyran walked up behind me.

"Please, don't be mad at me. You don't understand."

"No, I don't understand, and maybe I don't want to. I clearly see you are not the guy I thought you were. Just leave me alone." I started to cry again. "Where are they?" I continued looking for my keys.

"Please, you don't need to drive right now. You are clearly still upset."

"Oh, you're a fine one to talk," I retorted.

He chuckled with a slight grin and confessed, "You have a good point. I let my emotions get the best of me. Please don't act crazy like I did. Calm down for a minute, okay?"

Then he deviously held out my keys with one finger and said, "Promise me you'll calm down, or I won't give you these!"

I tried to snatch them from his hands, but he held on to them tightly, putting his hand behind his back.

"Uh-uh-uh," he said, moving the index finger of his free hand left to right, as if I were some child.

"Give them to me!" I said, standing my ground.

"Has anyone told you just how beautiful you are when you're mad?" he replied, still holding them behind his back as if this were a game.

After a few minutes of struggling and losing the battle to gain my keys, I gave up. I leaned back against my car and sarcastically stated, "Okay, I'm calm. Now can I have them?"

"I didn't hear 'please!'" he said smugly.

I rolled my eyes and complied, figuring it was the quickest way for me to be on my way to church.

"Please, can I have my keys?" I edgily asked while holding out my hand, giving into his request.

He immediately grabbed my suspended hand and intertwined his fingers with mine.

"Only if you can forgive me for acting so foolish. I didn't mean to hurt you in any way," he said so genuinely.

My eyes met up with his, the beautiful green eyes I was accustomed to, and I wondered how I could not forgive him. I mean, we all have our bad days, right? And who knows what that guy said or did to him. There really could be a long history with that guy that I didn't know about. I believed in second chances, so I had only one choice to make.

"Okay, Kyran, I forgive you. Now I really have to go, honestly. I don't want to be late."

He then put an arm on each side of me as if he had been planning that very move all along; with hands against my car he gently pressed his moist lips to mine. I stood absolutely still like a deer, aware of its potential hunter, and felt completely caught off guard by his bewildering, yet loving gesture. His lips felt so tender and smooth. As our mouths slightly parted, I inhaled his warm, minty breath, which he released simultaneously. I could feel my heart pounding through my chest. And though the intimate moment lasted a mere few seconds, I knew in that brief period that this little girl was starting to become a woman. An unexpected feeling of being broken came to me, reminiscent of a minuscule crack in fine china, hardly noticeable to the eye, but an awareness and sign of being damaged. I was consumed with mixed emotions and unsure of how to act or what to say. Kyran released my anxiety by breaking the silence first.

"Baciato da un santo," he whispered into my ear. "See you tomorrow, *la mia amore,"* and opened my door for me to get in, carefully placing my keys into my hands.

"Uh, Kyran," I said softly in my trance-like state. "May I ask what you just said to me?"

With a contented smile he said, "Kissed by a saint." Then he gently closed my door and walked away.

SIX

Planned Coincidence

The next day at school began as any other. The only thing that seemed different, however, was the knot of nerves that had found a resting place in the pit of my stomach. As I waited for Jamie to show up, I considered what I was going to say to her. Was I going to tell her that I was now the worst friend ever for falling for the same guy she so clearly liked? We had never faced such a dilemma before because of my previous lack of interest in boys. I looked at my watch, and it was almost time for the bell to ring. *Hmmm . . . I wonder what her holdup is today,* I thought, which was quickly followed by another. *I wonder where Kyran is . . . .*

I decided to call her cell phone to see if she was running late. After three rings I heard a weak voice on the other end.

"Hello."

"Jamie, is that you?" I barely recognized her voice.

"Hey, Ren," she whispered. "What's up?"

"I was just calling to see if you were going to be at school today. From the sound of it, I can take a pretty good guess."

"I've got a really bad case of the flu. Looks like I'll be in bed through the weekend. I gotta go. Talk with you later." And with that, she hung up the phone.

I felt terrible. Here she was, sounding like she was dying, and I had been having such a great time with Kyran. I even had my very first kiss, a moment I thought she would be the first to hear about. The recent memory came flooding to my head, and I couldn't help but get goose bumps all over my arms. "Kissed by a saint," he said. *I wonder what he meant by that* . . . my thought was interrupted by the school bell.

I headed toward class, and coming my way to meet me was Kyran. He was smiling at me with the same excitement to see me, as I was to see him. "Morning, *amore*," he said as he curled his arm around my shoulder. I was a bit mortified by this public display of affection. Things seemed to be moving so quickly with him, and my comfort zone hadn't quite caught up. Still, I let this natural flow of affection continue.

We walked into class, and I could feel the eyes of every single person in there right on us. We took our seats, and Miss Adamma began her lesson. I tried my hardest to concentrate on what she was saying, but found myself only thinking of last night's events, good and bad. Something seemed to still prick me when I recalled Kyran's sudden burst of anger and the way he handled himself. *We all have our moments, though, and I guess that was just his. I can't judge him by that one incident; it wouldn't be fair.*

The bell rang, and class was dismissed.

"Renee, may I speak with you for a moment?" Miss Adamma asked.

"Sure, Miss Adamma," I said as I grabbed my books and headed toward her desk. I could see Kyran waiting for me by the front door.

She looked right at him and said, "I would like to speak with Renee privately, please." Kyran walked out, and she waited until the door was shut before speaking.

"Something wrong?" I asked first.

"I was going to ask you the same thing. I noticed a slight change in you since last week. Is it a coincidence that that is the same time Kyran arrived at our school?"

I didn't say anything in return. I wasn't sure what to say, to be honest.

"Renee, you are my star student and very special at that. I knew from the moment I met you that you have been touched by God. You have many good works to do here. Don't get distracted by silly little boys. Okay?"

"I won't, Miss Adamma. Thanks for your concern."

"I know these days in America we are not politically correct in speaking of God in school, but I want you to know I will be praying for you, child."

"Thanks, I appreciate it."

I headed toward the door, unsure of what brought this on, but grateful at the same time to have her as my teacher and now, my ally.

I walked out the door, and Kyran was leaning up against the wall, waiting for me, arms folded as if he was agitated by something.

"What was that about?" he quickly asked.

"Nothing. She just noticed I wasn't myself and wanted to make sure I was okay."

I could see his expression change, but couldn't quite pinpoint why it did. He then put his arm around my shoulder again and proceeded to walk me to my next class.

"See you at lunch?" he asked.

"Of course," I replied, elated by his request.

The next two classes were hard to get through. I had to force myself to listen and pay attention to the teachers. *Remember your priorities*, I thought to myself. I was only .2 ahead on my GPA from Greg Saddler to get the valedictorian honor, and I wasn't about to put my guard down. *I've worked way too hard.*

The bell I had been waiting for finally came, and I rushed out of class to get to my locker. Walking around the corner and seeing Kyran leaning up against it only added to my excitement. He looked so handsome and captivating with his hands inside his jean pockets and a crooked smile, with those cute dimples planted on his face.

"I thought you'd never get here," he said.

I only smiled in return and put my books away, then grabbed my lunch.

"What's on the menu?" he asked as we walked toward the lunchroom, again with his arm around my shoulder. I was beginning to feel more comfortable with this picture.

"The usual—ham and cheese, chips, and an apple," I replied.

"Ahh! The apple. I love apples," he said as he reached in my bag and grabbed it, throwing it up in the air like a ball. "They are so temptingly sweet and hard to resist." He took a bite out of it.

"Hey! That was part of *my* lunch!" He tried to offer it back to me, but I pushed his hand away. I grinned at him and said, "It's yours now. So, what's on your menu? You owe me!"

"I'm sure the cafeteria will have the perfect array of steak, seafood, and caviar, a delicacy I love to eat," he teased.

"You're such a snob," I laughed. "Go get your food, and I'll meet you at the table."

As I was sitting and waiting for Kyran to join me, Beth came up with her little clan. They were all standing uniformly behind her.

"So, we've all noticed that you seem to be getting tight with Kyran. What's that all about?"

"Yeah, what's that about?" Heather repeated.

"We're good friends, that's all," I replied. As if I even needed to answer them.

"You two seem to be pretty affectionate to be just friends," she said incredulously. "Wouldn't you say, girls?" Of course they all agreed with her by shaking their puppet heads up and down, and saying their own various comments in an effort to validate their vicious leader's accusation.

I've always been one to be the peacemaker and never cause any trouble, but something came over me, and I found my blood beginning to boil. I stood up in order to raise myself to their level. "I don't think my personal life is any of your business. Now if you don't mind, I'd like to eat my lunch in peace, so please leave!" I snapped back in the firmest voice I had.

Surprised at my irritated response, Beth said, "Whatever, Renee. We all know deep down inside you're really not the little angel you pretend to be." With that being said, they walked away as I had requested. I couldn't believe it actually worked.

I could see them heading in the direction of Kyran, who was by this time carrying his lunch tray over to meet me at the table. Beth placed her hand around his neck and whispered something into his ear, glanced back at me, and walked away from him.

He came and sat down next to me and said, "What did you do to Beth to make her so mad?"

"Nothing really. I just told her to mind her own business, that's all."

I could hear a slight laughter underneath his breath as he shook his head and began picking at his food, not really enthused about eating it. I guess he found me to be funny for sticking up to her like that. I thought I was more daring than funny.

"So, what did she say to you?" I couldn't help but ask. My curiosity was beginning to kill me.

"Nothing for you to worry about, *amore*. Now let's talk about something more interesting, like the party at my house on Friday. I happen to know that Jamie won't be playing at the game, so now you have no excuse."

He had a good point, but bringing up Jamie's name brought back the guilty feeling all over again.

"I don't know, Kyran. I really have to get in some extra practices before my dance performance next month."

"You do as you feel necessary, but I want to leave you with

this," he said confidently. "If you will be my guest, I promise you an amazing evening you will never forget."

His tantalizing voice and beautiful accent made it even harder to resist, but it would be the right thing to do. *Dang it . . . if only I could tell Jamie how I'm falling for Kyran, too. I can't, though. I have to end this before it goes any further. He just makes it so hard to refuse him.*

"I'm sure I would have a great time, but I'm still gonna have to say no. Sorry," I said. I was surprised when he didn't argue or try again to persuade me to turn my decision the other way. He just looked at me and smiled.

"Whatever you say, love," he said, and left it at that.

When I got home from school, I noticed my mom's van wasn't in its usual place. *I wonder where she is?* I walked in the front door and went to the kitchen for a snack. I had a ton of homework to do before dance class. I was about to open the fridge door when I noticed a note from my mother:

Hey Sweetheart,

I ran out to look for a dress to wear to a party we were invited to tomorrow night by your father's potential new client. It's supposed to be a big, fancy ordeal, and your dad wanted me to look extra nice. See you after your dance class. Oh, a big package came for you today. I put it on your bed. I'm anxious to hear what that's all about, and I want every detail!

Love you, Mom

I quickly ran upstairs to my room and saw a huge pink box with a beautiful, hot pink satin ribbon wrapped perfectly around it with a note attached:

Renee,

Here is your late birthday present and an extra surprise for you. Think of it as another attempt to seek your forgiveness for my inexcusable behavior last night.

Love, Kyran

I opened up the box, and there was the $950 leather jacket I had both admired and felt disgusted with at the same time. I couldn't believe it, though, so I lifted it to my nose to smell the new, fine leather scent it released to make sure I wasn't just imagining this incredible gift. I had to admit it was fashionably delicious. I quickly put it on and stood in front of the mirror, admiring the perfect fit and the way it instantly turned my simple-girl look into that of a stylish icon. I found myself jumping up and down a few times with excitement. Just as I began to spin around and pose like I had seen the models do the night before, the phone rang.

"Hello?" I said, halfway out of breath.

"Do you like your surprise?" a thick Italian voice said on the other end.

"Oh my gosh, Kyran . . . yes, I'm stunned. You really shouldn't have, though. I already told you that I forgave you."

"Yes, well, my guilty conscience got the best of me, and I wanted to spoil my girl a little."

Did he really just call me his girl? I wasn't quite sure if I was ready for that title.

"How did you know I admired this jacket?" I questioned him.

"Let's just say a little birdie saw you looking at it."

"You realize this one jacket could feed twenty families in Africa, don't you?"

I had been planning to go on a mission trip with my church over the summer to a small village in Africa, and I couldn't help but think of them as I indulged myself with this beautiful piece of fashion.

"Yes, but what good is it to have lots of money if I can't make others happy with it? It's nice of you to think of the poor people in Africa, but you need to spoil yourself once in a while, too. You deserve it."

I guess he was right in a way. Not the deserving part, but the spoiling ourselves now and again.

"Did you try the dress on?" he asked.

"Not yet. I haven't had a chance."

"Don't wait too long. You need to make sure it fits for tomorrow night. I'm anxious to meet your parents."

That's when it all clicked. My mom's note saying they were invited to a fancy dinner party, and Kyran not pressuring me at lunch today to go with him.

"You little sneak!"

He laughed and said, "It happened to be coincidence, that's all."

"So your dad is my dad's new client he's been all worked up about?"

"Yes, well, we're always looking for a good lawyer to oversee our estate, and we heard your father was the best in town."

"I still can't help but wonder if you put your dad up to this," I accused.

"Perhaps it was just destiny. Have you thought of it that way?"

I guess I hadn't thought of it like that.

"Well, whatever you say. I still think you set this whole thing up just to get me to come over. I suppose I should just say thanks, and I'm looking forward to an enchanting evening as your special guest." I had finally succumbed to his master plan.

SEVEN

Unforeseen Encounter

I looked in the mirror, admiring the perfectly fitted classic black dress I was wearing, even giving it a twirl or two. I paid special attention to my hair and makeup, making sure I looked equal to Kyran's perfect appearance. I heard a honking horn outside in the driveway, so I grabbed my little black purse and quickly ran down the stairs and out the front door. The back door of a long, stretch limo was open, awaiting my entrance into its spacious and luxurious interior. I entered the vacant limo as gracefully as I could, acting the part of Cinderella being whisked away by her pumpkin carriage.

The door shut behind me, but I couldn't recall seeing anyone on the other side of it. The limo began moving and I glanced out the window, admiring the lovely home my parents had worked so hard to build for our little family. As the distance began to fade this dear sight from my eyes, I felt excited about the evening to come. Still a little nervous, I pulled my mirror from my purse for one more check. I reapplied some lip gloss and felt confident with my appearance.

The black tinted window separating me from the front seat prevented me from seeing the driver. I felt awkward sitting in this enormous car with no one to talk to or share the moment with. I scooted forward and tapped my carefully painted finger on the window, hoping to have a little company for the ride to the party. *Tap, tap, tap.* I tried to gain the attention of the driver, but got no response. I tapped a little harder, and the window began slowly descending. Excited for the future conversation with this complete stranger, I poked my head forward into the now open space.

Panic struck me when I clearly saw that there wasn't anybody driving the moving car. I was deafened by the fear-stricken screams bursting from my own mouth. I could faintly hear a muffled laugh within the walls of the car, but couldn't tell where it was coming from. I leaped toward the side door to try and open it, but it was locked. I tried with all of my might to unlock the door, but it wouldn't budge. The laugh was getting obnoxiously louder, and I could feel a heavy darkness begin to creep up my body, starting at the bottom of my feet. I started kicking my legs and screaming the words, "Leave me alone. Go away!" I moved around the traveling vehicle, trying to separate myself from the darkness that was trying to overcome me. With nowhere to go and nowhere to hide, I fell to my knees, tears gushing down my rosy cheeks. I began to pray with complete desperation as the darkness encircled me.

"Lord, help me. I am weak, but You are strong."

I could hear the screeching sound of the tires as hard pressure was applied to the brakes. The car came to a complete halt, forcing my body forward. The doors were furiously opened, completely taking them off their hinges and sweeping them away, as if the vehicle had been caught in a tornado. The bright light that shone through blinded my eyes, a sight I had seen once before, and the darkness released me from its hold. Just then, as if watching a movie in slow motion, this revelation of something remarkable began fading away. I somehow became conscious of the dream I was having and taking part in. I began to fight the process of awakening, hoping to stay in the dream a while longer. I had to know more about this light that entered my nightmare once again.

"I am no longer afraid," I found my subconscious mind telling myself, and the dream was allowed to continue. The vision was clear again, and the brightness continued to shine into the vehicle as I sat, waiting, somehow unafraid of what was to come. An urge to speak came over me, and I could hear myself say, "Who are you?"

The light began to transform into a more defined shape, one that was more recognizable.

"Don't be afraid," said the light.

And as clearly as if he had commanded me to him, I sensed him drawing me out of the limo, closer to his presence. Still a bit blinded, but able to outline a shape, I could visualize his statuesque build. He had amazing outstretched wings that were held still, yet they looked so bold, full of strength and power.

"I'm not afraid," I said once again, meaning it wholeheartedly. I felt such great comfort in his presence. "I'm Renee," I said in my stupor, almost regretting the silly introduction.

With a slight laughter in his sturdy voice he simply said, "Yes . . . it's a pleasure to meet you. I am Liam."

While I wasn't able to see distinct features in his face, I felt as if I had always known him.

"You have a very strong soul, Renee. It is because of this that your subconscious mind is able to see me or hear me. Of course, this is something I have known since the day you were born, but we'll save that story for another day. It is almost time for you to go."

"No!" I exclaimed. "I want to stay with you."

"I am always with you, Renee. I am your assigned protector," he stated.

"Did you save me tonight? What was happening to me?" I asked, cringing at the memory of the dark shadow.

"That is for you to figure out on your own," he answered, but not really answering me. "It is time for you to go."

"Wait! Will I remember you? Will you come and see me again?" I asked, frightened to lose him.

"I hope so."

And with that, I awoke in my bed to the sound of my alarm.

EIGHT

Confession Time

The next day couldn't go quickly enough. I was so excited about my date with Kyran and getting all dressed up in that beautiful dress he had bought me. With Jamie's absence from school, it made it easier for Kyran and me to hang out in between classes and at lunch, which helped the time fly by. I knew I would eventually have to face her, though, and reveal this new relationship I had developed but until then, I wanted to just enjoy the moments we were having. The last bell of the day finally rang and Kyran and I walked out to our cars, which we had parked next to each other early that morning.

"I can't wait to see you tonight," he said in my ear as he gave me a tight squeeze.

"I'm a little nervous," I confessed.

"What are you nervous about, *amore?*"

"Lots of things. For one, meeting your parents."

"Shouldn't I have the same concern then?"

"True, but you're probably used to this sort of thing," I replied.

"Trust me, it never gets any easier!" he chuckled. "Now don't worry your pretty little head off. I'll be at your house to pick you up at six thirty tonight."

"I was just gonna ride with my parents," I said innocently.

He shook his head a bit and said, "You're *my* date, Renee. I will see you tonight."

I smiled at him, and he gave me a small kiss on the cheek before walking away. I had to pinch myself to make sure I wasn't dreaming.

I rushed home so that I would have plenty of time to get ready for the amazing evening to come. My mother was sitting at the kitchen counter, a set of clear and pink polish in front of her, and she was blowing on her nails when I walked in.

"I see you got a head start for the party tonight," I said as I poured myself a glass of milk.

"Yeah, I figured since I didn't have to cook dinner tonight, I could spend a little extra time pampering myself."

"That's good, Mom. You deserve it. You always work so hard around here or helping others. You have to take time to spoil yourself now and again." Wow, Kyran was really starting to rub off on me.

"Is that what you think, huh? The Lord has blessed us in more ways than we could ever imagine or keep up with. I don't think I 'deserve' to be spoiled, sweetie. I just want to look nice; that's all."

She always had a way to keep me grounded and on track. I walked over to her, gave her a kiss on the cheek and said, "I love you, Mom. I'll be upstairs taking a nice, hot bath. I want to look nice too, ya know!" I began to walk away.

"Wait a minute, young lady. I still haven't heard the juicy details of who sent you a gift and what it was. Sit," she commanded as she pulled out the stool next to her.

"Okay, but I gotta hurry. I want to make sure I look perfect for tonight."

"Honey, what's the big deal? It's just a dinner party with some of dad's clients. I thought you would dread having to go."

"Well, there's a little more to it than meets the eye," I finally admitted. "Do you remember the new kid that I've been hanging out with at the coffee shop and the one I went shopping with?"

"Kyran, wasn't it?"

"Yes, that's him. Well, coincidently, he is daddy's new client's . . . "

"Mr. Dellamorte," my mother inserted.

"Yes, he is Mr. Dellamorte's son. When we went shopping on Wednesday, it was to help him look for an outfit for this party tonight, and he asked if I would be his special guest. At first I said no, because I was going to Jamie's basketball game. But when she got sick, and when you and Daddy were also invited, I finally agreed to be his date."

"You what? I must say this is an unexpected surprise. I'm a little hurt that you didn't ask us for permission first or even mention that you were supposed to be his date," she said disappointedly.

"I'm sorry, Mom. I really didn't agree to go until I found out you and Daddy were gonna be there."

"I can be understanding of where you're coming from this time, but let's just come to our own little agreement right now. Before you consent to any sort of date in the future, you seek our permission first. Okay?"

"Yes, ma'am," I said happily.

"So tell me about this mysterious pink box that arrived yesterday."

I cleared my throat a bit, almost afraid to tell her of the extravagant gifts Kyran sent me.

"When Kyran and I went shopping in Denver . . . " I tried to say it as quickly and casually as possible to not stir the pot any more, but it was too late.

"You what?" she asked, although she knew the answer. "You went shopping in Denver? How on earth did you go all the way there and back in time to make it to youth group?"

I had to clear my throat again, "Well, we kind of took his family helicopter."

"You what?!" She started to sound like a broken record with each bit of news, the next exclamation being louder than the one before.

"Renee Brianne Lewis!" Uh-oh . . . she used the full name. This wasn't good.

"What in the world were you thinking, going so far away in a helicopter with a boy your father and I have never met? Something terrible could have happened to you, and we wouldn't have known where you were."

I could see the hurt and anger she felt by the expression in her face and the wetness of her eyes. I had never been so irresponsible before and felt terrible that I let her down.

"It just all happened so quickly. I had no idea that he was taking me shopping in Denver until he ushered me into the helicopter."

"You should have called us anyway," she argued.

"I know, Mom. You're right. I just got so caught up in the moment that it slipped my mind."

"It seems that twice now this Kyran fellow has caused you to act irresponsibly. I'm not so sure I want you hanging around this guy."

"Don't say that, Mom! He's really an amazing guy. Just give him a chance. None of this was his fault; it was all mine. I promise I'll be more responsible in the future."

She looked at me, somewhat guarded, not really sure what to do or say next. I've always been a very trustworthy, dependable, and responsible person, so I'm sure she was weighing that factor into her decision.

Finally, after what seemed to be an eternity of silence, she said, "I'll allow you to be his guest this evening. But I will let you know after meeting him if this will continue. Do you understand?" she said firmly.

"I understand. Thank you so much, Mom!" I said, wrapping my arms around her neck. "You're gonna love him, just wait and see!"

"Your father and I will be the judge of that," she replied.

I began to walk off again when I heard, "Sweetie, I still haven't heard what was in that box."

Oh, no. Here we go again.

"Well, when I helped Kyran pick out his outfit, he sort of bought a dress for me, too. But it was a late birthday gift, so I couldn't refuse his offer," I quickly disclosed, before she had any objection to the gift.

Releasing a deep sigh, she said to my surprise, "You better hurry up and go get ready then. I suppose he'll be picking you up?"

"Yes, ma'am."

"Your father and I will be leaving a little before you. He said he had some things to discuss with Mr. Dellamorte before dinner. I will look forward to meeting you and Kyran at the party then."

"Sounds good, Mom. I love you!" and with that I quickly ran upstairs to get ready, thankful I didn't have to go into any details about the leather jacket.

NINE

Fish Out of Water

As I nervously waited for the ringing sound of the doorbell, I looked at myself in the mirror yet again, to make sure that I was perfect from head to toe. I noticed that the girl staring back at me was not the same girl from even a week ago. In fact, her appearance, my appearance, had changed, and I barely recognized who I was. I felt like I was looking at a young woman trying to sell a product in the prom edition of *Seventeen Magazine*. Honestly, I never thought that this "vanilla" girl could even compare to any of those models. Not that I think I'm this beautiful goddess or anything like that, just more surprised by how this fancy dress and some extra makeup on my face made me look so mature and sophisticated. I smiled to myself, pleased by the thought that perhaps I *was* finally emerging into a woman. Still enamored by my change, I had to give my beautiful dress one last twirl before pinching myself to make sure I wasn't dreaming.

"Ouch!"

I guess this really was happening to me. It just all seemed to be happening so fast with the unexpected arrival of Kyran. *I can't believe I'm going to his house as his date! Who knew?*

I peeked outside from behind the curtains to see if he was coming up the road, anxious for our date to begin. I could see the dust trailing behind the fancy black car that was coming up our gravel road, so I grabbed my little black purse, complete with breath mints, lipstick, and cell phone, then headed downstairs. I waited by the front door. *Weird . . . this feels like a déjà vu moment,* I thought to myself.

Before my mind could explore this peculiar feeling, the doorbell rang. I waited for just a minute, not wanting to look too anxious, and then opened the door. I couldn't see Kyran's face, the result of a huge bouquet of white long-stemmed roses in front of him. There had to have been at least two dozen, which let off an amazing aroma that brought a huge smile to my face.

The previously hidden Italian, finely dressed in his Chanel suit, poked his head around the beautiful flowers and said, "Some lovely white roses for my lovely lady."

"Oh my gosh, Kyran, these are so amazing! Come in so we can put them in some water."

We walked into the kitchen where I grabbed a vase from underneath the kitchen sink. Mom always kept a couple there for the times Dad would surprise her with flowers, usually a monthly occurrence. And by the loving, surprised look on her face every time, she never grew tired of it; twenty-seven years together, and they were still so much in love.

I filled the crystal vase with some water and carefully arranged the flowers in place.

"You know, I once read somewhere that white roses are a symbol of purity, innocence, and charm."

"Yes, I know," Kyran agreed.

"Well, did you know it has a secondary meaning?"

"No, please indulge me," he replied. I never seemed to tire of his smooth accent.

"Apparently they could also signify secrecy and silence. So, Mr. Dellamorte . . . keeping any secrets that I should know about?" I asked with my flirtatious voice, eyes still focused on the task at hand.

With a slight chuckle, he replied, "You are so very clever, aren't you, *amore?* Well, I suppose only time will tell, won't it?" He came closer to me. I could feel his fresh breath slightly brush my hair before he spoke softly into my ear. "Did you know they are also a symbol of young love and unity? Perhaps another option for your inquisitive mind to ponder."

I could feel the warmth in my cheeks as they instantly blushed. "Shall we go," I quickly asserted, afraid he might try to lay another one on me while I was caught off guard.

"After you," he replied, allowing me to step in front of him.

I lead him to the entry closet so I could grab my long, black coat. Being the perfect gentleman, he assisted me in putting it on, then twirled me around to face him, and began to button it up before I could start the process myself.

"I'm not a child, you know," I said with a half-smile, still not used to having so much attention with even some of the smallest details, "but thank you anyway." A girl could get used to this.

I could sense he wanted to kiss me, and before he could completely pucker up, I placed my index finger on his moist lips and said, "Kyran, I'm not ready for that yet. Okay?" I was afraid this motion of rejection would hurt his feelings, but he responded very well.

"Whatever you want, *amore.*"

We walked out to the limo where the driver was awaiting our arrival. A vehicle of this stature warranted a graceful entrance, so Kyran took my hand as I gently placed myself into this monstrosity of a car. I was thankful for the dance lessons all these years, leaving the clumsy girl far behind. The driver closed our door, and we began our journey down the long, rocky drive. I looked back at our house, admiring all it meant to me. Strangely, another *déjà vu* moment came. I felt as if I had done this all once before, but that was impossible.

Kyran grabbed my hand, interlacing his fingers with mine. "I hope to make this night very special for you, Renee," he said as he looked into my eyes, seemingly genuine.

"It already is. What more could a girl ask for?" I replied.

"Funny you should ask," he said.

"Why do you say that? What are you up to now?" I stated curiously.

"You look stunning tonight, but you seem to have something missing."

Oh no! What did I forget? I did so many checks in the mirror I thought I had it all covered. My hand instinctively went to my ear to make sure I remembered to put on my earrings. *Nope, they're there.* I smiled as I remembered the day my father gave me my first real diamond studs for my fifteenth birthday. I made sure to wear them only on very special occasions.

"What am I missing?" I asked, a bit confused.

Kyran pulled out a long, rectangular, purple velvet box. As he opened it, he said, "I believe this will accompany your beautiful smile perfectly."

"Ahhhhh!" I gasped out loud, shocked at what my eyes were seeing. "Kyran, I'm stunned! I don't know what to say."

"Say, 'Thank you, I love it, Kyran,'" he replied.

"Of course! I absolutely love it. It's just . . . just, too much."

He began taking the sapphire and diamond oval pendant out of the box. I instinctively turned and pulled my hair away from my neck so that he could place the stunning necklace around it. My heart was pounding. I was nervous for some reason, perhaps feeling a little guilty for accepting such an expensive gift, and not having anything to give in return.

"Nothing is too much for my girl," he replied.

"But you've already bought me this amazing dress and the gorgeous flowers. I'm just overwhelmed, I guess."

"Just relax, *amore*. I get so much pleasure from pampering you."

Our hands reconnected, and I laid my head on his strong, broad shoulder. The soothing notes from the classical music that filled the car helped me relax for the rest of the ride. I still felt like I was taking part in some amazing dream. *I must be the luckiest girl in the world right now.*

The limo pulled in front of the biggest house that I had ever seen in my life. Engrossed with Kyran on the way there, I didn't pay much attention to how we arrived at this American palace. I had no idea it even existed. I looked around and noticed it was neatly tucked away behind a forest of monstrous trees, allowing its owners complete privacy from the outside world.

The chauffeur pulled the limo around the circular driveway and stopped in front of a massive set of stairs leading up to the front door. The very diligent driver quickly opened our door. I couldn't help but feel like a real princess arriving at the grand ball as Kyran escorted me up the stairs, which were complete with a red carpet that stretched from the very top to the bottom. I took each step carefully as these high heels and a mountain of stairs were the perfect recipe for a tumble back down. Just prior to approaching the oversized, heavy door, a distinguished gentleman opened it for us.

As he stood there, stationary, he offered a greeting. "Good evening, Mr. Dellamorte and Miss Lewis. May I take your coat, please?"

Kyran helped me take mine off and gave it to the attentive man.

"Your parents are expecting you in the Sunset Room, sir."

We walked through the marble-floored foyer in between two grand staircases lined with hand-forged iron railings, which ascended to the second story. I looked around, completely astounded by the beautiful, museum-like house that Kyran lived in. I felt timid and uncomfortable as I took in the array of expensive paintings, furniture, drapes that reached from ceiling to floor, and artifacts that looked to be hundreds of years old.

"What are you so nervous about, love?" Kyran asked.

"Who, me, nervous? What gives you that impression?" I quickly responded, knowing he was right.

"I can feel the pulse of your heart beating uncontrollably through your sweaty palms. Relax, you're with me. Everything will be wonderful; I promise."

Embarrassed by the uncontrollable body fluid that was now pouring out of my hands, I snatched my hand away from his.

He stopped me from taking my next step and turned me toward him. I looked at his handsome face and felt reassured by his sincere expression.

"Take a deep breath for me," he requested.

I complied with his request, thankful for the breath mint I had inserted into my mouth before we got out of the limo.

He then gave me a tender hug before entwining his arm with mine as we entered the room. I immediately saw my mother among a group of ladies, looking bored by the conversation. I could always tell when she had her fake, polite smile on. She didn't break it out very often, so I was curious as to who those ladies were and what they were saying. Kyran directed me in a different direction, though, so my curiosity would have to wait a bit.

We headed toward another crowd of nicely dressed men and women, all surrounding the host and hostess of this fanciful gathering. I knew immediately they were Kyran's parents as their attractiveness equally matched his.

"Ah, my son has arrived, and accompanied by such a lovely young lady," the distinguished man said out loud. He extended his arms, waiting to affectionately greet his son.

"Father, this is the girl I have spoken to you about. This is Renee."

"Yes, Renee. My son speaks so fondly of you. I can see why."

He then proceeded to give me a bear hug with a husky laugh in his voice as if our attendance completed his night.

"And this is my mother, Richelle." Kyran introduced her with such poise.

I could understand why, too. She was the epitome of grace and beauty. She was much more reserved than Mr. Dellamorte, but at the same time had a way of drawing one to her.

I extended my hand forward to shake hers and said, "It's so nice to meet you, Mrs. Dellamorte. You have such a lovely home."

She took the tips of my fingers with hers and gave one gentle shake, yet held onto them firmly. She seemed very cautious, checking me over, and I wasn't quite sure why. After a few seconds, she spoke with a thick, sultry accent.

"Renee, the pleasure is all mine, I assure you."

"Mamma, if you don't mind, I'm going to take Renee to the balcony," Kyran interjected.

"Of course not; I look forward to seeing you again at dinner," she said to me.

"Yes, ma'am" was all I could think of to say.

Her demeanor was so strong, revealing an aura of both elegance and power, one not to be contended with on any given day.

The original conversation seemed to pick back up as we walked away toward some beautiful French doors. When Kyran pushed them open, the cool, crisp breeze brushed my face, giving it a slight tingle. For being 40 degrees outside, it felt surprisingly comfortable. Even so, there was a stack of cozy, plush throws on a nearby table, which Kyran grabbed and wrapped around us. We walked to the edge of the balcony, embracing each other's waists, and looked out at the panoramic view.

"This is stunning!" I commented.

He looked at his watch and said, "Wait a few more minutes."

"Okay," I said slowly, unsure of what he had up his sleeve now.

I could feel heat rising from the floor. I thought, *Either my blood is rising with excitement, making my toes feel toasty, or there really is heat coming from the floor.* The curious girl from within forced me to bend down and touch the ground. Sure enough, it was hot.

"We had heated decks installed on all of the balconies. Helps keep the snow and ice from forming when we want to come out here and enjoy the fresh air," Kyran asserted.

"Nice touch," was all this common girl could think of to say.

With a crooked smile and a quick nod of his head, he agreed.

"So, has it been a few minutes yet?" I asked impatiently, anxious to see what he had in store.

He squeezed me closer to him, holding the soft blanket tight, keeping us together like a rolled burrito. "Just look past the tree tops toward that mountaintop," he said, and pointed.

It only took my being still for a few seconds to see what was to come. It was the most amazing sunset I had ever witnessed. I marveled at this spectacular beauty that stimulated my eyes with vibrant colors, descending upon the white snow tops of the mountains in fire-red and orange, bringing these sleeping giants to life as if blood were running through their massive veins. I stood quiet, careful not to move, too afraid that I might interrupt this display of God's glorious work. My thoughts drifted away as I imagined what awaits us in Heaven. I visualized a place filled with indescribable beauty and where pain wasn't in the vocabulary because it simply didn't exist. It only took minutes for the life-giving sun to completely disappear behind the mountains, going on to its next job at the other end of the world, but still reminding us of its presence by illuminating the moon that was soon to follow. It was one of those moments in time that you wish you could freeze or rewind over and over. Completely entranced by the experience, I whispered to Kyran, "That was so incredible. Thank you for sharing it with me."

However, he stood silent, seemingly lost in his own thoughts or memories. I sensed he never wanted to let go of this moment, either. It was as if he was trying to hang onto something that had been taken from him, and if he could just reach out and touch it one more time, life could move on. The corners of his lips drooped, and anguish covered his face through his slanted eyes and the wrinkles in his forehead, but no tears were shed. No, instead, he held them in, trying to contain the pain inside. I rubbed his back and could sense his hurt. I remained silent, giving him his time, until he was ready to release whatever it was that grabbed hold of him. *What on earth could have ever done this?* I wondered.

After a few minutes, he finally looked into my eyes. "I'm sorry, I don't know what came over me. It was quite unexpected." He then cleared his throat and said, "Thank you for sharing the beautiful sunset with me. Your presence seemed to magnify its splendor, reminding me of something I lost long ago."

"You're welcome. And, hey, for what it's worth, I'm glad you were able to open up to me. I believe in being yourself, and you just showed a different side to who you are; that's all."

He cleared his throat again, finishing off the last of the lump there, and attempted to lighten the mood by saying, "Yes, well, don't ever speak of this to anyone; my manhood would be at stake if the guys ever found out!"

We both laughed and gave each other a nice hug.

"This has always been my favorite part of the house because of its perfect location. That is why I named the room off this balcony the Sunset Room," he admitted.

For once, Kyran looked so vulnerable to me. This was the side I completely loved seeing in him.

"Shall we go back into the house before we forget why we are here?" he asked.

"Wait a minute," I said, "lean up against the balcony and pose for a picture."

He complied with my request and posed like a pro, giving a bit of a sultry look.

"No! Give me a big smile," I said with one squinted eye and hands shaped like a square in midair. When the corners of his mouth appeared to reach from ear to ear, my right index finger pretended to click a picture before I tucked the invisible camera into my invisible pocket.

Kyran looked at me as if I had just completely lost my mind and said, "What was that about? I thought you were going to take my picture."

"And I did! I know, it seems a little crazy, but my mother has always told me that when I find myself feeling exceptionally happy to take a mental picture of it to look back on at times when I'm not so happy. You gave me something that I never want to forget!" I said genuinely.

I thought my frankness would please him, but I almost felt that it made him uncomfortable instead.

"Let's go in, shall we?" was all he had to say in return.

All the guests were called into the grandiose dining room where the enormous dinner table was beautifully set with several pieces of fine china, outlined with gold and neatly stacked upon each other. There were more bowls, plates, and utensils than I knew what to do with. Never mind the teacup resting upside down on its saucer and the three various shaped crystal glasses, patiently waiting for their time to perform.

Kyran pulled my chair out, which was next to his father and directly across from his mother. I looked around for my own parents, who were placed at the opposite end of the long table.

Once everyone was seated, Mr. Dellamorte firmly clapped his hands twice, which signaled the group of waiters and waitresses to enter the room with silver bowls and platters. They all had an assigned place they were to go to, and with no emotion on their faces, they uniformly took their designated marks.

Mr. Dellamorte stood up from his chair located at the head of the table, holding up the prefilled wine glass, and confidently announced, "To my renowned guests. It is an honor to have each of you in my home. I look forward to future relations with you. *Salute*, as we say in Italy." And with that, he raised his glass a little higher, then took a drink of his red wine as everyone followed suite. I had never been offered any sort of alcohol before and, quite frankly, never had any desire to test the waters. I looked around, unsure if this would be the right time to acquaint myself with this worldly pleasure.

"Go ahead and taste it, Renee. It won't kill you," Kyran urged.

Nervously, I took a sip of the oddly sweet, yet bitter wine. I couldn't help but cough as it reached the end of my throat. Kyran gave a slight snicker, perhaps amused by my lack of social skills.

"It's an acquired taste, love. After drinking it a few times, you'll begin to like it and enjoy all it has to offer," Kyran claimed.

Needless to say, the glass sat stagnant the rest of the evening. I didn't feel like I needed to suffer through any more sips, trying to acquire a taste for it.

"You may serve the food," Mr. Dellamorte commanded of his dutiful staff.

The first course was served, and the hired help immediately shuffled back out of the room. Just as everyone was about to partake of this fanciful, delectable food sitting before us, my mother cleared her throat. As loudly as she could, so that her voice would travel to our end of the table, she said, "Ahem . . . pardon me, Mr. Dellamorte. May I be so bold as to ask for the Lord's blessing upon this remarkable meal presented to us? After all, it is by His grace that we are blessed with such a meal."

After knowing my mother very well for sixteen years, I could tell that even though her voice stood strong with absolute confidence, she was somewhat annoyed at the fact that our host didn't think of this himself.

Completely shocked and somewhat embarrassed by my mom's sudden outburst, I placed my hand upon my forehead and slightly covered my eyes in disbelief that she would impose this request to this authoritative man in his own house.

As the entire room shifted their eyes from her to him, he quickly said, "Of course, Madame. Could you do the honors of saying grace?"

She nodded her head "yes" as she lifted her five-foot-one-inch body from her chair so that all could hear the prayer.

"If you would please bow your heads," she commanded of the room. I immediately noticed that her southern Texas accent found its way back into her speech. She's lived in Colorado for the past twenty-five years and lost her southern twang somewhere along the way, but every now and again, usually when she's trying to charm someone, it will slip back out.

"Our Dear, Heavenly Father. We humbly come before You to thank You for your love and mercy upon us. It is because of You that we sit at this incredible dinner table about to partake in such a splendid meal. Your continuous blessings show the boundless grace You shed upon us each and every day, and we would be nothing without You. Thank You, Lord, for this meal. May it nourish our bodies and keep us strong so that we may continue to do Your good work while we are here on this earth. Amen."

The rest of the room, some reluctantly, some quietly, said, "Amen."

As my mother seated herself, everyone commenced with eating, holding private conversations with those around them.

"So, Renee. I understand you are quite an intelligent girl, potentially the lead candidate for valedictorian of your class," Mr. Dellamorte said, seemingly ready to forget that my mother had just stepped on his toes.

"Thank you for the compliment, sir. I am trying my hardest to earn that top honor so that I will have a better chance of getting into Harvard on scholarship."

"Harvard, huh? My, my, aren't you rather ambitious? And what would you like to be when you grow up?"

"I want to be a lawyer, just like my dad. He truly inspires me to help others who really need the help, but don't have the means to get a good attorney on their side."

"Yes, I understand your father takes on numerous pro bono

cases each year. With his potential, he's giving up making millions by being a simple commoner's lawyer, don't you think?" he conceitedly asked.

I could feel the hair on the back of my neck rise, and I was quick to defend my father's honor.

"Pardon me, Mr. Dellamorte. Without sounding too presumptuous, there are more important things in this life than money. Our family has done just fine all these years, thank you very much."

"Forgive me, my dear, for making you feel a bit defensive. I just know from firsthand experience all the wonderful things money can do for you. Just think of how many people your family could help if you had plenty of money in your bank account to do so."

While his point seemed very logical, I still had to stick by my guns and reply with, "True, but Jesus was extremely poor and seemed to help millions of people. He still helps people everyday, and it doesn't cost a dime!"

Mr. Dellamorte gave his husky chuckle once again and directed his comment to Kyran. "You have a feisty one here, son." Then he looked over at me. "Very well said, my dear. Now please, let's enjoy this evening and lighten up the conversation. What do you like to do for fun, eh?"

The rest of the dinner seemed to go a little better after that. I made it a point to concentrate more on Kyran, which certainly helped.

After the five-course meal was finished, several men, including my father, disappeared into the wine-tasting room for an after dinner drink and cigar. Apparently, there was still some business that needed to be discussed. I excused myself from Kyran to freshen up in the powder room. My mother saw me walking in the direction of the bathroom and met up with me.

"Having fun, Mom?" I asked.

She gave me an "are you kidding" look before saying, "Are you kidding? These people must be from another planet because I feel like such an alien among this crowd."

"I sort of thought so by the fake smile I saw on your face when we got here."

"Yes, well, your father has been schmoozing with every Tom, Dick, and Harry in the room. Something has gotten into him lately, but I just can't put my finger on it," she said as she dabbed some powder on her nose and pulled out her lipstick.

The powder room was exquisite. Its gold-plated faucets perfectly fitted into the brown onyx sink, accompanied by a magnificent golden antique mirror that made you want to say, "Mirror, mirror on the wall. Who's the fairest of them all?"

I looked myself over as well to make sure everything was still in place. That's when she noticed it, the "it" I knew she would have a fit over.

"What in the world is around your neck!" she exclaimed.

"Do you like it?" I asked excitedly, holding it out so she could get a closer look.

"Whether or not I like it has no relevance, young lady. I have to ask you, where did you get such an extravagant necklace?" And before I could answer, she answered herself. "Don't tell me. Kyran is on a roll with spoiling my little girl. Well, I just won't have it."

She grabbed her purse as if she were going to storm out of the bathroom and straight to Kyran to tell him a thing or two.

But I grabbed her arm and pleaded, "Wait, Mom, please! Nothing like this has ever happened to me before. Can't you just be happy for me?"

"Renee, don't you see what these people are doing? They are dazzling you with their money so that you will let down your guard and be more vulnerable. Have your eyes already gotten so blinded by this boy that you don't see that?"

"You're wrong, Mother. He's not like that. He's sweet, caring, and attentive; he just wants to make me happy, that's all."

"And so you're only happy when you're getting extravagant gifts from him? Does he have nothing else to offer of himself other than what his money can buy?"

Ouch . . . that hurt. Only because she made a good, yet painful, point, and I knew it. But my pride wasn't about to let her know that. "You're not being fair to him, and I might add *you're* being a bit judgmental, don't you think, *mother?*" I said with a stern, sarcastic voice.

I don't believe I have ever spoken to my mother in that tone before. I could see she was not only shocked by this abrasive behavior, but a little hurt as well. The supersized powder room became very quiet, and the walls appeared to be caving in on us. Suddenly, the beauty it once held no longer held its intended appeal. It quickly became the holding ground of displayed anger between a mother and a daughter, a place I never thought we would be.

"I can see the Dellamortes have had an effect on two of the most important people in my life now, and as your mother, who is only here to protect you, I have to insist that you return the gift to Kyran . . . immediately."

"No, Mother . . . that's not fair. You have no right to make me give back a gift that was given to *me*," I stated as tears began strolling down my cheeks.

"Renee, sweetheart, you have to trust me on this. You may think it's just a gift, but that gift will eventually cost you. Now for your own good, this party is over. I suggest you pull yourself together and then go excuse yourself. You are going home with me," she demanded.

I grabbed my purse from the sink and ran over to where Kyran was standing among a group of men, all laughing as they conversed. He noticed that I was clearly upset and started to walk to meet me.

"What's wrong, love?" he asked with such care, looking deeply into my eyes.

"I have to go. My mom's not very happy about the expensive

gifts you've been giving me. She's taking me home with her."

He looked away from me into her direction where she was standing, carefully watching us. "Doesn't she know how hard I worked to get you here tonight?" he chortled in an effort to try and cheer me up. "Isn't there something we can say or do to make her change her mind?"

"You don't know my mom very well. Once she's made up her mind about something, that's it. And there's one more thing," I said as I began to unhook the clasp of the necklace. "I have to return this to you. I want you to know it's the nicest gift anyone has ever gotten me, and I really did appreciate it."

"Please, let me talk to her. I can be very persuasive, you know," he admitted.

"I don't think that's a good idea. She's not too happy with you as it is."

As Kyran and I were discussing this matter and saying our good-byes, I noticed Kyran's mom walking up to my mom. She was strikingly smooth and graceful, almost as though underneath her long dress she was floating somehow. They began to converse, both staying calm from what I could tell of their facial expressions. Then my dad, who finally came out of hiding from the wine room, walked up to them as well.

"I had a great night. I guess I'll see you in school on Monday," I said before giving Kyran a hug good-bye.

As I approached the trio, I caught the tail end of the conversation.

" . . . it will be fine. I promise you. We'll be home in a couple of hours," my dad said, assuring my mother of some deal they seemed to have made.

"What's going on?" I quickly asked.

All of their attention turned toward me.

"Your mother and I have agreed to let you stay here at the party with me, but just for another hour or so," Daddy said to my disbelief.

"Seriously?" I said with a smile on my face. I grabbed my mother's neck and said, "Thank you, thank you!" I ran back over to Kyran to tell him the good news.

"Somehow my dad convinced my mom to let me stay!" I said excitedly.

I grabbed his hand and walked back over where my father was saying his good-byes, so that I could finally properly introduce him to my mom.

"Mom, this is Kyran. Kyran, this is my mom," I said beaming.

"Mrs. Lewis," she quickly inserted.

He took her hand, gave it a gentle peck and said, "It's such a pleasure to finally meet you."

I could tell it was very hard for her to say, but she put her pride aside and said, "The feeling is mutual. Unfortunately, I am departing early, as I am feeling a bit tired. Your mother has generously offered the limo to take me home so that my daughter can go home with my husband. If you don't mind, I'm going to steal her for a moment so she can walk me out. I'd like to say good-bye to her in private."

"Not at all, Mrs. Lewis. And may I just say I'm very disappointed we didn't get the chance to spend more time together, but perhaps we can all meet again soon," he suggested.

"That would be lovely," she said as she tugged my arm.

All I could think about was what a gentleman Kyran was. Surely my mom was as impressed with him as I was.

TEN

Choices

We began walking toward the front door, arm in arm, and I expected a lecture would soon follow. The properly dressed man, still stationed by the door, had my mother's coat in hand. He was waiting to assist her. I was impressed with his efficiency. He helped my mother with her coat and offered me a nice throw blanket.

"It's still quite cold, Miss Lewis. You may wrap yourself with this blanket to keep you warm."

"Thank you . . . I'm sorry, I don't even know your name."

"You're welcome, Madame," was all he said before opening the door for us.

As we walked out, I started the conversation in hopes of keeping it on the lighter side.

"Thanks again, Mom. It really does mean a lot to me that you're letting me stay for the rest of the party. I am having such an amazing night."

She let out a heavy sigh and said, "I suppose I should be happy to see such a bright smile on your sweet face. But I still can't help but worry."

"Worry about what, Mom? I'm a big girl now, and I have

found such a great guy. You knew it was bound to happen sooner or later."

"Yes, well, I certainly hoped for the later."

"Mom," I said with a long, drawn-out breath.

"I know, but I can't help it. It's all gone by so fast. It seems like just yesterday I was holding your tiny body in my arms, and singing you lullabies to sleep. I guess I just don't want anything to ever come between us, and tonight I feared something may already have."

"No, nothing's changed between us, and it never will. You're my best friend, and I love you so much."

"Please . . . promise me that you will not forget who you are and where you come from. I just don't trust these people. God gives us instincts as a way to alert us to danger. My gut feeling tells me you need to be careful," she implored.

"I think you're just worrying too much because you're not used to seeing me with a guy."

"I wish that was all it was. All I can say is keep your eyes open, sweetie. Don't get blinded by money or sweet temptations. And I am only allowing you to stay here because your father will be here with you, so you really have him to thank," she said with finger pointed at me and one eyebrow arched.

The limo pulled around the circle and stopped at the bottom of the stairs. Still arm in arm, we slowly walked down the long descending steps. The chauffeur had the door open as we reached the car.

"Keep your eyes on God, not on what the world has to offer," my mom said before giving me a tight hug. "I love you. See you in a couple of hours."

"I love you too, Mom!"

The driver closed the door after she entered the limo. I stood there as the car drove off and waited until the red lights of the back end were only dots in the air. I felt sad at the thought of parting from my mom. All these years we have done everything together and could talk about everything. I didn't want to lose that, but I knew that it was all part of growing up. She couldn't be there for me every time I fell or got hurt anymore, and that probably killed her. I knew I had begun the transition of having to make my own mistakes and pulling my own self up when I stumbled. While I still yearned to be that little girl, I also yearned to be the woman I was becoming.

I could hear footsteps coming down the steps behind me. I looked back, and there was Kyran with his striking looks and over-the-top charm. I met him at the bottom of the stairs and looked up at him.

"Turn around, *bellissima*."

I instinctively complied with his request. I could feel a small, cold object gently hit my collarbone. It was the necklace I had returned to him on my mother's request. I touched it with my fingers. The large sapphire felt so smooth. I didn't reject his offer this second time around, just as I didn't the first time. I turned back to face him, and he held out his hand for me to take.

"Come, love. The night is still so young."

As we walked back up the stairs, hand in hand, I began to shiver. I could have easily blamed it on the temperature, but it was a different kind of shiver.

My mind was filled by a memory of me as a little girl, about four or five, when I was visiting Grandma J's house in Texas for a week. We had gone grocery shopping for dinner ingredients, and I begged her for some Neapolitan ice cream sandwiches for dessert, my favorite.

"I'll buy these for you, but you have to promise me you will eat all of your dinner first."

"I promise, Grandma J," I all too quickly agreed.

I should have taken better notice of what was on the menu before making such an agreement. Pot roast, carrots, mashed potatoes, and green bean casserole was what I had agreed to consume in order to wrap my mouth around the delicious tri-colored ice cream sandwich.

I found myself holding my nose at the dinner table every time I had to take a bite of a carrot or of the green mush that was called a casserole. Halfway through eating the gross "good for you" stuff, I started feeling like I was going to regurgitate all that I had managed to get down. I started gagging, trying to keep it all in so that I could earn that sweet, delectable treat that awaited me. Hard as I tried, I couldn't keep the orange and green mush down and threw it all up onto Grandma's freshly cleaned carpet.

"Can I still have my ice cream?" I asked her, giving her my most pitiful eyes I could.

"A deal is a deal, sugar. Now I only gave you small scoops of the veggies. Can't you try again to finish them off?"

I looked over at my plate as I was still slumped over, holding my stomach, and thought of the ice cream sandwich. Then I looked at the plate again and came to the conclusion it just wasn't worth all the suffering for one ice cream sandwich, which would equal about three minutes of pleasure.

"I'll pass, Grandma."

She gave me a look of slight disappointment that I didn't keep my word. I gave her one back, thinking grandmas are supposed to spoil their grandchildren and let them get away with more than Mommies and Daddies. Nope, not Grandma J. She was always trying to teach me lessons in life, and I knew this was just one of them.

Later on that evening while she was sitting in her recliner, crocheting a scarf for an upcoming charity event at the nursing home, I decided that my attempt at trying to eat half of the nasty stuff was worth half of an ice cream sandwich. So I snuck into the freezer, grabbed a sandwich, and found a hiding spot in the entryway closet. I slowly and carefully tore off the wrapping from my much deserved treat with every intention of just eating the half that I had earned. I began indulging myself in the frosty temptation and had a hard time stopping at the halfway point. Before I knew it, it was all gone. As I sat there in my dark hiding place, I began to shiver. At first, I thought the coldness of the ice cream made my temperature drop, but soon realized I shivered because I felt so terrible for doing something I wasn't supposed to do. Feelings of regret began to consume my mind for deceiving my grandma. It turned out to be *one* minute of pure pleasure and two days of extreme guilt.

As we reentered the party, the music was turned up loud, and everyone seemed to be really enjoying themselves as they danced on a makeshift dance floor in a cleared-out ballroom. There were chairs and tables along the walls for the less energetic to mingle. I also noticed most of them were drinking, several were smoking, and all were laughing and having a good time. These were the types of parties I had only seen on TV or at the movies, never here in Westcliffe. I was very surprised to see my father as one of the jovial participants. I can't recall ever seeing him drink anything other than a soda or glass of water before. I then witnessed Mr. Dellamorte hand him a cigar that he took out of some fancy box and assisted my dad in lighting it up. Now I understood what my mother was talking about when she said something strange was going on with my dad. The thought of walking up to him and asking just what he was doing crossed my mind, but I didn't want to make him feel awkward in front of his newfound friends. Besides, he's the parent, and I'm just the kid, so what would give me that right?

"Let's go dance," Kyran said excitedly.

I looked at the adults, who were already shaking and gyrating their bodies like they had no sense.

"I'll pass," I said, uncomfortable at the thought of just completely letting myself loose in front of people I really didn't know.

"Don't be ridiculous, *amore*. I know what a great dancer you are. Please, come and dance with me."

There he went and made that face again, with those pouty lips and sad eyes.

"Nope," I confidently said back, being strong enough not to give into his sucker move.

"Renee, have you ever been to a dance before?" he asked curiously.

"Not exactly," I said, still staying strong in my decision.

"Then how do you know that you don't like it?"

I pondered his question for a second. I hated to admit it, but he had a good point. *Dang it!* I sighed loudly, making it clear to him that I wasn't too happy about giving in to him. "Hhhh . . . okay, Prince Charming, but you're gonna have to lead the way. I would look a little silly doing a *pas de chat* out on the dance floor to this music!" He chuckled, a sound I loved hearing from him because it meant he got my quirky sense of humor.

He grabbed my hand and walked me to the dance floor, weaving in and out of the partygoers, who were proud to show off all their latest moves. I didn't recognize the song that was playing, but the tempo was upbeat and spunky; I kind of liked it. We landed in the middle of the floor. I was content with our spot because no one would notice me out there from the tables and chairs surrounding the dance area. Kyran began smoothly moving his body to the beat of the music, and I just stood there . . . motionless . . . watching him. Before attempting to mimic his moves, I looked around at everyone else out there with us to make sure that they weren't paying any attention to this girl who had no clue what she was doing.

Slowly, I began swaying my body, trying to connect it with this fast beat. Though very structured kinds of dance, years of ballet and jazz certainly made this new way of dancing much easier for me. I looked over at Kyran as he smiled at my attempt while snapping his fingers right on cue to the beat. I could tell he was naturally a good dancer, no lessons necessary. He placed his hands on my hips and instructed me to shake them a bit, forcing them to go side to side.

"You're too tense, sweetheart. Loosen up," he directed.

"I am!" I shouted back over the loud music.

He let go of my hips, and they continued in the motion they had been commanded. I looked around, still very conscious of what I was doing and how I might look to others. I glanced in the direction of my dad and was relieved that he was too involved in conversation with three other men standing by him to notice me.

I looked back over at Kyran, who was clearly enjoying himself as he so suavely moved to the music. Just seeing how much fun he was having made me smile. I decided to really try and loosen up more so I could get the full effect of this escapade. Before I knew it, I was laughing and enjoying myself right along with him. He would bust out a move, and I would follow suite. I even created a few of my own moves, one of which he later named the "Ren Spin." A few songs came and went before a slow, romantic melody was played.

"May I have this next dance?" Kyran asked politely as he bowed in front of me.

My heart simply melted as I watched him conduct himself in such a gentlemanly fashion while asking me for my first slow dance. "Yes, you may," I said indulgently.

He grabbed my waist as I wrapped my arms around his sturdy neck. Our bodies seemed to easily sway together to the beat of each note. My heart was racing, even though our movements had slowed. I still felt cautious and even a little nervous being so close to him. This influx of emotions was becoming a bit overwhelming. Why did everything seem so right and so wrong all at the same time?

"What has you so tense, *amore?*" Kyran must have sensed my conflict.

I tried to play it cool. "Nothing. What gives you the impression that I'm tense?"

"I can just tell," he said confidently.

For the five or so minutes that the song played, I consciously put my guard down so that I could relax and have a more natural flow to this romantic music. I laid my head on his hard shoulder and became lost in the setting. When the song ended, he pulled my arms from his neck and grabbed my hand to lead me off the dance floor. We strolled down the hall to yet another room that I had not been in. I noticed a big, beautiful fire blazing in the fireplace, perfect for this chilly evening. I looked around and easily concluded this was the library, as the shelves of books reaching from floor to ceiling and wall to wall gave it away. On the table next to the black leather sofa was a bottle of red wine and two glasses. To the left of the fireplace was another small table set up with two chairs and the classic game of chess sitting on top of it.

"Are you going to read me a story?" I asked with just a dash of sarcasm mixed with a pinch of flirtation in an effort to act as if all was well with me.

"I just thought you would be more comfortable away from the crowd and knew you had a passion for reading. What do you think?" he said as he began to pour some wine into the glasses.

I looked around and began reading some of the titles labeled on the spine of the books.

"I see you have some great classics here," I replied, quite impressed with the collection.

He walked over to me and handed me one of the glasses, filled with more of the sweet, bitter liquid that I didn't care for. I took it from him anyway.

He held his up and waited for me to follow his lead.

"Here's to a wonderful evening with a beautiful lady. I hope for many, many more to come. *Salute,*" he said. And with that, he tapped my glass and took a drink. Again, torn about what to do, I yielded to his offer. It didn't taste any better this second time around, and I gave a slight cough.

"What does *salute* mean, anyway?"

"It means 'cheers,' which is what most people would say in America before a toast," he patiently explained. "In Italy, we always say *salute.*"

"I see," I said as I walked over to the small table. I was intrigued by the exquisite chess set, which seemed to be calling my name. "Play much chess?" I asked inquisitively.

"I've played a round or two in my life. And you?"

"A time or two," I replied back with lips slightly slanted upward.

"Is that a challenge I'm sensing?" he asked.

"It is if you're prepared for a whipping!"

He pulled out the chair belonging to the white pieces and signaled me to sit in it. He walked around and took the black side.

"You first," I insisted.

"A gentleman would never . . . ."

"But I insist! A gentleman wouldn't deny a lady's request, would he?" I had to convince him to go first as I had my moves ready for whatever he was to throw.

He moved his pawn in front of the king two spaces forward. I mimicked his move. He concentrated for a minute before moving the knight to the right of the king up and over. Again, I mimicked his move, only I chose my opposite knight.

He looked over at me as if trying to guess what I would do next. He moved his bishop diagonally three spaces.

"You are falling perfectly into my little trap, Monsieur!" I said with complete arrogance.

"Oh, Mademoiselle . . . I think it is you who is falling into mine!"

I then moved my knight forward once again. Now he mimicked my move. I boldly moved my queen diagonally three spaces.

"What is this?" he questioned, surprised at such a bold move so early in the game.

"Your move!"

He concentrated a few minutes before delivering his next move.

"After all that time, you moved your knight forward again? I would have thought you could have come up with something better," I said arrogantly.

"I love this confidence you have. I didn't know chess could bring this out in you!" he chuckled.

I moved my queen forward two spaces and took his pawn. His next move was sliding his bishop over and placing it next to his Majesty.

"You know . . . greed causes many people to ignore defense," I continued to taunt to him. Quite honestly, I had never acted in such a pompous manner, but it certainly was fun.

He looked over at me while taking a sip of his wine. I wasn't quite sure if he liked being on the defense. He knew I had complete control over this little game. It must have made him uncomfortable as he took yet another sip before deciding to move his bishop back to also protect his king.

With a smile from ear to ear, I moved my knight over two spaces and forward one. "Checkmate," I smugly announced. "Death by suffocation!" I continued to egg him on relentlessly.

"I suppose you won this round, *amore*. But I bet I've got the next!" he said in a more serious tone than the current mood.

"Ahhh . . . not used to getting beaten, huh? Oh come on, Kyran, I learned these moves from my Grandpa J. He taught me how to play chess from the time I turned five. He called this the Kostics Trap. I was surprised you kept taking the bait. It was just luck, that's all. Don't get all serious on me! Loosen up. Isn't that what you've told me all night?"

I was surprised at what a poor sport he was. He definitely wasn't used to defeat.

He poured himself another glass of wine, and though I had only taken one sip from mine, he added some more to it as well.

"A toast then," he said as he lifted his glass. I followed suite to try and soothe things over.

"To a very clever girl with all the right moves." And with that, he clinked his glass to mine.

"Hear, hear," I said in return and took my third sip for the night.

The wine still tasted bitter, but I managed to cough less this time.

He carefully placed his glass down on the table along with mine. His expression reminded me of how he was planning his next chess move. He swiftly placed his hand around the base of my neck to pull me closer to him. He closed his eyes and leaned forward, ready to give me a second kiss on my lips. I looked at his spellbinding face and admittedly felt tempted.

The first time he caught me off guard, but this time I had a choice, and I was not ready for this. I knew where this could end up and so went with my gut feeling. I resisted his offer by pulling away.

"I can't, Kyran. I'm just not ready yet," I said apologetically.

I could tell by the look on his face he was not used to rejection either. His surprised face started to harden, and I could sense he felt frustrated.

"Renee, it's only a kiss. It's a way to express how you feel about someone. Can't you see how much I like you?" he asked before making another attempt.

"To you, it may be only a kiss. But for me, it's more; it's special and something I don't just give away freely. So, if you like me as much as you say you do, then you will have to patiently wait until I am ready. Okay?"

I was surprised by my own reaction and the firmness of my words. I felt confident about my decision and for once this evening had no mixed emotions about my actions.

I couldn't pinpoint Kyran's look on his face, though. He seemed a bit bewildered. I held out my hand for his and said, "I think this would be a good time for me to go. Can you walk me out to find my dad?" I asked, giving him a smile of truce. He begrudgingly took my hand.

ELEVEN

Time to Leave

The silence between us made the journey down the hall seem longer. When we finally entered the party room, I glanced around for my father. Kyran released my hand and headed toward a door off to the side. I quickly followed him, hoping he knew where my dad would be. He knocked on the door and waited a few seconds before entering.

The room was filled with smoke and a group of men and women laughing, having what seemed to be a good time. I immediately felt uncomfortable upon entering the room and couldn't find my father quickly enough. No one seemed to pay me any attention; they all just continued on with their clearly flirtatious gesturing. I hadn't noticed Mr. Lender, my school principal, before but he looked as if he had been a part of the scene all night. He was sitting on the couch, quite comfortably, next to a striking woman who I thought looked about ten or twelve years younger than he was. I had never met his wife before, but was quite impressed by her attractiveness and could tell by the way they were fondling each other that they must still be very much in love. He looked at me for an instant as I walked by him and noticed his huge, laughing smile fade. I didn't say anything; I just wanted to hurry up and find my dad.

I finally spotted him talking with Mr. Dellamorte. Kyran led the way to where they were standing. As I approached them, I could see in my dad's body language that he immediately became uncomfortable with my presence. Mr. Dellamorte didn't seem too happy either.

"Sweetheart! What are you doing?" Dad asked as he placed his beverage on the nearby table.

I looked at Mr. Dellamorte, whose eyes had narrowed while looking at his son, and then back at my father to say, "I'm ready to go home."

Nervously he replied, "I thought you were having such a good time with Kyran. Is something wrong?"

"No, Daddy. I'm just starting to get tired, that's all. Plus, I promised Mom we wouldn't be out too late."

"Oh, okay, sweetie. Give me just a minute to wrap things up with Mr. Dellamorte. I'll meet you in the foyer. Okay?"

"Sure, Dad."

I looked around for Kyran, who had mysteriously disappeared. On my way out, I passed by Mr. Middleton, Beth's father and an esteemed doctor, who was clearly inebriated. He was joyfully telling a story to a group of people that seemed to be very intrigued by what he was saying. Surprisingly, I was able to understand his slurring words: " . . . and she believes me every time. She just doesn't want to give up her lifestyle, I'm sure. What some women will do for a pair of Gucci shoes and a Louis Vuitton purse!" They all laughed, amused by the ignorance of the woman. He seemed to tense up as he noticed me walking by. I simply nodded my head at him, and he returned the favor.

After happily leaving the smoky room and then the party room, I decided I had better go to the bathroom before the journey home. I headed down the hall toward the powder room that I had used earlier in the night and passed by a cracked door just before it. I heard voices coming through it that seemed to be distressed. I wasn't usually the nosey type, but I felt alarmed, and the urge to find out what was going on ruled my decision. I slowly approached the doorway and began to peek inside, careful not to open it any more than it was.

"You imbecile! This was not how the plan was supposed to go. You said everything was under control, and that she was like putty in your hands . . ." These were the words I heard coming from a harsh, guttural voice around the corner from the door, so I could not see who was in there. The voice was faintly familiar, but I couldn't pinpoint its possessor.

Before the receiver could even respond, a sharp slap across a face followed by a heavy grunt as if all force was put into that chastisement filled the air. I gulped as my throat tightened; feeling frightened by what I had heard, I quickly ran up to the foyer, bypassing the bathroom. Thankfully, my dad walked up at the same time.

"Ready to go?" he asked as he placed his arms into his coat.

"Yes!" I exclaimed, gasping for breath, not wanting to tell him of my previous encounter.

"Renee!" Kyran called out, running up to us. He looked and sounded desperate. "Wait a minute," he instructed.

"I'll go get the car and pull around while you say your good-byes," my dad said as he walked out the front door.

I looked at Kyran's face and noticed his cheeks were bright red. His expression appeared to be somewhat empty. "Are you okay?" I asked, concerned. "What happened to you, Kyran?"

"Nothing . . . you wouldn't understand."

"How do you know I wouldn't understand? Please, give me a chance." I felt of his burning cheek, and he closed his eyes upon my touch as if it soothed the pain some.

"No, it's not that simple. Just forget about it, okay?" he urged.

"Kyran, is someone trying to . . . ."

"Don't go," he interrupted. "Why must you leave so soon? Were you not having a good time?"

"Yes, of course. I just think its time to go; that's all. And I told you already that I promised my mom we wouldn't be out late."

"I see. I suppose there's nothing I can do to make you change your mind, then," he said sounding conquered.

As I gently rubbed his warm cheek, I began questioning myself for just a moment, wondering if I was running away from him too quickly. There was so much more to Kyran than met the eye, and I couldn't help but feel drawn to him. He was so mysterious, like an unsolved puzzle waiting for me to piece it together . . . to make it complete.

He seemed to be everything a girl could ever want in a guy . . . in a boyfriend. I felt so torn with what my gut and what my mind were telling me. I looked into his beautiful green eyes, sympathetic to his plea, and said, "I'll see you in school on Monday."

I stretched my neck slightly so that my lips could kiss his still burning cheek. Although it was a short peck, it let him know that I did care for him. I looked at his face, hoping he would be pleased with my gesture, and saw his eyes were closed once again as if he were deep in thought.

Just as I turned to walk away, he grabbed ahold of my arm and said, "You remind me of someone I once knew a long time ago. She was very special, like you."

I didn't know what to think of this. He caught me by surprise.

"Thank you for being my date tonight. I will hold our time together forever in my heart," he announced, as if it would be his last chance to ever tell me his feelings.

"Kyran, you're acting like we'll never see each other again. I promise, I'll see you Monday." I took hold of his hand and said, "Listen, I want you to know that I plan to talk with Jamie this weekend and tell her everything that has gone on between us so that we can see what will happen next. Okay?"

He raised my hand up to his lips and gave me a loving kiss before walking away, not even saying as much as good-bye. I was confused by his conflicting actions, but knew my dad would be waiting out front for me, and I had a long hike down the stairs in these high heels. So I turned and walked out of the house, anticipating a private conversation with him on Monday.

When I entered into the passenger side of my father's car, I could instantly smell the lingering effect of cigar smoke and booze.

"Dad, why don't you let me drive, okay?" I asked cautiously. His actions tonight made me very concerned.

"I'm fine, sweetheart. Besides, there are a lot of narrow and sharp turns going down this mountain and you're still an inexperienced driver, young lady," he cautioned me.

We proceeded to leave the circular drive and move on to a two-lane road, descending downward on the mountain. I wanted so badly to lecture my dad on his behavior tonight, but thought against it.

"Everything okay with you, Dad?"

"Yes, honey. Why do you ask?"

"Just wondering, I guess. I was just a little shocked to see you drinking tonight. That is so unlike you."

"It was just business; that's all. Nothing for you to worry your pretty little head over," he said as he mussed my hair playfully.

"So are you officially Mr. Dellamorte's legal counsel now?"

"Still working on it."

"What's the hold up?" I asked curiously, assuming Mr. Dellamorte was being particular over several candidates he was considering.

"Well, I haven't quite decided I want to take him on as a client," he admitted.

That was unexpected. Here I thought Mr. Dellamorte still had the decision to make, and it was my dad who was holding things up.

"Really? Why?"

"I know that if I take him on as my client, he will be taking up a lot of my time. He has numerous businesses that he's involved in, and I'm afraid that I won't have time for the other cases I'm already working on."

I knew that most of his other cases were charity cases that he had taken on to help out some locals. I was happy to know that he wasn't ready to give those up.

"And, it would also require some traveling, which means I would have to be away from you and your mother at times."

While we were talking, I noticed he was having some trouble staying in his lane on the sharp curves and found myself clutching the door and my seat.

"Well, then, there's clearly nothing to consider," I assured him. "Why haven't you already just declined?"

"It's a little more complicated than just saying 'yes' or 'no' to him. He's offering a substantial amount of money that would really help us out and pay for your college. I have to also think about our future," he admitted.

"Daddy, you and Mom have always taught me that money is not the answer to anything. I still don't understand why you haven't flat out told him no," I replied impatiently.

"Dad! Careful!" I shouted, noticing he had gotten awfully close to the edge of the cliff we were turning on.

"I think you should let me drive," I implored.

"You're overreacting, just like your mother. I'm fine!" he said brazenly.

I was a little offended at the way he made that statement, as if he had been annoyed by us. It was becoming clearer to me what my mom had implied earlier in the evening.

"Daddy, if the ball is in your court with Mr. Dellamorte, why were you drinking with him all night? You told me it was business, so what was that all about?"

My father's eyes narrowed, and I could see he was not happy with my questioning him.

He looked over at me and said, "That is my business, young lady, not yours!"

His concentration was diverted from the road, and once again he got very close to the edge, so he turned his wheel, quickly overcompensating the turn.

"Daddy!" I screamed as our car careened to the other side.

I heard brakes screeching and saw lights heading our way, directly in our path. Our car was out of control, swinging back and forth on the treacherous road.

"God, help us!" I yelled as I covered my face, with my arms acting as a shield.

I've always heard that your whole life will flash before your eyes before you die. As the bright light blinded me, I was able to see some very distinct memories, seven of them to be exact, as if I were watching a movie right in front of me.

The first memory was of me at age four when my dad was teaching me to ride my bike without my training wheels. "Don't let me go, Daddy!" I said nervously as he pushed me down the driveway. But he did let go, knowing I would be fine. I caught on quickly.

Next, my mom was tucking me into bed. We had a nightly routine that we always abided by. She would read me a book before giving me our fun made up kisses. We had silly names for them like the Bouncy Ball, the Corn-on-the-Cob, or the Timber, which were all delivered with funny noises that coincided with their name. Then, I would say my prayer: *Now I lay me down to sleep, I pray the Lord my soul to keep. May angels watch me through the night, and wake me to the morning light. Amen.*

An odd memory flashed of the time I had gotten lost at the amusement park. A really nice man with bright blue eyes held my hand and took me to where my parents were frantically looking for me. After all the hugs, kisses, and exclamations of "Thank You, Lord," my parents looked around for the nice man to thank him for bringing me to them, but he was nowhere to be found.

I saw Grandma J teaching me how to crochet a hat with the yarn that I picked out to match my red winter coat. It was red and white like a candy cane, and I wore that knitted hat every day until it finally fell apart. Looking back now, it wasn't the hat that I cared so much about. It was the special time that Grams and I had together making it.

I saw myself getting saved during a Sunday morning service. I remember so well. I was twelve, and I had felt so convicted by the preacher's sermon that day and knew I wanted to live for Christ. That's when I truly understood what being reborn meant.

I saw myself in Grandma J's closet again when I had gulped down that ice cream sandwich and felt so guilty about it afterwards.

And last, I saw Jamie and me at youth camp, dancing around and banging our heads at the Skillet concert. She would play the air guitar and I would beat on the air drums totally in sync to the music. We probably looked like fools, but didn't care anyway. I was just so happy and felt so free. It had always been such a special memory for me.

After my seven flashes came and went, the bright light progressing toward us was all I could see anymore, and the tear drops that were welling up in my eyes began streaming down my face. I knew this was to be my final moment on Earth. I inhaled one last deep breath, ready for my destiny.

Suddenly, the light shone brighter than my eyes could withstand. I kept staring into it, though, determined to see what was in the midst of this spectacle that enraptured me. I wasn't sure if my eyes were deceiving me as I gazed upon a beautiful, extraordinary face with mesmerizing blue eyes looking right at me. White, feathered wings spread out, completely encircling our car. My ears were consumed by a loud crashing noise, metal to metal screeching as the two cars collided, sending our car spinning around. Everything became a blur and I felt dizzy . . . very dizzy. I could feel something warm dripping into my eye and down my face from the top of my head . . . then nothing but complete darkness.

TWELVE

Season of Rest

Everything was still pitch black when I heard a slow, beeping sound coming from a machine. Beep . . . beep . . . beep. Its high-pitched, steady sound was somewhat annoying to me. My eyes felt so heavy, but I wanted to open them so badly to see where I was and where that noise was coming from. With all of my strength and concentration, I could feel my eyes tremble as they slowly began to open. Once all of the struggling was over with, everything was a blur and very white.

"Oh, God . . . am I dead? Where am I?" I said in a weak voice.

"Shhh, don't get yourself all worked up, child. You're not dead," a familiar voice said.

"Grandma J? Is that you?" I asked, still unable to make out any clear images.

"Yes, sugar. Now you get some rest and we'll talk later," she requested.

Rest . . . that actually sounded really good to me. I didn't argue from feeling so weak and found myself fading back asleep to the beeping sound that had once awakened me. Beep . . . beep . . . beep.

"It will be extremely important that you both get your strength back before

returning. You will each have many battles facing you, but she will be a key to helping us win this battle," He said.

"I understand, Lord. My wounds are quickly healing, and I will do everything in my power to build her up as well."

"She's not going to understand everything that is happening. They will be attacking her from every angle, but you must allow it to happen. She will feel alone or abandoned and may even get very angry and feel like hating us. But I know her faith will overcome it all. Your job is just to keep her safe until then."

"I will not let You or her down."

"And, Liam, you too must stay strong. I know you have a special bond with her, but remember what happened to your brother. Angels can give into temptation too, when they are vulnerable and the temptation is strong."

Liam lowered his head, as he knew exactly what his Lord was saying. He also knew the battles ahead were going to be brutal in so many ways. But he had faith in God that everything that was to happen and that had already happened was all in His plan, which gave him great comfort and peace.

"AUGH!" I gasped for air as if I were suffocating. I sat up quickly in my white, sterile bed, feeling confused. I looked over to my right, and there was Grandma J, sitting in a rocking chair, crocheting a red and white scarf.

"Grandma? Where am I?"

"You're recovering from a bad car accident, sugar."

"What are you doing here, and where's Mom and Dad?" I said frantically.

"They're fine. Now settle down before you get your heart all worked up."

I laid back down and glanced around the room. It was an all white room with a sweet aroma in the air, which must have been Grandma's perfume. Her presence gave me a sense of peace, and I began to relax.

As I lay resting, still a bit groggy and confused, in walked a strangely familiar person. I could hear the heart monitor beep steadily going faster as I looked at a strikingly handsome blonde man walking toward me. He was all in white, so I was sure he was my doctor coming to give me my diagnosis. I had to admit I was astonished that such a young guy could be a doctor. I quickly concluded that he must have been a child prodigy, and I was undoubtedly impressed.

He swiftly came to my side and began to examine me. Although, I did find it odd that he had no stethoscope or any other doctor's tool. He was just looking me over as if he were assessing any damage.

I gave him a weird look back before saying, "Am I going to be okay?"

"Yes," was the only word he said as he continued the examination, and yet, with that one single word, I knew I recognized his voice.

I began examining his inviting, radiant face more attentively. Finally, our eyes united, and I once again saw those lustrous blue eyes that seemed to pierce my soul every time I saw them. I began to recall who was standing before me.

"You're the one who saved me, aren't you?" I asked.

"Something like that," he replied.

"Liam?" I asked hesitantly, not really sure where I knew this name from, but felt the impulse to say it anyway.

"Yes, Renee. That is who I am."

I looked over at Grandma J and said with accusation, "You said I wasn't dead!"

She smiled and kept on crocheting, rocking steadily in her chair.

"You're not dead, Renee," Liam said. "We simply have you in a resting place. As far as the rest of the world is concerned, you are in a deep coma."

"What about my Dad? Is he okay?" I asked, concerned.

"He's alive. Don't worry; right now you just need to concentrate on building up your strength. There is much work to be done. I'm going to leave for a little while, but Grandma will keep you in good company until I get back."

Before he could walk away, I grabbed his hand. I instantly felt a warm, tingling sensation that reached to the very depths of my soul. I looked at him with a weak smile, feeling such peace and comfort.

"Liam, thanks," was all I could think of to say.

I knew as soon as I grabbed his hand that he was the one who had been with me since the day I was born. I instantly felt that connection.

He quickly pulled back his hand before departing from the room. I was disappointed by the lack of a response. I wasn't sure what caused his abrupt departure.

I looked over at Grandma, putting it out of my mind, and took notice of what she was working on.

"That scarf reminds me of the cap we once knitted together. Do you remember that?"

"Of course, I do. That was such a special time for us. I always got such pleasure every time I saw that hat on you. Remember the picture of you that I always kept on the piano? You were lying in the snow, making snow angels, while wearing your red coat and striped hat," she said as she fondly recalled the memory. "It always reminded me of God's greatest gift to us."

"Huh?" I said confused. I mean, I always knew I was special, but God's greatest gift was a bit over the top! I just remembered everyone always telling me that I looked like Waldo when I wore that knitted cap, but I never cared one iota.

"Let me explain, my dear child. You see, the color white, like the snow or the base color of your hat, stands for Jesus' pureness and sinless nature. The red-colored coat that lay splashed atop the snow, or the stripes on the hat, stand for the pain He suffered for us while dying on the cross to save us from our sins."

"Oh, I see now. It reminds me of that candy cane story I heard in church when I was a little girl."

"Exactly," she agreed, "and some people choose to take that sweet story to heart and share it with others. Sadly, though, there are those who just try to make a mockery of it all. But that's how life is now, isn't it? It's about how you choose to see things."

"Yeah, I suppose so," I softly replied, pondering the lesson she was giving me. Some things will never change with her.

"So, if I'm not dead, how is it that I am talking to you here, face to face?"

"There is nothing that is not within the Lord's power to do. He allowed my soul to spend time with yours. He thought you would feel more at peace with me here."

How right He was. I had missed Grandma J so much. She passed away a month before my fifteenth birthday. I had been so sad, but I knew in my heart she went to Heaven. That was the only solace I had to hold on to, knowing that she had given her life to Him.

"So how is Grandpa?" I asked, remembering her always saying she couldn't wait to see him again.

"Grandpa is great. He said to tell you 'hi,' by the way, and to eat a Baby Ruth for him when you get back! He always said that was a small piece of Heaven all wrapped up," she said as she giggled.

"Tell him I'll do it . . . in honor of him. And can you tell him that I love him very much while you're at it?" I added my own request.

She gave me an assuring nod.

"So tell me about yourself. What have you been doing since I've been gone?" she inquired.

I began to think about that and had a hard time recalling anything prior to the last time I saw her. I thought as hard as I could, and the only thing that came to mind was Liam rescuing me from a crashing car. How I even got to that point was a complete blur.

"Gee, Grams . . . I don't know. I must have hit my head pretty hard or something because I can't think of what I've been up to this last year or so."

She continued to rock, keeping busy with her knitting, and simply gave me a smile.

"I suppose it will all come to you when it's time. Until then, you just get some more rest."

THIRTEEN

Place of Contentment

Time passed, but I couldn't really tell if it were hours or days. It seemed to have no relevance. I did know, however, that my strength was coming back to me. I couldn't help but wonder when Liam was going to come for a visit again. I felt that I had angered him somehow during our last encounter, and I was anxious to apologize to this man . . . this guardian who saved my life once again. I wondered where he went to when he wasn't with me.

Meanwhile, Grams and I would go outside of the room and walk around in this amazing and beautiful garden that had an array of flowers that were so exquisite. The pebbled pathway was made of sparkling gems. The first time I stepped onto this opulent walkway, I couldn't help but bend down and sift my fingers through these magnificent, tiny rocks made of diamonds, sapphires, rubies, emeralds, and so much more. They gave off a brilliant sparkle, not gaudy or flashy, just simple beauty to match their surroundings. There were flowers that were typically grown in the southern region, some in the northern, and my favorites, those grown in Colorado. There was no particular climate, and all of the flowers seemed to thrive with full, vibrant blooms. There were flowers and colors of flowers that I had never even seen or heard of. Their beauty and aroma was immeasurable, and I was at such a place of ease. I would slowly inhale the sweet perfumes that filled the air as we strolled, arm in arm, around the constructed pathway.

Each time we were here, I never failed to get excited when I would see the Rocky Mountain Columbine with their white small petals settled atop larger lavender ones; they almost looked like two flowers in one. I would always stop to smell this precious flower, which brought thoughts of home to mind. I always thought fondly of home, but oddly enough, didn't seem to miss it. Perhaps it was because I knew I would be back soon enough, and I was very much enjoying this time I had with Grandma J.

As we continued up the path, I saw him up ahead, standing with such strength and confidence. My heart started to race, and I was filled with excitement to see that Liam had come for a visit. Even so, I walked at a casual pace, trying to remain cool and calm.

"Good morning . . . or good afternoon," I said, a bit flustered. "Whatever it is. I'm not really even sure." I had to chuckle at myself, knowing I must look like such a high school, babbling girl to him.

"How are you feeling?" he asked.

"Great! I'm feeling great. How about you? How are you feeling? Great, I hope!" I said too quickly, ready to bop myself on the forehead after I said it. My nerves were causing my mouth to speak all on its own.

He gave me a pity laugh before saying, "Never better." And then he got a little more serious. "Renee, there's someone who wants to meet you. Care to walk with me further up the path?"

"Absolutely," I said. I was both curious and excited to see who it was that wanted to meet me.

"Grandma J, Grandpa is waiting for you. I've got this from here," he assured her.

I thought it was sweet how he called her Grandma J, too. I wondered why that was.

"That's what she likes to be called," Liam answered.

Huh . . . did I say that out loud? I questioned myself. I quickly forgot about it when he held out his bent arm, allowing mine to connect with it, just like Grams and I had been.

We continued up the pebbled trail until we came upon a wonderful playground filled with laughing children running all around. I couldn't possibly guess who it was playing in that magnificent park who had requested to meet me. I looked up at Liam with a puzzled expression on my face. Just then, a sweet little boy, who appeared to be about six or seven, came running over to us excitedly.

"Renee, this is Kevin," Liam said, looking at me with an excitement in his eyes. "He is your brother."

I gazed at the boy in complete wonderment, astonished by the unexpected surprise, but even more touched that he wanted to come and meet me. I didn't quite know what to say or what to do, so I held out my hand to shake his, but the innocent boy bypassed it altogether and endearingly wrapped his arms around my waist. I immediately followed his lead and wrapped my arms around him, too.

When we finally let go of each other, I bent down to take a closer look at him. I could see my father's smile and my mother's brown eyes as I looked upon his charming boyish face.

He gently rubbed the side of my face and said, "You're so pretty!"

"Thank you," I said in return, ready to release a gush of tears. "It's so good to meet you, Kevin." My voice quivered.

"Can you come and swing me?" he asked politely.

"Of course," I said. We took each other's hand and walked over to the swings. I felt so complete in that moment as I gently pushed his small back, swinging him high into the air. His honey-brown hair would wave around as he flew back and forth, going higher with each pass. I loved hearing his energetic laugh as he would kick his legs, making himself go even higher. Once we were done swinging, we ran over to the giant slide. I climbed the steps behind him, and he sat in my lap as we slid down. We must have gone down that thing a hundred times, never growing tired of it. I glanced over at Liam as he watched us with a pleased look on his face. I mouthed the words "thank you" to him, and he nodded.

Since the moment I had arrived, time had no relevance. It wasn't until Liam called out to me, saying it was time to leave, that I felt I was cheated from this method of measuring intervals. I wanted to know the precise minute or hour I got to spend with this precious boy who I instantly loved. I hated to end our time together; it seemed to go by too fast. However, I couldn't help but feel completely grateful for the opportunity to meet my brother. Kevin and I gave each other one last tight hug and said, "See ya!" to each other as if there would be a tomorrow or a next time. It was perfect.

When Kevin went back to play with the other children, I couldn't help but wonder why he was a young boy, since he was s upposed to be born before me.

"Liam, why is my brother a child instead of a grown-up? Realistically, he would be two years older than I am."

"All the innocent children who are called home before they've had the opportunity to experience a full life will remain children. Because your brother was at a point of not being self-sufficient when he passed, his soul came as the child that you saw so he could fully grasp the wonders and pleasures of Heaven. I assure you, though, the children are filled with immense joy, just as every other soul is."

As Liam and I walked further away, I looked back one last time in hopes of catching a glimpse of Kevin. I wanted to see his adorable smile that I cherished one last time. I was disappointed when I noticed the park gradually disappear from my sight.

"Where did the park go?" I asked.

"The children are back in Heaven. Kevin asked if you could see how happy he is when he met you, so I allowed your mind to see him in his favorite place."

"But he felt so real when I touched him."

"And he was. Your souls connected with each other, but the park and the other children were part of the illusion in your mind. It's all very tricky," he smiled.

"Yes, I see. It's kind of hard to wrap my mind around everything," I admitted.

"It's all part of God's greatness. Humans can't come close to comprehending all that He is and all He can do . . . no offense! At least, not until they make it to Heaven."

"Well, I'll certainly have a ton of questions to ask. It's a good thing we'll have forever!"

We both just laughed and continued our walk back down the sparkling pathway. I felt amazingly content.

FOURTEEN

Beauty Beyond Comprehension

Time continued to pass, and I would keep busy with the books that would miraculously show up on my nightstand; gifts from Liam, no doubt. I quickly read the books that I loved as a small child like, *Curious George*, *Because a Little Bug Went Ka-Choo*, and the *Junie B. Jones* series that I had treasured in elementary school. Then moved on to my favorite books of the present, like *The Sisterhood of the Traveling Pants*. I couldn't help but laugh and reminisce as I read each one.

After getting through the recent books left for me, I decided to go for a walk in the garden. Halfway through, though, I walked off the usual path, feeling the need to explore. I discovered a forest of big, beautiful trees that I had never seen before. I steadily marched through them as if I were in a maze, feeling insignificant next to their massive trunks. I didn't feel lost or scared, just curious as to what else I would find when I reached the end, if that ever came.

I continued to hike through the woods and started to think about Liam. I wondered if he thought about me as often as I thought about him. I wondered if angels got married or found soul mates, if they felt the same emotions or had any of the same desires. I wondered if they could taste and enjoy food like humans or play sports for fun.

He was so strange to me, not in the weird sense, but in the

unknown. I was deep in thought when I realized there was a clearing just up ahead. I quickly ran to it and found a beautiful pond filled with clear blue water. Sitting next to it was a large rock, perfect for me to rest on and splash my feet. As I anxiously dipped my toes into the cool, sparkling liquid, I instantly felt so alive and stimulated. I was enjoying myself tremendously when suddenly I saw a stunning reflection in the now still water.

"Beautiful, isn't it?" Liam asked.

"Yes, I love it. Why didn't you tell me about this place?"

"It was here all along. You just had to look past your usual surroundings to see it," he replied.

"I thought I had, but I never saw the enormous forest before which led me here."

"Renee, some things are just meant to be discovered by your own desire or curiosity. I knew you would find it eventually! Think of how you felt when you first found the Pond of Purity. Part of its beauty and magnificence came when you, by your own will, discovered it."

Wow, that was deep. I had to really contemplate each word as I tried to embrace the message. I stared into the luminous body of water once again and cherished my finding.

"So, what brings you here, anyway?" I asked curiously.

"There's somewhere I want to take you. Think you're up for another adventure?"

As if he had to ask. "Yes, of course," I said too excitedly.

"Good," he said as he helped me off the rock, drying my wet feet with his shirt. I loved how he was always so sweet and thoughtful.

"Ready?" he asked.

"Ready when you are," I replied.

"Now, for this little adventure, I need you to wrap your arms around my neck and hold on tight," he explained.

With no questions asked, I quickly complied with his request, surprisingly not feeling nervous. I had so much trust in him that he could tell me to do anything, and I would know it would be okay.

As soon as I put my arms around his neck, two enormous white-feathered wings spread out from his statuesque body as though emerging from an ethereal glove compartment in his back. They were so beautiful and soft looking, yet strong and powerful at the same time. A part of me wanted to stroke them to see if they were as soft as I imagined. *He's not a pet,* I thought, so I kept my hands to myself.

"They are what separate angels from humans," Liam stated. "They are our source of strength."

"You're amazing . . . I mean *they're* amazing," I admitted, red in the face for the slip in words.

He looked at me with a grin and said, "Let's go!"

Before I could even blink, we were lifted off of the ground and into the sky. But it wasn't the ordinary blue sky with white, puffy clouds that I had seen all of my life. We were traveling through the realms of a giant rainbow filled with an enormous collection of bright, beautiful colors at the speed of light, yet it almost felt as if we were standing still, suspended in air as the colors passed *us* by. It seemed like mere seconds before a bright light filled my eyes. And as quickly as we ascended up into the air, we landed smoothly and gently. The ground looked like white fog, which rested in place, giving off a pleasing aroma as a greeting to all who entered its domain.

Liam gently put me down. I kept waiting for my feet to feel the sensation of touching the ground, but it felt as if I were floating. I could hear mystical melodies in the air, bringing to me great joy and comfort. It was the most beautiful music I had ever heard, and I knew I never wanted it to stop.

I finally broke the silence and asked, "Liam, where am I?"

"You are outside the gates of Heaven," he proclaimed.

"Why am I here? Did God change His mind?" I asked with sincerity, okay with the decision if He had.

Liam laughed and said, "No, He wanted me to bring you here to fill your soul up. He knew it would give you great comfort and strength to help you endure what is to come."

I continued to look around and only saw the whiteness and simplicity on the edge of Heaven. I thought to myself, *How could something so ordinary seem so extraordinary? How could this unpretentious place of whiteness give so much peace to me?*

"It's the love that fills the air," Liam answered. "Come, walk with me. There's something I want to show you."

We began to effortlessly walk upon what seemed to be an endless sea of clouds. I realized something that hadn't dawned on me before: Liam was holding my hand as we smoothly strolled in what felt to be no particular direction.

"Don't let go," he directed.

I didn't say anything in return. I just knew I needed to keep ahold of him, and I was okay with that.

Suddenly, as if a mirage appeared before my eyes, I saw something so magnificent, so resplendent, just ahead. My eyes squinted a bit to try and get a better focus of the unbelievable sight. I began rubbing them to make sure I wasn't dreaming this. I was in absolute awe of what lay before me.

I had heard about the Pearly Gates ever since I was a small child in Sunday school, and there they really were. My body was so overwhelmed with emotion that I had the urge to fall to my knees and cry happy tears. The beauty was more than one could ever imagine or comprehend. The sounds of singing voices, accompanied by an array of musical instruments, grew louder as we drew nearer to the front gates. No song or sound could ever compare in beauty and richness. The melody was drawing me in with each note that went by. There was no sadness or pain in the resonance. I knew I never wanted to leave. I tried to move forward, closer to the majestic gates that were drawing me to them, but Liam kept me firm in my place.

"This is not your time," Liam stated, taking me out of my trance.

I remained silent, but still hopeful. At no time did the thought bring any sadness to me. It was as if sadness and despair did not exist at all.

"Okay," I said. It was all I could muster in return.

"Come, there is much to do before you awake." And with that, he placed my arm around his sturdy neck and lifted me up into his arms once again.

Before his swift departure he stated, "It will be very important for you to try and remember the feeling of love and happiness that filled you while you were here."

I looked at his uncomplicated, wholesome face and simply nodded. Off we went, quicker than the speed of light. This time, I tucked my head into his ripped chest. Not as a result of fear, but for comfort and tenderness. It reminded me of all the times I would fall asleep in the car, and Daddy would lift me from my seat and carry me to my bed. Even though I would be half asleep, the half that was awake always felt such love by the action. I would keep my eyes closed, arms loosely wrapped around his neck, breathing in his leftover cologne from the morning, feeling safe from the rest of the world.

"Okay, Renee. Open your eyes."

I looked around and instantly recognized where we were. "Why are we at my school?" I asked Liam, slightly confused.

"Tell me what you are seeing," he said.

I began to look around. We seemed to hover above it, and I was able to see the hallways that I knew so well. I saw various classrooms and the cafeteria. I saw the principal's office and the gym. While I was able to see every part of the school, I didn't see people. I noticed, however, there was an assortment of colors all around.

"I see shadows of white, blue, black, and red. Some of them seem to be blended together like they're not altogether white or black or blue. What are they, Liam?"

"You are seeing people's souls," he said with a smile, proud of my newfound ability. "God has blessed you with the gift to look into someone's soul, Renee."

I continued to look around at the colors, but I couldn't make out who the colors were. I looked at the cafeteria and noticed several of the souls were black and blue. How could that be?

"What you are seeing are those who have been saved, but are under severe attack by the devil. The blackness is the dark shadow of sin, slowly climbing up them in an attempt to consume that soul," Liam informed me. Was it just coincidence that he kept answering the questions in my head, or could he hear everything I was thinking?

"Why are some of the black shadows flat with various shapes and sizes, hovering on the ground, the walls, and ceilings, while others appear to be human shaped?" I asked, aloud this time!

"The flat ones are not human souls. Those are sinful spirits, waiting to find their opportunity to enter into the human souls. Meet pride, envy, doubt, and lust, just to name a few. The smaller ones are there to assist in making one lose hope, or feel loneliness or despair."

They were everywhere and appeared to move around quickly, jumping from place to place, never standing still. They were like fleas going from one dog to the next.

"Those you see in the shape of a human are the lost souls. They have completely rejected Christ and play key roles in assisting the devil. But, we do still have hope for them," he added.

There were so many of them all over. I wished I knew who exactly they were. "What about the red ones? They seem to have black shadows hovering all around them," I said.

"Those are the souls going through their own spiritual warfare. They don't know the Lord, yet, and have only been taught the ways of the world. They are conflicted, hurting, and confused, with no one in their life to guide them into God's path. They are red because they are still being protected by The Blood for now, but the dark shadows are keeping them blinded from the Truth. Deep within, though, they know their soul is seeking something far greater than anything imaginable. They just need to open their hearts and minds to it."

"Like how I discovered the Pond of Purity," I inserted.

"Exactly. Now, do you see the ones that are blue? They are confident in who they are and who they live for. They are the ones God will bless and use to help fight the enemy. They are chosen by His grace and have a place in Heaven waiting for them when it is their time. We call them our earthly saints."

I was intrigued by the white-colored shadows that appeared to be larger than the rest and staying very close to the saints. I looked over at Liam as he stood tall and proud. I didn't need to ask, but he offered the information anyway.

"The white ones—those are the protectors and warriors sent by the Lord. They are angels." I could see them striking at some of the various black shadows with something in the shape of a sword. The shadows would disappear upon being stricken. I thought for a moment I could hear cries of pain.

It was all so much to take in. I felt so heavy and saddened by what was before me. I would have thought I would have seen more of the blue souls. I mean, Westcliffe is such a good place to live, with good people who attend church regularly. Why was there so much evil around? I didn't understand.

"Satan is heavily attacking your family and your town. He knows it's getting close to the end for him and wants to take as many souls as he can. It's all a numbers game to him. He thinks that the more souls he takes to hell, the more he'll show God how great he is. Oh, he's very clever in his ways of getting humans to blindly follow him, but he has no idea what's coming," he boldly stated.

"Why are you showing me this, Liam? I'm just a sixteen-year-old girl. What could I possibly do to make a difference?" I asked genuinely.

"Why do you think of yourself as so insignificant?" Liam asked.

"Seriously?" I questioned back. "I mean look at you! You have wings and . . . and . . . and you can fly for Heaven's sakes," I stammered, still trying to grasp the fact that I was actually having a conversation with an angel.

"Yes, but you have the Lord living in your heart. You have a strong soul that is full of love and compassion. You must believe that through Christ, you *can* change the world."

He was right; I did have the Lord in my heart. And I had always thought of myself as a loving, compassionate person. But I lacked the confidence I needed to make a difference to anyone. Looking at all of the lost souls made me feel a tremendous amount of stress and burden. Where would one even start to try and help?

"You start by those closest to you, and the love will continue to spread from there," Liam said.

"Liam . . . can you hear . . . ?"

"Yes, Renee, I hear your thoughts. God gives us that ability, but there is a catch," he said.

"A catch? What sort of catch?"

"It's easier for us to hear your thoughts when you are close to God, trying to live your life for Him, and vice versa. You are able to hear Him more clearly as well. But when you allow sin into your life or leave God out, it makes it a little harder for us to hear you."

"Oh . . . I see." I briefly began to recall an incident that occurred before the accident.

"You were the one that said 'don't' weren't you? You could hear what I was thinking when I was out with . . . with . . ." My memory started coming back in full force. "You were the valet attendant in Denver, weren't you?"

"Yes, that was me," he confessed.

"But you looked different and seemed so human. Now I'm really getting confused."

"We are able to enter into a human body as needed. Of course, the body must have a pure heart, and there's a catch there, too. You see, this is how we are able to use people to help other people, but this weakens our powers, so we only do it when absolutely necessary."

I listened in fascination, trying to absorb what he was saying.

"Sometimes we can just put a thought into someone's head to deliver a message, too. And, of course, we've been known to appear before man in a human-like form, but that can only last temporarily. It just all depends on what we feel will best help our assigned human."

Wow, now I was really blown away. I had a hard time wrapping my brain around it all.

"The little boy who kicked a red ball out into the street the first day I had my car. Was that . . . ."

"Yes, that was me, too. I needed you to slow down for a few minutes. Had you not been detoured, you would have been hit by an oncoming truck. I'll leave it at that."

I shivered at the thought of where he left off. He really was my guardian, wasn't he? I was really freaking out! Seriously, who gets to meet their guardian angel?

I could hear a laugh coming from Liam. "Stop! Don't laugh at me," I said with my own chuckle. "Put yourself in my shoes, why don't you, and see what you would think!"

"Sorry," he said.

"I'm not so sure I want you listening to my every thought. It sort of, well, creeps me out."

"I don't listen to *every* single thing you think. It mostly happens when you're trying to make a decision that would impact you or someone around you or when you need my help. While you've been here, however, I've listened to every word. It's how I will know when it's time to send you back."

"Is it almost time?" I asked, hoping he would say "no."

He didn't answer, but instead said, "It's time to go back to your resting place."

"You're the boss," I muttered back.

I looked down one last time at all of the souls that were mingling with each other, still wondering where I would fit into all of this. Just before we took off again, I quickly noticed one additional color, a color I had not noticed before. It looked sort of grayish. I couldn't tell that it had any distinguishable color, really.

"Liam . . . there's one soul with a different color. What is that?"

I could tell he was not ready to answer that question, as he chose to ignore it altogether. "Come, Renee. It's time to go," he said. And with that, he lifted me into the sky once again.

FIFTEEN

Test of Wisdom

We were back in my room, and Liam gently placed me on my bed. He must have thought I needed some rest after the profound journey. "Liam, I'm still not so sure that I will be able to help. I've only ever had one best friend, only one friend, who ever really wanted to be around me. I'm just not . . . ."

"Renee, was it because you're not a likable person, or was it because that's what you chose for yourself?"

I pondered his question intently, reflecting upon my life. Sure, when I was younger, I was a bit geeky with my glasses and stringy hair. I didn't care much about being fashionable or popular. I was always so close to my mom that I didn't feel like I needed to have a bunch of friends. That was what I grew up knowing and was comfortable with. As I got older, I can admit that my appearance also matured, and the clumsy, geeky girl was no more. But, I had Jamie and the goal of being valedictorian so I could go to an Ivy League school; that's all I ever needed. *Huh?* Maybe Liam was right. Maybe it was by my own accord that I didn't have many friends.

"That's what I thought!" he said.

"Will you stop that? Can't a girl have a moment of thinking to herself? Geesh!" I snorted.

"Renee, when you leave here, you will need to trust that God chose you for a reason. He doesn't make mistakes. Even when it may seem like He's abandoned you and allows tribulations to enter into your life, He always has a plan. Do you believe that?"

"Yes. Absolutely," I exclaimed.

"You're going to have to believe that when you go back as well."

As I sat on my bed trying to grasp everything, I began to wonder if I was going to remember all of this. The tour to Heaven's Gate, the color of one's soul, meeting my brother, and the time with Liam—these would certainly make things easier if I did.

"You will need to keep your soul fed and stay close with God," Liam stated.

"Keep my soul fed?" I asked.

"Yes . . . 'Man cannot live by bread alone.' Sound familiar?"

"Mathew 4:4, 'but on every word that comes from the mouth of God.'"

"And where do you get the word of God?" he asked as if I were his student.

I raised my hand to be a smart-aleck since I was sure he heard my thought and quickly said, "The Bible—too easy!"

With eyebrows raised, he blurted out in question form, "Ephesians 6:10 and 11?"

"'Be strong in the Lord and in his mighty power. Put on the full armor of God so that you can take your stand against the devil's schemes.' Youth camp . . . 2004, got anything harder?" I challenged.

He then began to pace the floor, hand on chin, in deep thought. This was getting fun now. "Philippians 4:6 and 7," he said confidently, ready to stump me.

Hmmm . . . let me think about this one. Philippians was Paul writing to the church he started while he was in prison. He was trying to give them some advice on how to live a Christian life. I remember Grandma J reading this to me when my cousin John had to be put in the hospital because of severe pneumonia. We were both very upset and feeling uneasy about his condition. As we waited for Aunt Mollie to call from the hospital, she began to read Philippians. It happened to be those verses that really spoke to me that day. Got it!

"Okay, I may not get it exactly as it says in the Bible, but here it goes—'Do not be anxious about anything, but in everything, pray with thanksgiving, and give your requests to God. And the peace of God, which goes beyond all understanding, will guard your hearts and minds in Christ Jesus."

"Is that your final answer?"

"Yes, final answer," I said excitedly. For a minute there I thought the lights had dimmed and that I had heard "Dun, dun, dun!" in the background.

"Renee Lewis, you have just won one million dollars," he teased.

I was surprised that all those readings Grandma J made me listen to actually stuck. She knew what she was doing . . . "Didn't you, Grams?" I said out loud, assuming the message would get to her somehow.

"Seriously though, it is so important that you remember these things that you have been taught. Keep your eyes open. The Lord is always with you," Liam said in a more somber tone. "Things will be very difficult, but we believe in you, Renee."

Remarkable . . . *they* believe in me. *I can't let God down then, now can I?*

"That's the spirit!" he said.

I smiled, proud of the newly formed faith in myself that I had discovered. I was determined to help in any way I could. *There are lost souls out there that desperately need my help, people I know and love. I'm just going to have to figure out who they are and what I'm going to do help them. Without any recollection of my stay here, I know I will have my work cut out for me.*

"The time is drawing near. Get some rest, and I will be back soon," Liam promised before slowly walking out the door.

"Okay . . . good night," I blurted out, knowing that even though he was gone, he could still hear me. And with that, my soul fell soundly asleep.

When I awoke, I saw two bright, cheerful faces looking down at me. I recognized them, and yet I didn't. "Grams? Grandpa J?" I said, unsure.

"Hey ya, kiddo," Grandpa said.

"You look so different, both of you. Grams, I just saw you, and you looked as I had always remembered . . . old and plump!"

"That's because at that time it was important for you to see something familiar. This is what I really look like now. It's my heavenly body," she explained, and gave me a cute model pose.

I couldn't believe how breathtakingly beautiful my grandmother was. I recalled an old picture of her in one of my mother's photo albums; she looked about my age. I thought she was beautiful when I saw it, but looking at her now, I was truly blown away.

"Wow, you guys look so amazing," I admitted to them.

They looked at each other, and both smiled, simultaneously saying, "We know!"

"So, what's going on?" I questioned.

"We know it's almost time for you to go back," Grandpa stated, "and we asked if we could visit you for just a moment. It's so good to see you, kid! Now how about a good old-fashioned bear hug?" He opened his arms wide for me to jump right into them. It was so good to get to see him, too. "Want to take a walk in your favorite garden?" he asked.

"Yes!" I said excitedly.

As we walked out of the room, the aroma instantly satisfied all of my senses. I could never tire of it.

"You two look so happy," I said, watching them holding hands as they strolled along the path, just smiling at each other in complete bliss. "I always knew you would make it to Heaven!" I admitted.

Both their faces lit up even more. I still couldn't believe how young and healthy they looked. It was really nice to see, especially since before Grandpa died from heart failure, he looked so frail and sickly on top of his balding head and all the wrinkles. Now he had a head full of sandy blonde hair, no wrinkles or aging spots, and was toned with muscles. I was impressed that I came from such good genes!

They separated, and each came to my side, putting their arms around my waist and shoulders as we continued our walk. As usual, the day was stunningly beautiful, with perfect weather and an array of fantastic colors surrounding us to stimulate our eyes; having my grandparents with me only added to its perfection. I had missed them so much.

We stopped in a small clearing that had a white wicker couch and two wicker chairs set up around a table waiting for us. On it was a teapot and cups waiting to be filled. Grams and I sat on the couch, and Grandpa poured us a cup before taking a seat in one of the chairs. It was a place of simplicity, and I felt that I could genuinely relax. I never wanted this time to end. We were all so quiet because there was a sense that no words needed to be spoken. We were all content to just be close to one another and felt that clouding the air with endless chatter would only take away from the moment. I closed my eyes to capture a memory of this flash in time. Grams always knew exactly what I needed, and for right now, this was it. I could feel my soul filling up with such love and peace. I opened my eyes and sipped some more of the tasteful cinnamon-flavored tea.

I began to think of Liam. I was ready to see him again. I missed him when he wasn't near me. I hated the thought of losing the memory of our time here. I couldn't help but wonder what it was going to be like when I went back into my body. I thought again about how he said things were going to be very difficult. For an instant, I allowed that thought to weaken me. But I reminded myself that I knew I would be able to handle anything that came my way because I had faith in the Lord and He in me. I let out a heavy sigh, and the silence was broken.

"What's on your mind, kid?" Grandpa asked.

"Just trying to figure out some things," I said. I gave such a broad answer, not wanting to show any insecurity I still had.

"Talk to us, sugar. Maybe we can help you sort things out," Grandma J urged.

I hesitated, but easily caved when I looked into her caring eyes. "Liam said things were going to be very difficult when I returned. I guess I was feeling a bit concerned with what's in store for me; that's all."

They looked at each other, not quite knowing what to say. It was as if they knew, but could not say. Grams put her arm around me and squeezed me tightly to her. She smiled and looked into my eyes and said, "You will be strong, Renee. Remember Isaiah 41:10?"

Not another quiz, I thought. Hmmm . . . Isaiah 41:10. *She has obviously given this verse to me before by the way she asked the question, so I had better get it right, or I'll get that look of disappointment from her.*

I started off slowly, picked up my confidence midway through, and ended with a strong finish. "So . . . do . . . not . . . fear . . . for . . . I . . . am . . . with . . . you; do not . . . be dismayed . . . for I am your God. I will strengthen you . . . and help you; I will uphold you with my righteous right hand."

Quite proud of myself, I raised both arms in the air with hands made into fists as if I had just won a marathon. As I pranced around the couch, pretending to wave to the cheering crowd, I heard a real sound of clapping behind me. Before I turned to see who it was, my cheeks instantly red from embarrassment, I already knew. I could feel him there with me. I smiled.

He walked up to our little tea party and asked, "Will anyone mind if I crash this party?" His brilliant smile stretched almost ear to ear; of course, no one could resist his joining us.

"I see you're still testing our girl," he commented to Grandma. She gave him a wink.

"Well, Renee. As much as we hate to part from you, I believe it's our time to go," Grandma said. They both stood up, arms opened wide, waiting for me to give them a hug. "Don't forget about that Baby Ruth," Grandpa reminded me. Silly man! Nothing on earth could compare to this. But I told him I would oblige his request if it made him feel good. Maybe he just wanted me to think of him back on Earth, and this was his way of doing it. After our hugs were complete, they began to walk off into the garden, hand in hand, and then disappeared into thin air.

"Thank you, Lord," I said out loud. I was so grateful for the time I got to see them. I turned to Liam and smiled. "What's next?"

SIXTEEN

Remember

I expected another amazing adventure with Liam, one filled with more flying through the air, going to the next lesson to be learned. I secretly hoped for another glimpse of the Pearly Gates, but I was quickly disappointed when he spoke.

"It's time, Renee. While there is no time lapse here, much has passed on Earth, and we need you in place." He stretched his arm out to me, and I grabbed hold of his hand. I squeezed my eyes closed as tightly as I could and waited, not knowing what to expect or how this was done. An instant passed, and I opened one eye to see where I was. We were exactly as we were. I was confused and looked at Liam, who seemed to be on the verge of laughing out loud.

"What?" I asked innocently.

"You look like you just bit into a lemon. Why the sour face?" he said, pleased with his little pun.

"I thought you were sending me back. I wasn't quite sure how that was going to work."

"In a hurry?" he asked.

"Well, no. But you said it's time."

"It is . . . almost. I thought we could talk some more. Is that okay with you?"

Uh, let me think about it for a split-second. "Yes . . . sure. Why not," I said, saying it casually, as if he couldn't really sense the excitement in my mind.

"Good, let's walk then."

We began to leisurely walk atop the jeweled pathway. I didn't pay much attention to where we were going; I was just thankful for the extra one-on-one time with my personal angel. We held hands, just like Grandma and Grandpa J were earlier. It was nice, and the thought of going back didn't enter my mind. I was in the here and now and wanted each second that passed to count. I sensed, for some reason, that my return was going to be hard for Liam, too.

"I've enjoyed our time just the same, Renee," he muttered.

It didn't make much sense to me, though. I'm just a geeky girl from Earth, and he's this incredible angel who completely takes my breath away every time I look at him. The comparison is almost nonexistent.

"There you go again, not giving yourself any credit for the person, the soul that God created. Why is it that I see in you what you cannot see in yourself? Do we need to have this whole conversation all over again?" he asked with a hint of frustration in his voice.

"No! Sorry, I'm still trying to get used to this 'confidence thing' that I'm supposed to have now. Habit . . . sorry!" I apologized again.

"I know it is impossible for you to remember this, so I will create the memory for you of our very first meeting. You were not the first human I've been assigned to. As angels, we are all given assignments according to rank. We start off with smaller tasks or are used as backups when a guardian is being attacked at the same time by several demons. Think of it as someone in the military who is a new recruit. As they accomplish assigned tasks, they get moved up in the rankings. Some of us are naturally better warriors and move up quicker than others."

"Oh, where are you in the rankings, then?" I asked curiously.

"I would be considered a colonel in your world. I have a band of angels that I am in charge of and will assign tasks to. If there are any angels or saints under severe attack, we will intercede and plan the best course of action, which often means going into heavy battle.

"I had been in this role for quite some time and was called by the Lord for a meeting. He specifically requested I be your protector. I was a little perplexed by the demotion, but accepted the task without question."

"Gee, thanks!" I snorted.

He gave a quick smile and said, "Let me finish before you start drawing your conclusions!"

"Okay . . . I'm waiting. Carry on," I ordered.

"As I was saying, I never asked the Lord why I was once again being used as a guardian because of the complete trust I have in Him. I took the assignment with pride and came to Earth on February 17, 1993. I entered into the room where your mother was in great distress. Nate—he's your mother's protector—was doing all he could to save her from dying. The Lord had not given the word that it was time for her to go to Heaven, so he had to find a way to keep her alive. He had tried guiding the doctor's mind by whispering instincts into his thoughts, but the room was all in a horrendous panic as your mother's heartbeat continued to decline. He had no choice but to enter into the doctor's body and take over the situation altogether. Once Nate did this, things moved along smoothly, and before anyone knew it, you made your grand entrance. The nurses carried you to the baby crib to examine you as you were screaming at the top of your lungs. Feisty little thing you were!"

"Yes, I've heard. When my mom tells me the story, she said that I came to an abrupt stop though."

"Yes, that's right; as I walked up to where you were lying, before I could even touch you to give you some peace, you stopped and looked right at me with those pretty, little blue eyes. You instantly sensed my presence. That was the first time any of my humans had done that. I understood immediately why I was assigned to you. Your soul was able to connect with mine. So you see, my little soul mate, you are significant. Don't ever think of yourself as less than I am just because I have different powers than you. We are both from God, and we will fight together to help bring more souls to their rightful home."

"Liam, may I ask a silly question?" I should have known he already knew what it was.

"Because God gives us free will—all of us. We have the choice of where we will spend eternity. He will never force anyone to love Him the way He loves all of us. The only way He knows where someone's heart lies is by the choices he or she makes. He allows the devil to tempt us for several reasons. Mostly, He wants to make sure we love Him more than self-gratification and the things of the world, even more than other people. God wants us to make the choice that He is first priority in our lives."

"Why do you say 'us?' Aren't angels already in Heaven?"

"Well, we do have a head start that way," he said, and gave a slight chuckle before getting very serious again. "But the devil will tempt us, too, trying to bring us down with him. There are fallen angels, you know. That's why Satan is so determined to try and win this battle. He wanted to be equal to God, so God kicked him out of Heaven. There *is* no one equal. He is Almighty. He is Love, and Peace, and Hope. He *is* the Great *I am!*" Liam stated this so sternly, with such focus. I thought I saw moisture build in his eyes.

"I wish everyone could see how much He loves us. It brings great pain to me to see the rejection He endures every single day."

I didn't know what to say or what to think. Liam showed me the colossal range of emotions and feelings he had, emotions and feelings just like mine. I was taken aback by the vulnerability he allowed me to see. I was moved.

I wanted to wrap my arms around his waist and give him a hug to try and console him, but before my action could catch up with my thought, he stiffened up, wiped a tear away, and said, "Forgive me. I have never found myself in this position before. It will not happen again. I need to be strong." He said this as if he were convincing himself more than anything. He puffed his sturdy chest out to show he meant it.

"It's time, Renee."

"Wait! Not yet. I want to spend . . . ."

"Too much time has already passed," he said, and with that, he placed two fingers over my eyes, commanding them to shut. Everything went completely black. "I'll never leave you," he said, his voice fading. "Remember." They were the last words I heard.

SEVENTEEN

Awakening

Beep . . . beep . . . beep . . . beep, beep . . . beep, beep . . . beep, beep, beep. The unsteady noise began to awaken me. As I tried to open my eyes, everything seemed so blurry . . . so bright. It took blinking them several times before I could find the strength to keep them open. I could see shadows standing around me and hear mumbling voices.

"Get the doctor. Hurry!" a nervous, muffled voice said.

"Renee, sweetheart, it's Mom. Can you hear me?"

I tried to focus on her, judging by the direction I heard the voice coming from. My focus was steadily coming back, but I could not find a way to answer her.

"If you can't talk right now, it's okay," she said. She grabbed my hand and held it tightly in hers. "Thank you, Lord Jesus, for bringing her back to us. Thank you."

Just then, the doctor came into the room. "If everyone could please step away from the bed for just a moment . . . Renee, it's Dr. Middleton, can you hear me?"

I focused on him, but still couldn't find a way to answer.

A bright shining light crossed my eyes and made me squint. I could feel cold fingers pull them apart as the bright light continued to blind me.

"Renee, if you can understand me, please tap your finger twice."

With concentration, I was able to barely move my right index finger, tapping it twice on my stomach where my hand lay. I could hear a sigh of relief fill the room.

"Sometimes, when someone has been in a coma for any length of time, he or she has a hard time speaking at first. Since she was able to understand me, I don't think we have anything major to be concerned about right now. We'll have to do a thorough exam and scan her brain again to make sure."

"Yes, I understand, Jack. Thank you!" I recognized the deep voice immediately. It was my dad. I was surprised to hear him address the doctor in such a casual way though. I saw them shake hands, and the doctor was off again to his next patient. He ordered the nurse to bring me some water and make sure I was able to drink some on my own.

My dad stepped up to the end of my bed. His form was still a bit hazy but I could tell it was him. "Thank God, you pulled through," he said with such relief in his voice. I kept trying to focus on him, but all I could make out was a black suit that covered his body. His usually shaggy hair seemed to be slicked back, away from his face.

My mother was immediately back to my side and holding my hand. I saw the tears streaming down her face.

"Mom," I said. I was able to barely whisper. My throat felt so sore; much like it felt when I had strep throat in the sixth grade. The word sounded so raspy, I didn't even recognize my own voice.

"Yes, sweetie, I'm here. I'm here. Try not to speak. You need to rest and build your energy back up."

I was so confused, though. I wanted to ask why I was in the hospital and why her hair seemed to be much longer than what I remembered. I felt sore, exhausted, and weak, so I took her advice for the time being and closed my eyes. I knew I would need this rest while I could get it. I just had a feeling.

With my second awakening, I found it easier to open my eyes. And, of course, there was Mom, right by my side as if she had never left. I saw a glass of water on the bedside table and tried to reach for it. My throat was as dry as the Sahara. I still felt weak and struggled to get my hand to reach it. My mom gave me a helping hand and put it up to my lips. I took a small sip through the straw and then another. "Thanks, Mom," I whispered.

I could feel her warm hands rub across my face and through my hair, stroking me gently like she used to do when she would put me to bed at night as a little girl.

"How are you feeling?" she asked with concern in her voice.

"Sore," I whispered back.

"That's understandable. Your body has been through quite a lot."

"What hap . . . " It was enough for her to understand.

"You were in a severe car accident. You've been in a coma for some time now."

I had a hard time comprehending what she was saying. As hard as I tried, I couldn't remember being in a car accident. She must have seen the look of confusion on my face.

"Try not to think so much about it right now, sweetheart. We're just all so thankful that you're here and alive. That's all that matters right now."

I pointed to the glass of water, anxious for another drink to soothe my throat. I wasn't done talking yet. After a few more sips, I managed to speak again. "What happened?" I asked again, looking straight into her eyes. I needed to know.

She was hesitant in speaking. She looked down in order to start the conversation. "Do you remember anything at all?" I shook my head no. She let out a heavy sigh.

"We had all been invited to a party up in the mountains. I had decided to leave early, feeling a bit tired, while you and your father stayed behind. I guess you were both having a good time and weren't ready to leave."

She let out another sigh. I could tell having to relive the story was hard on her, but I had to know.

"About an hour later, you were ready to come home as well. Your father was driving down the steep road a little too fast and lost control of the car. The limo driver that had dropped me off earlier was headed back up to the Dellamorte house . . . well, you can imagine what happened next."

I envisioned each word that came from her mouth, but it still didn't make sense. There was something missing; she wasn't telling me everything. It was like reading a book with half the pages torn out and trying to guess what led to the tragic ending.

I gathered that my dad made it through just fine. When I saw him after my first awakening, I couldn't tell he had been hurt.

"Who is Dellamorte?" I asked first.

"Mr. Dellamorte is your dad's client. As a matter of fact, he's now your dad's only client," she blurted out with frustration.

"Dad's okay?"

"Well, he is now. He had a broken arm and a few broken ribs. His face looked like he had just lost a boxing match to Muhammad Ali, but as you can see, he recovered nicely."

This was so shocking to me; given the time it would have taken for him to look that good. Fear struck my heart as I asked the next question.

"How long . . . ."

"A long time, sweetie," she said as tears welled up in her eyes. "You have been in a coma for eleven months. It is now January, 2010." She held my hand tighter as she gave me this shocking news with a shaky voice.

Tears began strolling down my face, and every ounce of me wanted to scream at the top of my lungs *"No!"* My body began shaking violently; perhaps from having to hold in this anger from the deplorable news I had just received. I tried to look at my mom's face, but the tears were too heavy, and she was a colorful blur. "No . . . why?" I said with all the strength that I could pull together. I didn't understand.

"Nurse . . . nurse," I heard my mother's panicked voice yelling out.

My body was still trembling, and I was feeling very cold.

"She's going into shock," an unfamiliar voice stated. "Get the doctor!"

Those were the last words I heard before blacking out once again. Another day lost.

I didn't know how much time had passed after my third awakening. I opened my eyes and looked around the room. There was Mom sitting on the recliner with the Bible resting on her chest. She was sound asleep. I began to recall the information I was given during my last awakening. I still had a hard time believing I had just missed out on eleven months of my life. I couldn't help but start to cry once again. My mother woke up and saw me wiping away my tears. She was quickly by my side once again, holding my hand.

A few minutes passed before she could say anything. "Don't cry," was all she could manage, as she was crying herself.

"I'm sorry, Mom," I said as I was trying to fight the tears.

"Sweetheart, don't be. There's nothing for you to be sorry about." Her silence was a signal that she was trying to think of what to say next. I could tell it was hard for her to find the right words to soothe me, but that didn't stop her from trying.

"The Lord saved you and that's all that matters now."

My crying stopped almost immediately; it was odd, but I felt a presence of peace in the air, and as I took long, deep breaths in, I felt it come over me as well.

She was right. *I am saved, and I will get through this.* I truly began to believe that. Right then I decided that I would not lie on this bed and feel sorry for myself one second more. I had already lost another day of my life, and now I needed to do whatever it took to get out of here, and that would be what I would focus on.

I looked at her and said "I love you" in an almost normal voice now. She was surprised by my quick adjustment in attitude. She looked around the room and just said, "Thank you," to no one in particular; but she knew whom she spoke to.

"The doctor said with some physical therapy, you should be back to your old self in no time," she assured me.

I smiled in an effort to comfort her. I could tell in her voice and the weathered look on her face she had been slowly dying with worry herself. If I had to guess, she probably only left my side to use the restroom and shower. I knew with her by my side, I was going to get through this.

EIGHTEEN

Confusion Sets In

I began thinking about my life as it was all those months ago. Certain things would pop into my head like Jamie and I hanging out at Cliff Lanes; Miss Adamma giving her testimony about how she came to the US; riding my horse, Tex, on our ranch; and finally, the red Explorer I got for my birthday, bringing with it a smile to my face. Yes, I remember now, walking out and seeing Mom and Dad in front of that exciting surprise. That was the day . . . the day . . . Kyran came to town, the day he came into my life.

Yes, it was all starting to come back to me. Not only were the Dellamortes Daddy's new clients, but one of them was my almost, would-have-been first boyfriend. My eyes lit up as the flurry of thoughts rushed through my head. I slowly reached for my neck to see if the beautiful necklace he gave me was still there. My hand came up empty. I remembered the night he gave it to me, the night of the party. It was such an amazing night. Then, as quickly as my smile came, it left me once again. I remembered finding Daddy to go home. He had been drinking, and I asked him to let me drive. In his frustration, he lost control of the car, and that's when it all went black again.

I looked over at my mom, tears in my eyes once more. She knew it was all coming back to me. She knew that I knew the entire story now. She lowered her head, shamed, although I wasn't sure what she had to be ashamed about. It wasn't her fault Daddy acted irresponsibly. I grabbed her hand, which rested on the railing, and whispered, "I remember. I remember everything, Mom. Isn't that great?" She was shocked at my response. I don't think the word "great" coming from my mouth was what she had expected.

"Yes . . . that is great, sweetheart. But aren't you a bit, oh, I don't know, mad?"

"Mad? You mean mad at Dad for being human and acting stupid?"

"Well, that too. But mad at me for not telling you everything all at once."

I thought about it for a moment. "I'm sure you were just trying to be gentle and not overwhelm me with everything at once. I forgive you, Mom!" I said with a smile.

"I have to admit; you're taking all of this much better than I ever expected."

"Would being mad at the world change the circumstances? If I'm going to get out of this joint, it's gonna have to start with my attitude. Yes, deep down inside I am a little ticked off at Dad, but I'll have that talk with him later."

I didn't understand the concerned look my mother still showed on her face; something else was eating at her. I thought my positive outlook and attitude would help her in healing from this tragedy, too, but apparently I was still missing something.

"Speaking of Dad, where is he?"

She sighed deeply before speaking. "He's off on another one of his out-of-town business trips. He said to tell you that he loves you very, very much whenever you woke up again."

I had to admit, a wave of disappointment drenched my mind. I would have thought he would have stayed here by my side this whole time, too. I could tell by looking at my mom, I wasn't the only one who was disappointed.

"What about Jamie? I'm sure she has just been worried sick about me. Did you let her know I was back?" I asked optimistically.

"Yes, well, I left a message with her dad. She's had a lot going on, too, so I'm sure she will try and visit soon."

"What do you mean she's had a lot going on, too?"

"Oh . . . you don't want to get into all that right now. Let's just concentrate on getting you well so you can come home."

I could see how much she wanted to avoid speaking about the other two most important people in my life. I didn't quite understand. Huh? The "loss of understanding," that must be a disease I picked up while in my coma because it seems to be happening a lot since I woke up.

"What about Kyran? Has he at least been concerned about me?"

"Kyran's been here a few times checking in on you, yes. But after the first few months, I just told him that I would call him when anything changed."

"Why did you do that?" I asked confused. Dang disease! Again, I didn't understand.

"I don't know, truthfully. I just always felt awkward when he came around you. I got an uneasy feeling, so I just told him I would keep him updated."

"So . . . did you call him yet?"

"Well, not quite. I wanted to make sure you were stable and feeling good before bringing anyone in to see you."

I let out a big sigh in an effort to understand her reasoning for everything. Honestly, I was still quite weak and wouldn't want for him to see me like this anyway.

"Mom, if I'm feeling up to it tomorrow, can you help me get myself together so that he can come for a visit? I really would like to see him."

"Sure, honey, if you're feeling better. Let's just take it one day at a time. Okay?"

"Yeah, I guess so."

"You must be feeling very hungry. Want me to get you something to eat?"

I was still lost in thought over Jamie not coming to see me and my mom telling Kyran not to. "Uh-huh . . . that sounds good, Mom."

"Great. I'll run down to the cafeteria and get you some hot, fresh soup. I'm sure it's best to start off with something light. How does that sound?" She seemed so happy that she was finally able to do something.

"Yeah . . . great. Thanks," I said still lost in my own thoughts. I just knew if it had been Jamie that was in this bed, no one would have been able to keep me from seeing her. I couldn't possibly understand what would keep her away. Dang disease!

"I've been made aware that the girl is back."

"Yes, master."

"Although our attempt to destroy her failed, you have done well while she has been away. You will still need to attack with a vengeance, my young servant, as I can feel the time is near."

"Yes, I understand, master."

"You must gain her complete trust so all our work is not lost. Do you have a plan?"

"You do not need to worry. I will have her under control."

"We are counting on you. I knew you would be of great use to us one day; now is that time. Do not let us down or . . . ."

"You have my word. I understand completely."

"Good. The reinforcements we brought in have also done well, and everything is falling into place. The rest will be up to you."

"Is that all?"

"Yes, go. We will be watching you."

"Jamie? It's Ren!" I said excitedly over the phone.

"Oh, hi, Renee; I heard you woke up," she replied too casually. She hadn't called me Renee since the third grade.

"Yup, I'm back! I would love to see you, I mean, if you're not too busy and all."

"Ummm, okay. I'll try and stop by before Aden picks me up. Give me an hour to get ready, and I'll just have him meet me up there."

"Great! I can't wait to see you!" I said elatedly.

"See ya."

Just then, my mom came through the door with my first meal in eleven months. I wasn't really hungry, though.

"Guess what? Jamie's coming up for a visit. I can't wait to see her!"

"Really?" She sounded shocked. "Well, that's great, honey." She pulled out the bowl of soup from the brown bag and lifted off the top. Then she dug around inside the bag, looking for the spoon, which she then peeled the plastic wrap off of. "Where did those crackers go," she stated as she was now digging in the bag again. "Ah-ha, here we go." She opened up the crackers and set them on a tray next to the soup before carefully walking it over to me and setting it on the shifting table attached to my bad. "Here you go, sweetheart. A nice cup of chicken soup; good for the soul!"

"Mom! Aren't you excited that Jamie's coming for a visit?"

"I said that was great, didn't I?"

"You said it with as much excitement as when you found out you needed to start wearing reading glasses. 'Well, that's great,'" I mimicked.

"I'm just not so sure you're ready for company is all. You are still recovering from a major head injury. I don't want to see you get too worked up," she said as she began to try and spoon feed me like a baby.

"M-o-m," I said stretching this one syllable word into three. "I think I can manage to feed myself."

"Okay, but if you start feeling tired, let me know. I don't mind, you know."

"No, but I do!" I said taking the spoon from her hand. I put the spoon into the bowl and lifted out my first bite. My arm felt shaky. I barely managed to get the spoon to my mouth, spilling a few drops on the way. I was much weaker than I thought, but I wasn't about to let her know she was right. I guess my stubbornness was still as strong as ever. I kind of felt bad, though, about taking away her chance to help me.

"Hey, Mom, if you really want to help, how about grabbing a brush and a headband for me so I can fix myself up a bit." Knowing my mom, I'm sure she had a bag with all of my things ready for this moment. She reached underneath my bed and unzipped my blue bag with the bobcat, our school mascot, on it. I knew her too well.

"Can you sit up some more? I'll brush the back of your hair."

The shifting bed made it easier with the push of a button. It straightened me up even more than I was, and I found enough strength to pull myself forward. I was almost out of breath just trying to shift myself around. *Boy, do I have my work cut out for me.*

"Mom, can you please tell me what's been going on with Jamie? I need to know."

"For starters, Brenda left her dad." Wow, she just jumped right into that one without me having to beg and plead for it. Oddly, this time I wished she would have eased in to it a bit more. Jamie's parents were like an extension of my own, and the news was quite shocking.

"What? Why? They seemed so happy before . . . well, you know, before . . . ."

"Yes, well, things seemed to change quickly. Apparently, she just wasn't happy anymore, and Paul couldn't give her the things she wanted out of life."

"Poor Paul, he's such a nice guy, too. It must be hard having two women pack up and leave you." I couldn't believe it. Paul didn't remarry for five years after Jamie's real mom left when she was two. Brenda has been the only person Jamie ever knew as a mother.

My heart bled for her. I know this must have been very hard on both of them.

"So you said for starters. What else is going on?"

"Well, she's got this new boyfriend . . . ."

"Aden, is it?"

"Yes, how did you know?"

"She said she was going to stop by here before he took her out tonight."

Mom rolled her eyes a bit. I could tell she didn't approve of this guy either. I had never even heard of him.

"Who is he?"

"He's one of Kyran's cousins. Their family seemed to expand once school let out—college boys, apparently. To make a long story short, Paul didn't approve of Jamie's going out with someone that much older and their fighting never seemed to stop. So, she moved out."

"What?" Okay, now things are really getting freaky. I would never have imagined anything like this happening in a million years. I stuttered my next sentence, a side effect from the LOU disease I picked up. "Where is . . . who is she . . . wh . . . wha . . . what?"

Miraculously, my mom understood my gibberish. "She's living with the Middletons."

I could now feel my heart racing and my breathing getting out of control. This just couldn't possibly be. She disliked Beth Middleton more than I did. I didn't understand.

NINETEEN

Hope

The news of Jamie was shocking to say the least. My head felt warm as I continued to breathe at a fast pace. It was a lot to take in.

"Calm down, sweetie. Now you know why I wasn't quite ready to tell you everything. Don't get yourself so worked up. Breathe gently," she said. She took slow, deep breaths in herself, hoping I would follow her example, which I did. I knew I needed to regain my composure before I hyperventilated and went into shock. After a few minutes passed, my racing heart began calming down, and I sat quietly, trying to absorb this new information once again.

"Renee, are you sure you're really ready to see her? She is not the same Jamie you remember."

I had a hard time processing that. How could she not be the same Jamie that I had known and loved like a sister since the third grade? How could eleven months change a person that drastically? I knew I needed to see her, now more than ever. She had lost the only mom she had known, and I'm sure having a best friend lying in a hospital bed half dead was hard on her, too. Perhaps if she saw me alive and well, things would start to go back to normal. I needed to look, act, and be positive for her sake. I had to do something. I had to hope.

I impatiently looked at the clock on the wall, waiting for her arrival. I felt nervous, unsure of what I was going to say, unsure of what I was going to see. All I could think to do was say a quick prayer.

"Lord, please be with me. Keep me strong and give me the right words to say, the words she needs to hear. Amen."

My mother went home to change out her bag of clothes. It was her way of giving us some space to try and sort things out. A few minutes later, Jamie walked in. It was the first time I had seen her since the day I dropped her off at the gym after school. That was the day Kyran and I connected.

I gave her a big smile. She looked just as nervous as I felt. "Jamie, it's so good to see you!" I said excitedly. I felt some tears well up in my eyes. It had been too long.

"Hey, Renee. Good to see you, too," she said, keeping it casual. She stayed near the door, unsure of how close she wanted to get to me.

"Please come in. Sit here," I said, patting the bed. I wanted to be near her. I had missed her so much. She reluctantly obliged to my request; however, the silence between us was deafening. I looked into her sad eyes. Mom was right; she was not the same Jamie.

"I see you colored your hair," I said nonchalantly to start the conversation. She had dyed it a bleached blonde color. I liked her natural color much better, but she didn't need to know that.

"Yup, I wanted a new look. Aden likes it a lot."

"So you mentioned him on the phone. Tell me about him."

"He's everything a girl could want and more," she said a bit smugly. She seemed to have some spitefulness in her voice. I wasn't quite sure where it was coming from.

"Well, of course, I wouldn't expect anything less from you," I responded, still trying to figure her out.

She began to fidget, twisting her hair around her finger over and over. Her black fingernail polish really stood out against her new 'do. She sat quietly, with the exception of smacking her gum, just waiting for me to say something. "So, my mom mentioned he's Kyran's cousin. I bet he's just as cute!" I said with a smile, trying to lighten up the air around us, not realizing it was going to backfire on me.

"Of course he's just as cute as Kyran. What? Did you not think I could get someone just as good-looking as he is?"

I couldn't believe how she was acting. Where was this coming from? "No, Jamie, I would never think something like that. I don't understand why you seem so condescending toward me."

"Oh, don't act so innocent, Renee. I figured you'd be happy that I had to settle for Kyran's cousin. You knew how I felt about him, and you didn't hesitate to take advantage of me being sick, did you?"

"No, Jamie, it wasn't like that. It was all accidental, I promise. I would never intentionally hurt you. I was going to tell you everything that weekend. It just all happened so fast." Tears began streaming down my face as I began to feel desperate for the right words to say. I knew by the look on Jamie's face she had felt betrayed by me, and that was the very thing I had tried to avoid.

"Sure you were. If you really wanted to tell me, you would have done so before it had gotten too far with him."

"You had been sick in bed, Jamie. I didn't want to upset you because when I did talk with you on the phone, you sounded so weak and awful."

"Good excuse," she retorted.

I knew she was right, too. It *was* my excuse. I had been too much of a coward to face her regarding my feelings toward Kyran. What could I really say to that? We sat silently for a few seconds, though it felt like hours. She started to get up to leave, and I grabbed her hand.

"Wait, Jamie. Don't go, please," I begged.

When I grabbed her hand, I instantly felt pain, not pain from my own body due to my accident, but pain from her. Colors of blue and black flashed into my eyes for a brief moment. I wasn't quite sure what I was experiencing, but what I did know was that my best friend in the whole world was about to walk out that door, and I knew I needed to stop her.

"Jamie . . . forgive me!" I shouted in desperation.

She stopped in her tracks, hand still in mine. She didn't say anything in return, but rather waited to see if there was more.

"Please," I said on a softer note. "I was wrong for deceiving you in every way. Please, can you forgive me?"

I felt as if my words caught her off guard. They weren't what she was expecting to hear. She slowly sat back down on my bed. Her eyes filled with tears. She looked into my eyes, checking for their sincerity. She had been through a lot in the past year. Trust had dissipated from her spectrum of emotions, and it was obvious I had lost hers a long time ago. "You hurt me," she finally admitted.

"I know, and I am *so sorry*. I never, ever wanted it to come to this. I can't even explain how it got to this point. It just all seemed to happen so fast. I promise, I tried to stay away from Kyran, but everything just kept falling into place for us. That's why I knew I just needed to tell you about everything, but I never got the chance."

The tears began spilling over, streaming down her face. I could tell she wanted to say more, but her cell phone rang and cut her off. She quickly wiped her finger underneath her eyes in an effort to regain her composure.

"Hello," she answered. She listened to the voice on the other end intently.

"Okay, I'll be right down," she said, and hung up the phone.

"I gotta go. Aden's waiting for me down in the lobby. Just give me some time to think, okay?"

If that was all she was ready to give, I was going to take it. "Okay, take all the time you need. I'll be here when you're ready," I said in a low, crushed voice. I didn't want her to leave yet.

She walked toward the door, and as she began to walk out, she turned halfway around. "See ya, Ren," she said, before walking away.

That's when I knew there was hope.

TWENTY

Wishful Thinking

As I lay in my bed pondering all that had happened with Jamie, there was a knock on my door. I figured the nurse wanted to just check on me, like she always did.

"Come in," I shouted out.

The door swiftly opened, and the only thing I saw was a huge bouquet of white, long-stemmed roses.

"I have a delivery for a Miss Lewis." While he tried to hide his accent and pretend to be a delivery boy, I knew exactly who it was.

"You're a terrible actor," I said in return.

A bright, smiling face popped out from around the flowers. "Yes, not one of my talents, unfortunately," Kyran admitted. He carefully placed the beautiful vase filled with the delightful flowers next to my bed. After my earlier conversation with Jamie, I didn't know what to say, think, or feel. I decided to keep things generic. "Thanks, they're beautiful."

Kyran had such a huge smile on his face. He made it very obvious that he was happy to see me. I only wished I could have said the same about him.

"It's so good to see you, *amore*. It's been too long." He stretched his neck out and gave me a kiss on my cheek. "I was overcome with joy when I heard the news you had awakened . . . ."

As I looked at him talking, carrying on, I thought it strange how everyone in my life that I had seen up to this point had changed; Mom with her long hair and weathered face, Jamie with all of her changes, and even Dad, with his fancy clothes and his hair combed back. But not Kyran . . . he looked exactly the same. Perfect.

"Renee?" he said, waving his hand in front of me. "Sweetheart, what's heavy on your mind? You didn't hear a word I was saying."

"Oh, sorry, just thinking. So much has happened, and I guess I'm still trying to take it all in."

"I understand; no apology necessary. Do you want to talk about it?" he asked.

"Not really."

"Is it about your visit with Jamie that has you down?"

"How did you know about that?" I asked.

"I guess you could say it's one of the perks of her dating my cousin. He told me she was coming by for a visit. Did everything go okay?"

"Why don't you ask your cousin?" I sneered.

"Whoa, whoa, love. Where is this coming from?" he asked genuinely.

"It didn't go very well, obviously. I may have lost my very best friend because of you." I knew I was also to blame, but it felt good to share it with him right now. After all, it does take two to tango.

"I thought she had gotten over this," he said dubiously.

"So you two have talked about this?" I asked with some frustration.

"*Amore*, you've been in a coma for eleven months, and she's now dating my cousin. We have spent time together, so yes, the subject did come up. She came to me about it first after Beth had told her everything."

"Beth!" I shouted. "Why is Beth involving herself with all of this?"

"Because of her jealousy," he answered.

"Her jealousy? Of who?" I asked, confused.

"Of you, *bellissima*, who do you think?"

Now that didn't make any sense. Beth has never liked me for reasons I've never understood. "Why is Beth, the most beautiful and most popular girl in school, so jealous of me that she has to butt her nose into our business?"

"Think about it. She's always wanted to be in your shoes, Renee. You have a good stable family; she doesn't. You are smart and content with who you are; she's not. And once she found out that we had a thing going, which she had wished for herself, it made her even more spiteful. She took complete advantage of your being in the hospital and slid into your place with Jamie, hoping this would infuriate you."

"Yes, I heard Jamie was living with her now. Unbelievable!" I commented, throwing my hands only halfway into the air. All of this drama was taking any strength I had away. "I'm surprised she didn't try to steal you away, too."

"Oh, but she did . . . try, that is. I told her I only had eyes for one person," he admitted before taking my hand and kissing it gently. It was so easy to get distracted by him, but I had to remember what Jamie was feeling and going through, the sadness that had spread upon her face as she spoke of the betrayal she felt.

"So, what did you say to Jamie when you spoke about us?"

"I told her the truth. I let her know how we felt about each other," he replied.

"Oh . . . and how do *we* feel about each other? Tell me, because I don't really know anymore."

I could tell by the look on his face that my blunt question offended him. "If I remember correctly, the last time I saw you, you were to tell Jamie about us so we could move forward in our relationship. I've told you how much I like you, Renee, and I thought you felt the same. Tell me if I'm wrong, and I'll walk out of that door right now and stay out of your life."

His face seemed so sad and almost desperate. I felt terrible for hurting his feelings. Besides, I was madder at myself for betraying Jamie; he didn't have anything to do with my falling for him.

"No, of course I don't want for you to completely walk out of my life. You have to understand, though, that this has been so completely overwhelming. I don't want to lose her."

"Don't get so worked up, *amore*. Everything's going to work out just as it should," he confidently assured me. "In the meantime, you need to get some rest so you can get out of this place. I am planning the perfect going home dinner—just you, me and a couple of kings and queens waiting for a rematch."

"Kyran, I don't think . . . ."

"Shhhh," he said, placing his finger on my lip. "Don't think right now. Too much has happened, and you'll only get yourself confused and worked up. Just rest and I'll be back tomorrow." He leaned forward on the bed and kissed my forehead this time. I sensed he was in a hurry to leave, but wasn't sure why.

"Kyran . . . ."

"*Domani*," was all he said before quickly walking out the door.

I found myself in the same place I was before Kyran had unexpectedly arrived. I lay on my bed and continued to ponder all that I had learned, with even more information to think about since the last time. The scent from the beautiful roses grabbed my attention. I looked over to gaze at the origin of the pleasing aroma that was filling the air around me and noticed an envelope attached to the vase. I reached over and took it off, immediately feeling something bulky inside. I anxiously ripped it open, and out fell my beautiful sapphire necklace. My eyes widened with delight, as it was just as exquisite as I had remembered. There was also a note from Kyran.

These last several months without you have been torturous. I've missed you. We have a lot to make up, so get well soon, mi amore. Kyran

I sighed as I placed the note on my bed. What was I to do? What choices did I have here? Resume my friendship with Jamie just like it used to be and completely forget about Kyran? Or get more involved with Kyran and lose Jamie forever? Or, more ideally: Jamie would get completely over Kyran and realize that she cared more about our friendship than letting her old feelings get in the way, and everything would work out. I could have both my best friend back and my first boyfriend. I had a feeling that was more wishful thinking on my part, but it never hurt to wish!

TWENTY ONE

Alek and the Dellamortes

I was so completely lost in my thoughts that I didn't even hear my door open.

"Hey, sweetheart!"

I jumped. "Mom! You scared me; I didn't hear you come in."

"Sorry . . . you seemed lost in thought. Everything okay?"

I was just about to answer when right behind her another visitor arrived, one I had never seen before. I had a confused look on my face, which triggered an introduction from my mom.

"Oh . . . Renee, this is Alek. He's our new ranch hand. I tell you what; he has certainly been a Godsend. He came shortly after . . ." My mom's voice drifted off as she continued to mumble about Alek. I couldn't help but stare at him, feeling a sense of familiarity as he looked right over at me. He looked down, as if to blush privately, and then looked at my eyes again. I sensed some sort of yearning, like he wanted me to remember who he was. Had I met him before? Where? When?

" . . . and so with your father gone so much, he's really come in handy," my mom finally finished up. She had to snap her fingers to wake me from my stupor. "Renee, you're lost again. Sorry, sweetie, I never gave you the chance to tell me if everything's okay."

"Yeah, Mom, everything's fine."

She then noticed the roses sitting on the table and gasped, "Oh, my! Those are absolutely beautiful. Your dad is so thoughtful sometimes." She assumed too quickly they would be from him.

"I hate to disappoint you, Mom, but they're not from Daddy. They're from Kyran."

She immediately stopped sniffing them as if now they had some sort of distasteful smell and said, "Oh . . . how lovely. So when did he come by?"

"Actually, he just left a few minutes before you got back. He seemed in a rush to leave. He said he just wanted me to get my rest so I could hurry up and get out of here."

"How coincidental," she smirked. I knew my mother had a strong dislike for him, I just wasn't sure why.

"He brought me this, too." I held up the necklace to show her, but it slipped from my fingers onto the floor.

Alek was quick to recover it for me, knowing that I wouldn't be able to just hop right off the bed to get it. He looked at it for a moment and said, "Someone must be trying to impress you with this beauty. Is it working?"

He handed it back to me and I sat silently, not really sure how to answer that.

"I think we've discovered what Renee was lost in thought with, Mrs. Lewis," he commented with a smile, looking right at me, but talking to my mom. He broke our gaze when he turned toward her and said, "Need anything else before I leave, Mrs. Lewis?"

"No, dear, these suitcases should keep us for another week. Thanks for the lift."

"Anytime. It's nice to have the company," he commented back.

"Renee," he said as he took off his straw cowboy hat, and that was when I noticed he was looking at me with bright, magnetic blue eyes. "I'm sure we'll see you soon."

"Um-hmm," was all I said, nodding my head back and forth. He smiled again, adding a wink this time, and put his hat back on.

Mom waited until the door closed completely before chiming in, taking the opportunity to tell me what an amazing guy Alek was.

"What a nice gentleman. Don't you think so, Renee?" I could tell she was up to something.

"Yup, he seems really nice, Mom."

"Oh, and so handsome, too . . . don't you think?"

Oh, no . . . the twang was coming on thick now. She must really want me to be as impressed with this guy as she is. "He's a looker alright," I said, really meaning it, but saying it without feeling. I didn't want her to sense that I did have an appreciation for the whole cowboy look with his boots, jeans, and hat. He was rugged, unpretentious, and charming all rolled into one . . . and I liked that.

"I'll tell you what. Our ranch would be in serious trouble had he not shown up. God always has a way of working things out. He was only going to stay through the summer, but when his scholarship fell through and he needed to earn some extra money, your father made him a really nice offer to stay through the following summer. I'll tell you, he has been such a blessing." Her eyes seemed to light up when she talked about him.

"That's really great, Mom. I'm glad he was there for you. Sounds like Daddy hasn't been around much; are you ready to talk about that yet?" I knew she had been avoiding the subject, but I needed to know everything that I missed while I was gone: the good, the bad, and the ugly.

She released a heavy sigh, trying to muster up the courage to tell me about my father. "So, I told you that he was pretty banged up from the accident."

"Yeah . . . and?"

Another sigh. "It took him about six weeks to fully recover from everything. He had to give a few of his cases to Mr. Peterson. At first he kept his pro bono cases because Mr. Peterson only wanted the money-making ones, but then Mr. Dellamorte came into the picture.

Your dad had been worried about all of the hospital bills that were racking up between the two of you, and Mr. Dellamorte made him an offer he couldn't refuse. Or at least it was an offer that *he* thought he couldn't refuse. I told him not to do it. I didn't get a good feeling about it from the get-go. But, your father seemed to be in a different place mentally. He was so guilt-ridden from the accident, he no longer thought straight. So, as soon as he was fully recovered, he officially became Mr. Dellamorte's personal attorney and advisor. With that came many long hours and out-of-town trips. Your father completely threw himself into his work."

"Where does he go?" I asked curiously.

"Everywhere. The Dellamortes seem to have businesses all over the world."

"What kind of businesses do they have?"

"Apparently, mostly things in the entertainment industry. Your dad doesn't discuss too much with me. He comes home a couple of days at a time, and then he's off again. I suppose I can't complain too much. I've spent every single day here with you, so I haven't really been there for your father either. The day you first awoke, he happened to be back in town and had just come to see you. It was such a blessing from God that he was able to be here when you came out of your coma. I could tell there was such a sense of relief from him."

I remembered having the conversation in the car with Daddy about him taking the job with Mr. Dellamorte; that was when he got really upset with me and lost control. A sense of disappointment fell upon me when I heard he chose to take the job.

"I talked with him on the phone last night when you were asleep. He said to tell you that he loves you very, very much, and he hopes to be home soon."

I couldn't help but wonder if that were really true, or if she was just trying to make me feel better. My face reads like a book sometimes, and my mom is always quick to pick up on things. I'm sure she sensed my disappointment. Not only in his taking that job, but the fact that he wasn't here with me. I gave my mom a smile in an attempt to make her feel that her little antidote worked. I was feeling weary and needed to get some rest. It had been quite a long day. I knew the days ahead were going to be even longer.

"Mom, I'm going to get some sleep. I'm really tired."

"You get your rest and don't worry about me. I'll be right over here reading," she said, pointing to the cot setup in the corner with its twin-sized flowered comforter and matching sheets. It was very obvious in glancing around the room that this had been her home for almost a year now. I looked at her thankfully. She had been a great source of my strength.

I turned over and whispered softly, "Thank you, Lord, for my mom." And with that, I went fast to sleep.

TWENTY TWO

Beguiling Proposal

A week went by, and my recovery was coming along, but not as fast as I'd like. I had several visitors, which certainly helped brighten my days.

Mo brought me some great CDs to listen to and said she was ready for me to get back out on the stage. Miss Adamma came by, asking if she could pray with me, and brought some sort of African sweet bread with custard filling for us to try. My Aunt Mollie flew in from Texas for a few days to visit and help out with whatever my mom needed her to do. It felt good, seeing how much they all cared about me.

I was in physical therapy several hours a day trying to rebuild my strength. The muscle tone that I had built from years of dancing was a thing of the past. My favorite part of therapy was going into the swimming pool for an hour each day. I felt so weightless, as if I were floating in the air. This made it much easier for me to control my muscles and move around—not to mention, it was so relaxing.

Mom was always right by my side, but today she needed to go back to the house and change out our suitcases again and take care of a few things. Apparently, that had been her routine for the last year.

I had just started my swim time when *he* finally showed up. He had told me he was going to be back the next day, but had never shown. I noticed him, complete with swimsuit on and towel in hand, after I had emerged from holding my breath underwater. He was the epitome of what a perfect body should look like, with ripped abs, a toned chest, broad shoulders, and muscular arms, complete with the perfect Italian tan. It made me nervous. I was grateful that Jack, my therapist, was there with me. Kyran splashed into the water and swam to where we were. He was a very good swimmer.

"What are you doing in here?" I impatiently asked with teeth clenched.

"I've got this from here, Jack," he said in a cool, calm voice, making it obvious that he had this preplanned.

"Sure man. I'll see you tomorrow, Renee," Jack said casually as he walked away.

"What?!" I shouted with outrage. "Jack! You can't leave me here alone! Get back over here!" I demanded.

He looked back and said, "You're not alone. Don't worry, it's going to be okay."

"Augh! You are so fired, Jack! Just wait until I tell my mom!" I threatened like a four-year-old. Kyran just laughed at me while I was throwing my tantrum. "This isn't funny, Kyran. You set this up, didn't you?"

"It's amazing what a couple of Benjamins will do," he said arrogantly.

I started to try and walk away, not quite able to really swim on my own yet, but Kyran had ahold of my waist where Jack had left off. My heart beat faster.

"Just relax, *amore*. I'm a very good swimmer and teacher."

"I know how to swim, thank you very much. I'm just not strong enough to do it yet, you . . . you . . . you big jerk!" He continued to laugh at me, paying no attention to the pitiful name I so stupidly came up with. "You said you were going to be back last week. A little late, don't you think?" I scoffed. Not that I should care anyway.

"Sorry. I should have called. I had to go out of town for a few days. It was an unexpected trip that I couldn't get out of."

"What-ev', it really doesn't matter anyway," I said with my arms crossed and body stiff.

"Look, I was wrong not to call and tell you, but I'm here now, and I've got a surprise for you. So quit being a big baby and loosen up a bit."

"A surprise? What kind of surprise?" I asked suspiciously.

He turned away toward the door and whistled loudly like he was at a baseball game or something. That's when the door sprang open, and in came a crowd of people, all in swimsuits. And just as suddenly, the air was filled with lively music, and people were splashing into the pool, laughing and hollering at each other. They were all people from my school. *Unbelievable, he's giving me an impromptu party.* I was in such shock that it took me a minute to see the big poster that someone put on the wall saying, "Get better soon, Renee. We miss you."

I looked around, only caring if there was one specific person there. There were so many people everywhere, splashing and tossing around beach balls, that I wasn't able to spot her. That's when I felt a tap on my shoulder coming from behind. Kyran helped me turn around, and there she was. A huge smile spread across my face.

"Hey, Ren! Surprise!"

I held out my arms, and we gave each other a tight, long hug. Tears instantly ran down my face from happiness, although one couldn't tell since I was already soaking wet.

"This is the best surprise ever," I proclaimed. I couldn't believe this was actually happening. It was the happiest I had felt since coming out of the coma, and there was one person I had to thank for it. I turned back around, still smiling, and wrapped my arms around Kyran's neck. "Thank you," I whispered in his ear and gave him a peck on the cheek.

"Anything for you, love," Kyran gently replied. "Now come on, we've only got this place for an hour."

"How did . . . ."

"Don't worry about how." He cut me off. "Just enjoy the moment. Now come, let me help you get around so you can visit everyone."

"Wait, let me talk with . . ." And before I could turn back around to talk with Jamie, she was gone.

He dragged me around the pool while I kind of just floated. It seemed like everyone from the eleventh grade was in attendance. People who I wasn't even sure knew I existed before came up to me and gave me their best wishes. Even Beth was there, and while her greeting didn't seem as genuine, I appreciated the fact she came anyway. This was such a great time for me that I didn't even want to think about her trying to steal my best friend. There would be time to get things out in the air later.

Kyran was so sweet and gentle with me, constantly checking to see if I was having a good time. I loved it when he put me on his back and would dive under water and swim while I just held my breath and held on. My body would float behind his, as he would go up and down like a playful dolphin, coming up for air and then back down again. I was impressed by his boundless strength and endurance.

He noticed that I was getting tired and offered to help me out of the pool to rest.

"No, I'm fine, really. You've made me so happy right now, even after the way I treated you. How can I ever thank you?"

"Say you'll be mine?"

"Do what? What do you mean?" I asked naively.

"Will you be my girlfriend?" he asked, giving me those irresistible dimples and gazing into my eyes.

I looked over at Jamie and saw her splashing around and playing with some guy that I assumed was Aden. I released a sigh, still cautious of what to do.

"Why do you always keep me waiting?" he said playfully. "Just say yes, Renee. What more can I do to prove to you how much you mean to me?"

"Okay . . . yes. I'll be your girlfriend," I replied impulsively.

Kyran lifted me up, forcing my arms around his neck and spun me around as much as possible with the water resistance. The next natural move seemed to be to give him a kiss. He obviously felt the same way because our lips locked together simultaneously. My head began to spin as if he were still twirling me around in circles. Although our lips had connected once before, it was different this time; I was an equal participant. I had waited sixteen years to find the perfect boy to give myself to, and Kyran did meet the description of picture perfect. But was he perfect for me?

As we continued our embrace, the arguing thoughts going on in my head were interrupted. Everyone around us started clapping, whistling, and even yelling, like our home team had just hit a home run. I quickly pulled my lips away from his and blushed from embarrassment. As I looked around and saw the cheering crowd, I felt unsure that I was on the same team that had just gained a point. Confusion made its way back into my head because Kyran was so amazing, and yet I felt so strange. I mean, really, who is this guy? Who on earth can find a way to rent the St. Thomas More Hospital rehabilitation pool for his own private party? Oh God, what have I just gotten myself into?

And then I remembered as clearly as if I were still lying in my bed pondering my choices; it was my wish come true. I didn't even think it was a real option to consider, yet here it was, and the choice seems to have been made for me.

As my mind drifted into this quandary, Kyran placed his finger under my chin so I could look at him once more. "Love, stop your worrying. You're going to fit into the family so well. Just relax and have a good time."

"Yeah . . . okay, Kyran. You're right. I do need to just enjoy this, huh?" I said, more as an attempt to convince myself. I could feel my heart racing, and my breathing was getting heavier. "I mean, any girl would be on the top of the world right now, right? Right? This should be such a happy moment for me . . . right?" I said, stuttering.

"Are you okay, Renee? You look flushed. Renee . . . Renee . . ." were the last words I heard Kyran say. I wonder if every girl fainted after accepting her first commitment proposal.

TWENTY THREE

A Different Kind of Happy

I awoke in my bed to the sound of my mother shushing Alek. Her attempt at trying to not awaken me failed miserably.

"Hey, Mom," I said a bit wearily.

"Oh, hi, sweetheart! We tried not to wake you. Jack said you were really tired after your session today. He must have really worked you hard, huh?"

"Um-hmm," I fibbed. I wasn't ready to tell her everything that had occurred. Kyran must have brought me up to my room and left before she got here.

Alek didn't seem as easily convinced for some reason. "Hey, Renee," he said, and casually strolled my way.

"Hey," I said nonchalantly.

"Have a good time?"

"Yup, um-hmm," I said, looking away from him. "I always enjoy the pool part of my therapy." Which was true.

"Anything exciting happen?" he questioned.

"Like what?" I asked in return, trying to figure out why he was curious about my day.

"Like perhaps a visitor or two coming to see you."

My eyes widened. How did he know?

"You know," he whispered closer to my ear while my mom was busy calling on the nurse asking for fresh, dry sheets, "I saw a stranger carrying you into your room. It's not right to lie to your mom, you know."

I sat silently, unsure of how to respond. I knew he was right, but I was also a bit perturbed that he was meddling in my business.

"Did she see, too?"

"No, she was busy talking with Jack and asking how your session went. He seemed to be filling her ears with lies, too. I know it's not my business, but if you have to lie about who you're with, is he someone you should be hanging around?"

Just then, my mom's attention was back on me.

"They're going to bring you some fresh sheets, sweetie. How about we get you out of that wet swimsuit? I can't believe Jack let you crawl into your bed soaking wet. Alek, can you help me get her to the bath?"

"Mom! No! That's so embarrassing."

"Oh, get over yourself. I just need someone strong to get you there, and I'll take care of the rest. We need to get that chlorine washed out of your hair before those fumes make you lose any more of your brain cells."

"My pleasure, Mrs. Lewis," Alek replied.

He looked at me and said, "Ready?" before lifting me off of my bed. My arms were wrapped around his sturdy neck. This all felt so familiar, so comfortable. I kept seeing flashes of white; I thought I was getting ready to pass out again. I squinted and blinked several times, trying to stop it. It seemed to work.

"Just place her in the tub, Alek, and I'll take care of the rest," my mom said.

He gently placed me down and said, "See you tomorrow."

What did he mean he'll see me tomorrow? What was going on tomorrow that I didn't know about? *I bet I know who does though.* "Mother . . . what's going on tomorrow?" I asked in a somewhat accusatory tone.

"I've got to run some errands, and I asked Alek to keep you company while I'm away."

"I'm not a child, Mom; I can take care of myself."

"I know you're not, but it will make me feel much better. So don't argue the point because you're not going to win this one." She then looked up at him and said, "Thanks again, Alek."

He tipped his hat at my mom and smiled at me. "Renee, see you tomorrow," he said, and with that, he walked out the door.

I felt anxious when I awoke the next morning. I wasn't sure how the day would play, having to spend time alone with someone I had just met. I could hear my mom in the shower getting ready. She said she had an appointment at ten this morning, but was secretive about where she was going. I didn't pressure her for any more info than what she had wanted me to know.

My room phone rang. "Hello!"

"*Buongiorno, amore!*" an Italian voice said on the other end.

"Huh?" was my response.

I heard a slight chuckle before he replied. "That means good morning, love."

"Oh . . . sorry. I should have guessed as much. Good morning back to you."

"How are you feeling today?"

"A little better and a little stronger each day," I replied.

"That's what I want to hear. What's on the agenda? More therapy?"

"Yup, same ol' routine. Mom's going to be gone for most of the day, though. I'm a little bummed about that, but don't get any crazy ideas because . . ." He cut me short before I could say she found a replacement to watch over me.

"Why am I still on the phone then? Give me an hour, and I'll be there." Click.

"No! Kyran . . ." But it was too late. I tried calling right back on his cell, but it went straight to voicemail.

"Augh! That's just great," I sighed.

My visitor arrived, and I was so embarrassed that I hadn't even had the chance to clean myself up or brush my teeth. This day was starting off just wonderfully.

"Morning, Renee. I brought you a vanilla chai latte," he said as he handed me the cup. That was very thoughtful of him, although I didn't really know that I liked vanilla chai latte. Sure smelled good though.

"Thanks," I said shyly, and sniffed the sweet aroma coming through the lid. "Smells really good."

He sat in my mom's usual spot and sipped on a cup of his own.

"Yes, smells heavenly," he replied.

I took a sip and began to enjoy this slightly sweetened beverage with a hint of cinnamon and clove. It reminded me of Grams for some reason.

"So, what time is therapy?" he asked.

"Jack usually gets here at eleven."

He looked at his watch. "How about I take you for a nice stroll and get some fresh air?" he offered.

I rubbed my hand over my hair, remembering I probably still had bed head and was still in my pink flannel jammies, which were covered with hot pink hearts and red kisses. *Geez, Mom, couldn't you have brought me something a little more grown-up?* I thought. Funny . . . they didn't seem to bother me until now.

"Ummm, maybe another time. I'm really not dressed to go anywhere."

"Oh, come on. I'll help you put your robe on. You look fine exactly the way you are. I think the fresh air might do you some good."

I realized the shower had been stopped for a few minutes and called out to my mom. "Hey, Mom!"

"Yeah," she shouted back.

"Alek's here. Can you help me when you get a chance?"

"Yes, give me just a minute to throw my clothes on."

A few minutes passed, and she came out with her towel wrapped around her head.

"Hey, Alek," she said.

"Good morning, Mrs. Lewis."

"What's going on, Renee?"

"Can you help me freshen up? Alek wants to take me out for a stroll."

"Absolutely! I think that would be just lovely," she said with a too-big smile.

Alek rolled the wheelchair up to my bed, and they both helped me into it. My mom rolled me into the bathroom so I could make myself more comfortable with my appearance. She helped me put on my favorite pink headband after brushing out my hair, and helped me get my robe and matching slippers on. I looked in the mirror and stared at the inch-long scar that sat at the top of my forehead.

"Remind me when I get out of this place to get bangs. This scar is so ugly," I said to my mom.

"Oh, it's barely noticeable," she said in a motherly attempt to make me feel better.

"It's always the first thing I notice when I look in the mirror, though." I continued whining like a child.

My mom looked at me with a gratitude that I didn't understand. "Sweetheart, you look gorgeous. When I first saw you after the wreck," she started to say, and then lost her words as her lips began to quiver. I looked at her with sorrow as her expression turned to agony.

"I'm sorry, Mom. I shouldn't . . . ."

"No, let me finish, please. When I first saw you, I barely recognized who you were. I thought surely there had been some sort of mistake. Surely this poor girl, lying on the table lifeless, was not my beautiful Renee. I wondered if you would ever look normal again, that's how bad it was. Every single part of your face was swollen and black and blue, but look at you now. It is a miracle and a blessing from God that you have merely a small scar on your forehead. I hope you can see it as that."

I will never complain about my scar again.

After we hugged each other and cleaned ourselves up, my mother rolled me back out to the room. I felt much better about the little adventure now.

"Ready?" he asked.

"If I have to," I said casually, not wanting to give any hint of being excited.

He gave me a crooked smile and said, "Let's go, then. What are you waiting for?" We simultaneously laughed as he rolled me out into the hall.

The ride to the elevator was quiet. I wasn't really sure what to say, and I guess he didn't, either. When we entered the empty elevator, I had to break the ice.

"Uh . . . thanks for helping my mom out so much. She seems to really like you."

"No problem. The feeling is mutual."

"I hate that she forced you into watching me today. Sorry about that."

"Nobody forced me to do anything. I'm glad to be here, so don't sweat it."

The silence between us was painfully obvious again. What do I say next? He decided to fill the air by whistling the tune "Take Me out to the Ball Game" until the door finally opened, and out we walked.

"It's a perfect day for a walk. The air is a bit chilly and crisp, but I think you'll find it refreshing."

How right he was. As soon as we went through the double sliding doors, the fresh air instantly felt so invigorating, as if I had been locked up in a cell all this time. My mom had been so overprotective about letting me go out before now. It felt liberating. The bright sun smiled, casting its energizing rays upon all that my eyes could see. Everything seemed so happy. Perhaps it was just because I was happy in this particular moment that it gave the magical illusion that everything around me was, too. I could hear the birds singing their little hearts out, especially as we got closer to the park situated across the street from the hospital.

Alek hadn't spoken a word. He allowed me to just take it all in and have some peace and quiet. I closed my eyes and took a few deep breaths. He stopped me just a few feet away from a swing set and put the brakes on the wheels.

"How about a swing?" he asked.

"I don't know if I'm strong enough."

"I'll help you, Renee. I'll never leave you."

"I'm sorry, what did you say?" He had spoken so softly I barely understood the last part of what he said.

"Nothing. I just said I'll help you, and you can lean on me for support."

"Okay, if you're sure."

"Positive. Now just put your arms around my neck, and I'll do the rest." He tenderly lifted me up into his arms and placed me onto the swing. "Think you can hold on?"

"I think so," I replied, hoping I had enough strength to follow through with it.

He walked around me and started gently pushing me. It was nice.

"So, do you remember anything about being in your coma?" he asked curiously.

"No, not really, why?"

"Just wondering. I've heard that when people go into a coma, sometimes they get a glimpse of Heaven. I was wondering if you had that same experience."

I thought about it for a minute, trying to recall any memory whatsoever from my deep rest, but nothing came to mind. "I can't say that I can recall anything. You gotta remember . . . I hit my head pretty hard!"

"Perhaps it will come back to you one day when the time is right."

"Perhaps," I replied.

He continued to slowly swing me, and my hair waved through the air. I felt just as happy as I did yesterday when Kyran gave me that surprise party, yet this was so simplistic and unpretentious. I liked being around Alek. I found something very comforting about him.

"Getting tired yet?" he asked.

"It's starting to get a little hard holding on to these chains. Maybe we can go for a stroll around the park," I suggested.

Once again, he lifted me from the swing and placed me back into the wheelchair. The thought crossed my mind while we meandered around the park that I didn't know much about this "Godsend," as my mom liked to call him. Where was he born, what college was he attending, what did he want to be when he was finished with his education, etc.?

Before I started asking him a million questions, I saw Kyran walking toward us. He didn't look too happy. "Alek, it's time to get going," I said hurriedly.

"Yes, I spotted the stranger walking into the hospital ten minutes ago. He must have figured out where we were."

"It's Kyran, and he's not a stranger. He's my . . . my . . . friend." I stuttered when trying to get "boyfriend" out and couldn't do it. "So, you saw him earlier and didn't say anything to me?"

"Why ruin the good time you were having? I knew he'd figure it out eventually," he smirked.

"Alek! That wasn't very nice. Now he looks upset with us."

"He'll get over it, I'm sure. Just relax, and let me smooth things over with him."

He began to walk toward Kyran before I could object. I kept a careful eye on the two as they exchanged words only thirty feet away from me. I could hear low mumbling, but couldn't make out what they were saying. I noticed Kyran with his puffed-out chest, much like he was in Denver with the valet attendant. Surely he didn't have a past with Alek as well. I was concerned that that side of Kyran was going to come out again. Their exchange was taking much longer than what I thought was necessary, and I was really starting to worry.

"Excuse me," I yelled, "can someone come take me in? It's getting close to my therapy session." They acted as if they couldn't hear me, and their harsh arguing continued.

"Guys, *please!* I need to go in now," I shouted even louder this time. It finally grabbed their attention as they both looked over at me. Then, they marched toward me. My heart was racing at this point.

"Renee, what is this guy doing here with you?" Kyran asked in a jealous voice.

"I tried to explain over the phone, but you hung up on me too quickly."

"So please explain now why my girlfriend of one day is spending time alone with a stranger."

I thought it odd that both of them referred to the other as a stranger, as if I were with some dangerous person that I didn't know or something.

"Look, Kyran, my mom set this whole thing up because she was going to be gone most of the day. She felt better about leaving me with Alek because she trusts him."

"So have you told her about us then?" he asked.

"Not exactly. I have to wait for the right time, Kyran."

His heavy sigh deflated his puffed-out cheeks. I could tell he was disturbed by the fact that I hadn't told anyone about us. "Well, can you at least tell 'Alek' over here to leave now," he said, using his fingers to make quotation marks in the air when he said Alek's name.

"What do you mean, tell him to leave? My mom asked him to be here; I can't just make him leave."

"Renee . . . *amore*," he said in a more soothing voice as he bent his knees so he could look into my eyes at my level, "you have to make a choice here. Is it me or him?"

"That's not fair, Kyran. Why would you put that on me?"

"You know I will take care of you and watch you just the same. It's time you tell your mom about us, don't you think?"

I had to think about it. He was right. He was my boyfriend now, and I couldn't keep hiding that from my mom. It was deceitful. I felt terrible about having to choose, but it was clear that these two wouldn't be able to coexist in the same room.

I hesitatingly looked over at Alek. It was harder than I thought to send him on his way. "I'm sorry, Alek. I want to keep the peace here. Do you understand where I'm coming from?" I asked him.

"Renee, I understand you have a choice to make. We're all faced with choices every day. If you ask me to leave, I will; just be careful about the decision you're making."

"You heard her . . . she made her choice. Now if you'll excuse us," Kyran said with a pompous grin and rolled me away from Alek. I looked back at him with an apologetic stare. He slightly raised the corners of his lips and simply waved.

TWENTY FOUR

Angels All Around

The next week of therapy was intense. I was bound and determined to get out of the hospital and back to my life. I tried to reach Jamie several times, but always got her voicemail. I was disappointed she had not come back to see me. Perhaps not all was forgiven yet.

I did finally tell my mom of the newfound relationship I had with Kyran. She wasn't overly joyful about it to say the least, but she confessed that I was at the point in my life where I had to learn how to make my own decisions; it was my time to grow. Telling her about us opened the door for Kyran to come see me every day. He always brought me sweet surprises, like a stuffed teddy bear, chocolates, and more flowers. Mother always watched him with a careful eye, but he didn't seem to mind. I think he took it as a challenge and scored major points when he brought her a beautiful bouquet of flowers as well. Of course, the points were with me, not my mom. He definitely played the role of storybook boyfriend to a T. He still had a way of making me feel special by giving just the right compliments and undivided attention. He even knew how to make me laugh uncontrollably when I needed it most. And though I did enjoy our time together, every now and again Alek would cross my mind.

The phone in my room began ringing. "Hello," I answered.

"Hey, princess! How's my girl doing?"

"Daddy! Oh my gosh! I'm great. How are you?"

"I'm about to get on Mr. Dellamorte's private jet, but I wanted to call you before takeoff to let you know I'll be home next week in time for your birthday." That's right; my seventeenth birthday was coming up. I had forgotten all about it.

"That's so awesome, Dad. I've missed you so much."

"I've missed you, too. So we've got a date next week, then?"

"Yes! Of course, I always have time for you."

"Oh, they're signaling me to get off the phone now. I love you, pumpkin. I can't wait to see you!"

"Bye, Daddy. Love you, too."

I noticed my mom waiting nervously in the corner of the room for our conversation to end. Her hands were in the prayer position up to her mouth, and I thought she had tears in her eyes.

"Did you hear that, Mom? Dad's gonna be home next week for my birthday. I've got to get better. Get Jack on the phone. I want to see if we can bump up my therapy an extra hour a day."

"You're already pushing yourself pretty hard, Renee. I think you shouldn't overdo it," she responded.

"But, Mom, I want to be out of here for my birthday. I need you on this. You've been my greatest supporter. Don't stop now. Come on, please?" I begged relentlessly.

"I just don't know. Let's talk to the doctor first and see what he thinks."

"I'll tell you what. Let's do one extra hour tomorrow, and if it's too hard on me, I'll back off and not say another word about it. Deal?"

She thought about my negotiation carefully before answering. "Okay, Renee. I know how stubborn you are, and how much this means to you. Just promise me that you won't overdo it. Promise?"

"Oh, thank you, thank you! I promise," I said, giving her my pinky finger so we could do the pinky swear. She happily obliged as she intertwined her pinky with mine, sealing the promise.

While my mom got Jack on the phone and was getting everything set up for me, I called Alek from my cell phone. I don't know why, but he was the first person I wanted to tell about my dad coming home and the added purpose for getting out of the hospital. I also needed someone else to help give me support. I knew this next week would be tough.

"Hello," he answered.

"Hey, Alek! It's Renee," I said in my most positive voice possible. I wasn't sure if he was still disappointed with me from our last visit.

"Hi, what's up? Calling to check on Tex?" he asked.

"How *is* Tex?"

"You've got a great horse there. He's anxious for you to come home!" he chortled.

"Well, tell him I'm anxious too, which is sort of why I'm calling you."

"Oh, yeah? Why is that?" he asked curiously.

"My dad just called me and said he'll be home for my birthday next week."

"That's great news!" he replied.

"I know, which means I need to do everything I can to get out of here. I talked Mom into bumping my therapy up to an extra hour a day. She wasn't too happy about it, but she knows how strong willed I can be."

"So how is it that I can help you, Renee?"

"Well, for starters, I thought you could say a prayer or two for me. I need all the support I can get, and something tells me you would know just what to say to God on my behalf."

I couldn't see his smile, but I could hear it in his voice through the phone. "I think I *am* just the guy who could do that for you. I'm glad you thought of me. Anything else?"

"Since you asked, a vanilla chai latte sounds pretty good this morning," I admitted.

"Small, medium, or large?" he asked.

"Hmmm . . . I'm feeling a little risky today. Let's go for the medium," I laughed in response.

"No . . . not the medium. You are living on the wild side! I'll be there in forty-five."

"Great! See you then." I was really excited for the chance to see Alek again. I could make the excuse that I still felt terrible about having to choose Kyran over him and this was my way of trying to make it up to him, but it was more than that; I just didn't know what it was yet.

"Who was that, dear?" my mom asked inquisitively.

"Alek. He's bringing me a vanilla chai latte."

"And what, may I ask, brought that on?" She sounded pleasantly surprised.

"I don't know. He crossed my mind, so I called him. I thought he would be good for prayer support to help me get through this next week."

"I couldn't agree more. So what's Kyran going to think about you spending the morning with him?"

"Well, I kinda didn't think that one all the way through. I just hate how he is so jealous of Alek that he can hardly stand to be around him."

"Is Kyran coming for a visit today?"

"He said he needed to work on some family business today, so I don't think so. I'll cross my fingers and hope they don't run into each other again."

My mom crossed hers, too. "Well, I better get ready myself. I'm going to the beauty shop to get my hair chopped off, and then I have another appointment to go to."

"You sure have been having a lot of appointments lately. Everything okay?"

"Everything is fine. There's absolutely nothing for you to be worrying about. You just need to concentrate on getting yourself better."

"Okay," I said, unconvinced. I had noticed my mom hadn't been looking as vibrant as she always had. She really ran herself down looking after me. At least now I was able to get out of bed on my own, though a bit clumsily at times, and get myself dressed.

I dabbed some makeup on, added a little extra over the scar, and fixed my hair. I wanted to make a good impression on Alek. Perhaps it was still my guilty conscience from our last meeting and departure. At least he *seemed* happy over the phone to talk to me. That was a good sign; perhaps I was forgiven.

I was even more excited than I had anticipated when he finally walked through the door. "I have a delivery for Miss Lewis. One hot chai, a medium no less, for you," he said as he handed me my warm drink.

"Thanks," I said and took a sip. "Ummm, that hit the spot!"

"Where's your mom?" he inquired.

"She said she had another appointment to go to. I'm starting to get a little worried about her."

"Your mom is a strong woman and has a lot of faith. I wouldn't worry too much about her."

"I guess, but it's hard not to."

"When you start to worry about her, pray. He'll take care of it."

"Yeah, you're right. I've sort of lost that since my awakening. I used to pray all the time for everything. Now I seem to have too many other things on my mind," I replied.

"Believe me, I know. People get so caught up in their own little worlds that they forget about talking to the very One who created the world for them in the first place. But He's still there, waiting, loving, caring for you."

"How'd you get to be so spiritual and connected with God?"

"I pray and read His word every day. That's what keeps me strong."

I considered what he said, how praying and reading the Bible made him strong. This has been what's missing in my life lately. I've seen my mom reading her Bible plenty, but I had yet to open mine. Between therapy and Kyran, I had been pretty distracted.

"You're right. Would you mind sharing some verses with me right now?"

"Okay, I think I've got one for you. Psalms 34:17 and 18," he said as he handed me my Bible. He even pretended to wipe off some invisible dust from it. I thought to myself, *What a smart-Alek!* I chuckled aloud, cracking myself up with that one.

I quickly turned to Psalm and found the verse he wanted me to read.

"Read it out loud," he suggested.

"The righteous cry out, and the Lord hears them; he delivers them from all their troubles.

The Lord is close to the brokenhearted and saves those who are crushed in spirit."

"I have another for you. Read Psalms 91:11 and 12 now."

I flipped over a few pages and found it.

"For he will command his angels concerning you to guard you in all your ways; they will lift you up in their hands, so that you will not strike your foot against a stone."

I thought about the two verses Alek chose for me to read. What I gathered was that God is always listening to our needs and because of our faith in Him, He would see us through our troubles, big or small. I began to ponder the second verse some more. *"He will command his angels to guard you in all your ways."* Huh? I wondered if I had angels around me that very minute. Where were they when I clumsily got out of bed and stubbed my toe on the chair last night? It hurt so badly, I thought that I had broken it. I cringed at the painful memory and looked at my toe to see if it was swollen or bruised. Nope. Okay, Renee, that's not the point; focus here on the message.

Meanwhile, Alek seemed to be chuckling to himself.

"What? Why are you laughing over there?" I asked curiously.

"Just waiting for you to say out loud what you're thinking, that's all. You have a funny look on your face as you muse over these verses."

"Well, I was just wondering about my own angels watching over me. I wonder when they try to protect me."

"When you cry out to the Lord and ask for help. He knows best how to help you and sometimes it will require an angel or two to intervene."

"So all I have to do is ask for help, and they're there for me?"

"Yes, but you must also do your part in trying to stay out of trouble in the first place."

"What do you mean?"

"By making the right choices and doing right by God. When you don't keep Him in your life, in your heart, it's harder for Him to keep you from the evil one, the one who comes to steal, kill, and destroy."

"Hey, I know that one. John 10:10."

"Grams taught you well!"

"How did you know . . . ."

And before I could ask him about Grams, he interjected by saying, "There's somewhere I want to take you; up for another walk?"

"Sure, I guess."

Mom must have filled him in plenty about our whole family these past eleven months. Maybe that's why I felt like we've known each other so long. I'm sure she bored him to tears telling him every detail about my life from the time I was born 'til the time I landed in St. Thomas More. Oh, man! I hope she didn't pull out any of those embarrassing baby pictures of me naked in the bathtub. *Note to self: find and destroy any naked baby pictures for elimination of future embarrassment.*

We walked out to the hall and into the elevator, but instead of going to the first floor, Alek pushed the number five. "Where are we going?" I asked, a bit confused.

"You'll see."

As we exited the elevator, I noticed right away that the walls were covered in murals of various children's storybook characters. It was very enchanting, looking at all of the happy characters and children laughing and playing around them. It was obvious that we were in the children's ward but what wasn't as clear was why. We passed by the nurses' station where the red-haired nurse said, "Hey, Alek. Good to see you again."

"Thanks, Bridgett. I brought a friend this time. This is Renee. Renee, Bridgett." We both nodded our heads at each other while saying it was nice to meet one another.

As we walked away, I started to ask, "Alek, what are we . . . ."

"Just trust me on this, okay?"

We slowly walked down the hall, mostly because that was the pace my body allowed me to go, until we got to room number 512. Alek gently knocked on the door, and I heard a faint voice say, "Come in." As we walked into the room, I noticed a young girl sitting on the bed and a lady who, thanks to her dried out, bleached hair and weathered face, looked more advanced in years than she really was. She paid no attention to us as she stared into the television in some sort of trance.

"Alek!" the child cried out with glee. Her big brown eyes got so bright when she saw him; they were all you noticed on her balding head.

"Momma . . . look who's here for another visit!" she said to her unresponsive mother.

"Uh-huh," her mother replied.

Alek walked right up to the excited child, took her right hand, and gave it a gentle peck.

"Ellie, I brought a good friend to meet you. Is that okay?"

"Yes, of course," she said with a big smile on her face as she looked at him fondly.

He summoned me over to them, and I slowly walked up—this time out of cautiousness. Looking at her coconut skin and gaunt eyes made me feel nervous. It was painfully clear she was a very sick little girl, and I wasn't quite sure how to act or respond to her.

"Renee, this is Ellie. Ellie, Renee."

I felt the urge to gently take her hand from his and looked deeply into her eyes, which were full of determination. She was so desperately hanging onto life. Flashes of black, blue, and white pierced my eyes, so it took me a moment to focus on her beautiful features. "Nice to meet you," I said as the flashes continued to taunt me, finally leaving altogether when I released her hand.

"Any friend of Alek's is a friend of mine," she replied. She looked so angelic, with her delightful smile casting a glow upon her face.

I looked up at Alek, not really sure of what I should say next. Thankfully, he bailed me out.

"Ellie has Acute Myeloid Leukemia. She has been undergoing very intense chemotherapy."

"Uh-huh, and we're gonna beat it this time. Right, Alek?" she said enthusiastically.

"That's right!"

"What does she mean by 'this time?'" I asked.

"Ask her," he suggested.

Of course, I didn't have to ask again since she heard me the first time. But I looked back at her as she began to explain.

"When I was five, I got so sick I nearly died," she said dramatically. I loved to see the expressions on her face when she talked. Everything she said had so much zest and passion. "When Momma was able to take me to the doctor, they ran so many tests to see what was wrong with me. They finally said I had AML. I went through chemotherapy like I'm doing right now, and my cancer went into remission. The doctors couldn't believe it. They said it was a miracle! It's been four years since I got better and now it's back, but this time we're gonna beat it for good. I just know it!"

I was impressed by the overwhelming faith this little girl was projecting as she stared death right in the face. Yet, she seemed so full of life. Alek must have read a few scriptures to her, too!

She continued on. "The doctor said that if I can get a match on a stem cell donor, I'll have a bone marrow transplant, which will give me the best chance to beat this stupid disease."

She was a tough little thing; that was for sure. Her will to live was much stronger than the body that carried it. On the outside she looked so frail and vulnerable, but on the inside, it was a whole other ball game.

"Renee," she called out to me with a gentle tone.

"Yes, Ellie?"

She waved her little index finger, beckoning for me to come closer to her. With her voice slightly hushed, and earnestness in her face as she looked directly into my eyes, she said, "*Acts 2:25-28. I saw the Lord always before me. Because he is at my right hand, I will not be shaken. Therefore my heart is glad and my tongue rejoices; my body also will live in hope, because you will not abandon me to the grave, nor will you let your Holy One see decay. You have made known to me the paths of life; you will fill me with joy in your presence.*' That's what keeps me going. I just thought you might need a little encouragement, too."

It was as innocent as picking a freshly bloomed flower in the garden, and it smelled just as sweet to me as I breathed every bit of it in.

"Ellie," I said as a tear rolled down my cheek, "I have this feeling you're gonna do great things in your life." This sweet little angel had touched my soul.

"Really? That's what Alek says, too!"

"Well, I hope you believe it!" I replied.

"Oh, I do! When I grow up, I'm gonna be a doctor so I can help other kids like me. I'm gonna work everyday to help find a cure so that no one else has to hurt and feel sick all of the time," she said so confidently.

She continued to amaze me, and I began to wonder how Alek found this precious child. "So, how did you two meet anyway?" I asked her.

"I prayed to God for him," she replied.

"Really? How'd you do that?"

She put her palms together in the prayer position, closed her eyes, and showed me exactly how. "I said *'Lord, please give me strength to get through this once again.'* The next day, Alek came to me," she said so proudly now looking over at him. I could see the sisterly love she felt for him. They must have had kindred spirits.

"Ellie, we have to go, but I'll see you again soon. I'll be praying for you," Alek promised as he gave her a hug and whispered something into her ear.

She smiled at him, and said, "I love you, too!"

"Hey Ellie, I'm in room 207 if you ever want to call me or come by for a visit, okay?"

"Room 207 . . . got it! See you soon," she said with a wave good-bye.

Alek cleared his throat a bit and said, "Good bye, Miss Brewer," to Ellie's mother.

She must not have heard him as she continued to stare at the television.

"Momma, Alek is talking to you," Ellie said in a polite manner, hoping to get her attention.

Miss Brewer just waved without saying a word, still focused on some show she had been watching.

Ellie looked at us with an apologetic expression and slightly shrugged her shoulders. We both just smiled back as if we didn't notice her mother's rudeness. I personally didn't want her to feel that she needed to apologize for her.

When we walked out of the room and closed the door, I asked about the lack of interest from Ellie's mother.

"She's completely lost," he said.

"What do you mean 'completely lost?' Her child is lying there with a very deadly disease, and you think she's just lost?"

"Yes, that's what I know. She has no faith that her child will survive because she doesn't know how to have faith. Her whole life has been one tribulation after another, which gave her the excuse to drink, smoke, and take drugs. If you think she was in a trance-like state because of some show, you're mistaken. She is addicted to crack, Renee. She thinks that will get her mind off of everything and take away the hurt."

I was stunned by the revelation of this. I don't believe I had ever seen anyone high on drugs before. It was sad for me to realize that she was completely missing out on precious time with Ellie just to avoid any pain.

Alek continued on. "She got pregnant with Ellie when she was drunk and isn't even sure who her father is. She hasn't spoken to her own parents since she was seventeen, when she ran away from home, never to return. This is how she has dealt with things her whole life instead of seeking God and turning her life over to Him. That's why I go and see Ellie; to try and bring a sense of hope into her life, and to let her know there is another way."

I leaned up against the wall, feeling weak and overwhelmed with sadness for her. This poor girl has had such a tough life, and yet she was trying to encourage me. *Me!* I should have been the strong one in there. I should have given her words to help her get through her cancer treatments. I mean, I've had a charmed life compared to hers.

Tears were streaming down my face as I continued to grasp what had just happened.

Alek tried to wipe them away with his fingers and said, "Hey, it's okay. You didn't know."

The tears kept coming anyway, even more uncontrollably. I couldn't help but think how blessed I was to have my mom and dad, who constantly loved me and supported me all of these years;

a grandmother who taught me about Jesus and faith and hope; a grandfather who would take me fishing, and talked to me about life—like to beware of boys, snakes that rattle, and Grandma's cabbage stew. Who did Ellie have to lean on? Where was her father? More importantly, where was God? *She's an innocent little girl!* I shouted in my head.

"Hey, calm down. Listen to me," he said as he grabbed my shoulders with his hands to give me the support I needed to stand straight. "God *is* with her. And do you know why?"

"Why?" I said through my tears.

"Because of people like you."

"Huh? You're not making sense, Alek," I said, unmoved, still crying in an ugly, childlike way, and wiping away the clear snot dripping from my nose. Embarrassment may have set in had I not been so afflicted with pain for the innocent child who lay dying behind the closed door.

"Listen to me," he demanded, still holding onto my shoulders. "When Ellie was going through her first battle at five, there was a young man who came to the hospital with his youth group to sing Christmas carols. He saw Ellie lying in her bed, unaffected by the uplifting songs like the rest of the children had been, so he went into her room and started talking to her."

He had my attention now, and my tears began to slow.

"He asked her if she was okay, and she said no; she was dying, and no one seemed to care about her. He told her that he cared, and so did Jesus. She sat up on her bed and asked who Jesus was. This young man told her all about Him and how He could heal her if she had faith. The young man then promised he would come see her as often as he could until she was out of the hospital. He kept his promise, and two months later, she was in remission. For the first time in Ellie's young life, she understood what hope was, and never let go of it."

My breathing finally slowed as I calmed down. I began to wonder how he knew so much about Ellie and her mom. I had to ask. "How do you know all of this?"

He thought about it for a minute before he answered. "Let's just say I was that young man four years ago. The point is that there are a lot of people just like her, Renee. People who need to know that they are loved and cared for. He . . . I mean, I . . . didn't do anything that anyone else couldn't do."

He was right. I felt ashamed because I had been so consumed with myself and my life. Meeting Ellie was exactly what I needed to heal, get strong, and approach my second chance at life with purpose. It was amazing how a complete stranger was able to do that for me.

Alek took my hand, and we began to walk down the hall to the elevator, leaving room 512 and all that it held behind us. Yet never, ever was it to be forgotten. We shared the silence together, still taking in all that had happened, hanging on to the raw emotions that consumed us. I knew from that moment on that I wanted to help her in any way I could. Perhaps helping her, and others like her, was my calling in life. Perhaps they were my purpose.

TWENTY FIVE

Preparing for the Battle

"The time is drawing near. Are you ready?"

"Yes, Lord. I have prepared my best troops for the moment to come. Daemon will be waiting close by for my word. I have stationed Ezekiel, Gideon, Benjamin, and Hakim with him. Gunner, Herick, Boris, Chazz, Armand, and Cavan will be stationed on top of the mountain, also waiting for the word. We don't want the enemy to sense our presence. And there are still plenty of prayer warriors in Westcliffe that the enemy has not deceived yet. Their protectors are giving them whispers on what to pray for."

"Do you think she will be ready as well?"

"I have much hope that she will be strong enough to remember. She must in order for us to attack."

"I can see her heart is still in the right place. But the enemy has many plans of their own. We will continue to allow them to attack. They must feel they have the upper hand."

"May I confess something, Lord?"

"Yes, Liam, please do."

"I must confess it has been very difficult for me to see her in any pain. The enemy uses that to weaken her. I am afraid she will fall into their trap out of confusion. My fear is that I will follow in the footsteps of Kristar. Will you give me strength, Lord, to keep the faith that I will not fall like he did?"

"*Liam,*" *the Lord said as He laid His hand upon his shoulder,* "*you should not be afraid of your feelings, so long as you do not lose what you already know. Hope, Faith, and Love are strong in your heart. The greatest of these is Love. I asked you to be her protector because I have faith in you. I know you will do right by Me and by her.*"

"*Thank you, Lord.*"

"*The time is drawing near. Are you ready?*"

"*Yes, master. Everything is going according to your plan.*"

"*Good. The others have been working around the clock preparing for this. Those who have not been cooperative with our temptations have been dealt with in other ways. The prince is anxiously waiting to see our work. He longs to stake his claim on the land that has been protected by the Sangre de Cristo. Soon, darkness will consume this town, and it will finally be ours! Humans from all over the world will be drawn to it, and we will thrust their wildest temptations upon them, stealing their very souls. Do not let that stupid girl mess anything up for us, or there will be hell to pay.*"

"*She will be under my control; I assure you.*"

"*If she does not cooperate, we will attempt to kill her once again. Perhaps this time He will allow it. If not, we will strike her with more suffering. Her pain will be so agonizing that the tremendous grief and despair she is consumed with will make her wish to die!*"

"*Master, I want this girl for myself.*"

"*Oh, so we've grown attached to her, have we? I should have seen that coming. Very well, you can have her . . . for now. But if she tries . . . .*"

"*Don't worry, master. She will be under my supervision at every moment.*"

"*Very well, begone. And remember, we're still watching you.*"

TWENTY SIX

The Nightmare Revealed

It was two days until my birthday, and I was expecting to get out of the hospital tomorrow. Kyran had been planning some big party as a double celebration, so he hadn't come around as often this past week. All he would tell me was that he was making big plans and it would be "the event of a lifetime."

I didn't quite feel the same excitement as he did because while I seemed to be getting better, my mom was noticeably looking worse. I had to ask her what was going on. I couldn't allow her to ignore me any longer. She had been protecting me from something, and I knew it wasn't good.

It was still very early in the morning. She was usually up ahead of me, but today I was abruptly awakened before the sun rose. One of my terrible nightmares had returned.

Darkness hovered over Westcliffe and I, somehow, was right in the center of it. My arms were stretched out, being pulled in both directions. I could see everyone I knew or cared about crawling on the ground, barely able to breathe, suffocating from the thick blackness that surrounded them. I saw my mom and dad, Jamie and her parents, Ellie, Mo, Miss Adamma, and even Kyran, who was at the farthest edge of my sight. I tried to reach for them, but my arms were frozen in the air. "Run!" I screamed to them. But they, too, were held captive by the chains of fear, which stole their sense of hope. My heart suffered tremendous pain, ripped apart.

Then out of nowhere, a loud, thunderous noise filled the air. Lightning struck down from the sky straight into the darkness, yet always careful to miss the people suffering on the ground. The bolts severed their chains around them, but still they lay there, too afraid to move.

As light began to emerge from the sky, confusion and panic, once used to torment all the innocent people, were turned against the shadowy haze. All the evil spirits began emitting horrendous screeches as they were undoubtedly filled with tremendous pain. The vile noise pierced my ears as it echoed from east to west. The darkness began to break up, scattering about, no longer able to withstand the torment that had been thrust upon them by the light.

Only one last veil of dark smoke, with stabbing, yellow eyes that were consumed with hatred, was seemingly unaffected by the attack. It slowly began taking on a massive, grotesque form, creating loud, dreadful noises of its own. It glided toward me, giving off a brazen laugh. I was drenched in sweat; the temperature was rapidly growing hotter as the beast drew nearer. My breaths were small and rapid; the air felt nonexistent. Now, standing next to me, it breathed out a cloud of horrific fumes through its protruding nostrils, leaving a sulfuric cloud around me. I began to cough profusely as I inhaled its discharge, further suffocating my every breath. Then, it pompously showed its large sharp fangs, covered with slime that stretched from the top to the bottom of its mouth, and gave a snarling growl into my ear. The prince of destruction was infuriated.

That's when I awoke, my heart pounding erratically like the rumbling of an earthquake, and I could barely catch my breath. The nightmare was over, but the fear it brought to me had not departed. I whispered a prayer to God. "Lord, give me strength. Keep your angels around me and the ones I love. Protect us from evil so that

I may go out and be a light in the darkness. In your name I pray. Amen."

I climbed out of bed to change my wet clothes. The dream was heavy on my mind. *What did it mean?* I wondered.

I walked over to the window and waited for my mom to wake up, gazing at the last of the scattered, faraway stars. The moon was faint in the background, as she patiently waited for her friend to make his grand entrance. And then, there he came, his powerful rays lighting upon the morning dew and settled snow left over in small patches sprinkled on the ground. How glorious it was to watch. And though it brought a sense of serenity with it, I still had to wonder what this day would bring.

My mom began to stir. I sat next to her on her cot. *What an amazing woman,* I thought. *She has slept on this uncomfortable bed since the day I was brought here.* She was the most unselfish person I had ever known.

She must have sensed me watching her as she opened her eyes. She quickly sat up and asked, "What's wrong, sweetheart?"

"Nothing, Mom. I was just watching you sleep."

"Oh." She paused and glanced around as she thought about it. "Why?" she asked curiously.

"Because we need to talk," I answered softly, looking down at my fingers, which were playing with a hanging thread on the blanket. I was still working up the courage to discover what she had been hiding. My mother waited patiently for me to finish. "We need to talk about you," I finally said with a firmer voice.

"Oh," she stated like a child who had been caught taking a piece of candy. "Well, there's nothing really to talk about."

"You can't keep ignoring me, Mom. I know something is going on with you. Please tell me. I need to know. We've never hidden anything from each other. Don't start now." I felt like the mother in that instant.

Evelyn knew the day would come when Renee would figure out she had been keeping a secret from her—from everyone, really. She remembered the day she found out she had breast cancer like it was just yesterday.

It was October 10, 2009, and Renee had been in her coma for eight months. Evelyn barely left her side, always afraid she would miss her awakening, or worse . . . that Renee would leave her forever. Her energy level kept dropping even though she wasn't doing much other than reading, praying, and helping Renee's lifeless body with physical therapy. Alek had noticed how Evelyn always felt tired, so he insisted she go see a doctor. He promised to stay and watch over Renee while she was gone.

She went to see Doctor Lee, and through a series of physicals and tests, he discovered she had stage two breast cancer. The words burned through Evelyn like acid on her skin, and she threw up all over the floor. The shock and disbelief from the news made her physically sick; she just couldn't believe this was happening.

"You need to start treatment right away, Evelyn," the doctor strongly urged, but she had to think about it. The thought of leaving Renee to go to chemo sickened her even more. She knew the treatment would make her weak, almost useless, for days at a time. If she were in the hospital herself, how could she take care of Renee? Secretly, she thought if Renee were never to wake up on Earth again, she was okay with going to Heaven right behind her. She knew that sounded selfish or stupid to some, but it's how she felt all the same.

Once Renee awoke and the doctor confirmed she was going to be fine, Evelyn began her chemo sessions. Her will to live was back full force, but now she had to wonder if she didn't start them too late. Now, as Evelyn looked upon her beautiful daughter's face, she dreaded telling her the news. She knew exactly how Renee was going to feel, and she had never wanted to cause her any pain.

She took ahold of my hand, and there they were again—flashes of blue and black filled my eyes. Why did this keep happening? I had to really concentrate to focus on my mother's face as she let out a heavy sigh.

"There is no easy way of telling you this, but I knew the day would come that I had to. So, here it is . . . I started going through chemotherapy last week." She released a heavy breath, hoping for the courage to continue. Saying the words would never come easy, but saying them to her precious daughter was a hundred times harder. "Renee, I have breast cancer."

"What? No, that's impossible. You're the healthiest person I know. There has to be some mistake. You always take such good care of yourself. Did you get a second opinion?"

"Yes, sweetheart," she said as she threw her arms around me.

I couldn't believe this was happening. This had to be some horrible, horrible dream. Hadn't we all already been through enough? I began to feel angry, very angry. Why was this happening? If it wasn't enough that my dad was never around anymore, that Jamie was no longer my best friend or even the same person I once knew, or that I was in a coma for almost a year and lost everything I had worked so hard for, now my mom had a disease that could forever take her away from me.

I stood up and began pacing around the room. The anger that consumed every ounce of my body gave me a surge of energy that was hard to contain. I held onto it as it gave me the power I needed to refuse the tears that threatened to fill my eyes. It kept me strong, and strength was what we would need to fight this. There I was, going back and forth, back and forth, from one side of the room to the other, trying to figure out what to do. My face was bright red as the fiery blood rushed through my veins.

"Why, Lord, are you letting this happen to us?" I shouted out loud with my hands balled up into fists. I had never in my life been so infuriated. I had never put such blame on God, but who else could

I blame? Wasn't He the one in control?

My mom got out of bed and stood firm in front of me. "Renee, stop this," she said as she grabbed me. "Stop this at once! Our God is a loving God. He did not do this. But if we have faith in Him, He will make it right according to His will. Don't let anger consume you. That's when the enemy wins."

"It's not fair though," I shouted. "You don't deserve this, Mom. You're a good person." I was filled with resentment.

"Listen to me. Being good or bad has nothing to do with this. And why this sickness fell upon me is not for us to understand or resent. But what I do know is that what the devil intends for evil, God will use for good and for His glory. I trust Him with all of my heart, and I hope you do, too."

My mother enveloped my shaking body. I quickly became powerless within her circle of tenderness, giving way for the tears that had gathered to flow—the tears that I had purposely blocked like a logjam in the rushing river. Now they covered my face with their salty essence. I needed her to be with me for a long, long time. The thought of losing her made me feel nauseated.

"I don't ever want to lose you. I need you, Mom. Don't ever leave me, please! Promise me; promise me right now you won't die!" I begged shamelessly.

"That's not something I can promise, Renee," she said as she put her hands on either side of my face and looked into my eyes. "We must all leave this place one day. God has said 'You are dust and to dust you shall return!' No one knows how or when they will part from this world. But I hope it will give you some comfort to know that I have the Lord Jesus in my heart, and there is a miraculous place awaiting my soul."

I continued to weep in her arms. The sadness that consumed me was almost unbearable. I began to think of my dad. Why wasn't he here, helping her through this?

"Does Daddy know yet?" I asked.

"No, I haven't told anyone. I didn't want anyone else having to worry about me needlessly."

"You should have told me! You should never have to go through something like this on your own."

"What I needed more was for you to get better. I didn't want to distract you from your progress, and look at you now. You're getting out tomorrow," she said with a smile, caressing my face in her hands with a proud look on her face. I realized that my getting out was not only an accomplishment of my own, but one she had set out to achieve as well. It shouldn't have surprised me that she put my health before her own.

I wrapped my arms tightly around her, resting my head upon her shoulder. I didn't want to let her go. We both stood there and cried in each other's arms. My heart felt broken . . . shattered into a hundred pieces. I just wanted to wake up from this horrible nightmare.

TWENTY SEVEN

A Needed Distraction

Moments passed. I couldn't tell how long we had been standing there when the knock at my door broke our embrace.

"Daddy!" I said out loud. He must have come a day early to surprise me. *His timing couldn't have been better,* I thought. I ran over to the door, leaving my mom standing. I opened it quickly in anticipation of seeing my father standing on the other side, ready to give us his love and support in this time of need

"Good morning, *amore,*" Kyran said. His expression quickly changed to concern when he saw mine.

He must have noticed my smile disappear when I saw that it was him. I didn't mean to show my disappointment; it just happened.

"Hey, Kyran, come in, please."

"Did I do something wrong?" he asked.

"No, why would you think that?"

"Because, when you first opened the door you looked so happy. Then you saw that it was me standing there, and your smile vanished."

"No, it wasn't because of you. Sorry. I just thought you were my dad; that's all. Of course I'm glad that you're here." I stood silent for a brief second and said, "So, why are you here this early anyway?"

"If you two will excuse me," my mother said as she grabbed a few things and went into the restroom. I could tell she was not pleased about his spontaneous visit.

Kyran walked up to me and gave me a big hug, lifting my feet off of the ground. He smelled so good. It was actually really nice, getting such an affectionate hug from him. "You've been on my mind all night. I couldn't wait to come and see you today. I thought we might have breakfast together, and I know how you like to eat early," he said so genuinely.

"That's so thoughtful of you. You know, your timing couldn't have been better, actually."

"Why is that, love?" he asked, finally putting me back down.

"Well, I got some bad news this morning. It's still too painful to talk about right now, so if you don't mind, I'd like to just save it for another time."

He looked into my eyes, placing his hand behind my head. "I am here whenever you need to talk. Okay?"

"Thanks for understanding. Let me freshen up a bit so we can go down to the cafeteria."

"No need . . . breakfast is on its way as we speak."

"Really? That's so sweet. You really know how to take care of a girl, don't you?" I admitted.

"You're not just any girl, Renee. I've told you all along. Trust me . . . I will take care of you."

"I know. I'm just not used to having someone else besides my parents and Jamie so close to me. I'm still getting used to this. I have to say, though, you're not too bad for a first boyfriend," I grinned.

He smiled back at me, pulling me over to him for another tight hug. It felt equally as good the second time around.

There was a knock at the door. Kyran released his affectionate grip so I could answer it. "Good morning, Madame. Your breakfast has arrived," an older gentleman with a dark mustache stated.

"Come in, Pepe. Set the table up over there," Kyran ordered as he pointed to the only empty corner in the room. Before I knew it, there was a whole entourage of men dressed in uniforms bringing in an entire table. Food had already been placed on silver plates, with large, silver dome-shaped lids keeping it warm.

"Wow! You really go all out, don't you?"

"Nothing but the best for you," he replied.

And as quickly as everyone came, they all left. I noticed the table was set for three. I thought that it was so considerate on his part to take my mom into account. "I would still like to freshen up and tell my mom about this nice surprise. Give me just a minute, will you?"

"Take your time. I'll be here."

I knocked on the door before entering into the bathroom, where I could hear the shower still running.

"Hey, Mom! Kyran brought us some breakfast. You almost done?"

"Just about," she replied.

I began brushing my teeth and washing my face. I couldn't help but stare at the scar, which was a constant reminder of the day my life changed forever. I still couldn't fathom why all of this was happening to us. Our family had been so good to this community, constantly giving of ourselves. Now look at us—look at me. My life once seemed so perfect.

"Hand me that towel, will you?" my mom shouted out. I gave her the towel and waited while she dried off. I noticed when she came out with it wrapped around her she looked so thin. I turned back to look at myself in the mirror. I didn't want to think about her sickness right now. It hurt too badly.

"So, are you gonna join us?" I asked, hopeful.

"Ummm, you two go ahead. I'm not all that hungry this morning."

"Come on, Mom. Kyran was so thoughtful in bringing us some delicious food. Won't you just give him a chance?"

"The truth of the matter is I have another appointment. Maybe next time, okay?"

"Let me go with you. I'll tell Kyran that we appreciate it, but . . ."

"No, I want to go alone. I don't want you there right now. Please, this is my wish, so don't argue."

I sighed, knowing I couldn't get into some wicked fight with her right now. For whatever reason, she wanted to be alone, and I had to respect that.

"Okay, I won't fight you on it this time. But when I'm out of here, it's my turn to help you get better. Deal?"

"Deal," she replied. "There is something that you could do for me."

"What? Anything—you just tell me what, and it's done."

"Pray for me."

"That's it? Just pray?" I said, puzzled.

"Yes . . . pray," she responded seriously.

"Okay, I'll do it. I love you, Mom," I said. I gave her a hug before I exited the bathroom to give her some privacy.

Kyran was sitting at the table, waiting for me. "Come, *bellissima*, the food is getting cold," he said. He signaled me to come over, waving his hand towards him.

He rose from his seat and pulled out my chair like the true gentleman he was. Pretending to be my own personal butler, he placed a white linen napkin across my lap and began lifting the silver domes from the various plates on the table. There was enough food to feed a small village.

"Your breakfast is served, Madame!" he announced so formally, and then sat back down.

"Ummm, it smells so good," I said, even though I really wasn't very hungry. I realized I was going to have to force myself to eat so I didn't hurt his feelings. I could tell he put a lot of thought and effort into this. I looked more carefully at the plate directly in front of me, as the smell was very familiar. I couldn't believe my eyes. "Ahhh! How did you know my favorite breakfast was German pancakes?" I asked, completely shocked.

"Why wonder about small details? Just eat and enjoy. Pepe makes the best German pancakes in the world."

"My mom would probably beg to differ," I countered.

"I'll let the food speak for itself," he said while placing the perfect bite onto my fork. "Open up," he smiled as he carefully placed it into my mouth.

"Oh my gosh!" I blurted out with my mouth still full as I savored every ounce of the bite. "This is amazing. It's *almost* as good as my mom's!" I said with a slight laugh, wiping the drop of syrup that managed to escape. *Great, now I'm gonna have a sticky line down my chin,* I thought. I kept trying to wipe it with my finger, but it only made my finger gooey in the process. I was slightly embarrassed because only I could ruin such a romantic setting with childish antics. Kyran came to my rescue.

"Here, love, allow me." He dabbed the white linen cloth that had lain upon his lap into the glass of water and gently wiped the shiny, sticky streak from my lips to my chin. Then he took my hand and placed my now maple-flavored finger into his warm mouth, leaving no sticky residue behind. Part of me thought, *Oooh, gross,* but the other half tingled a bit at the warm, soothing feel of it.

"There . . . good as new," he said, flashing his pearly whites.

The breakfast turned out to be a breath of fresh air, and exactly what I had needed. Kyran and I ate, laughed, ate some more, and talked about nothing significant; it was all so comforting. My mom had left for her appointment, and barely even acknowledged Kyran as she walked out the door. I was surprised she actually let him stay in the room with her gone. She must have had a lot on her mind.

It did make me sad to see her leave, though, knowing what she was about to endure. But, that's how she wanted it, for whatever reason only known to her. I was uncertain of so many things in my life at this point, so I decided to just get my mind off of everything altogether, and this crazy Italian—this "shampoo model boy" sitting next to me—was the exact antidote needed to do the job. On the outside, he only saw my smile as I recalled some of the nicknames I had once given him when we first met, but on the inside I was laughing hysterically. *I was so annoyed by him in the beginning, and now I'm so enamored.*

Kyran scooted my chair closer to him, forcing me to concentrate on only him. The room fell quiet as he tenderly pulled back my hair and cupped his hands around my head, staring deep into my eyes. I looked into his passionate green eyes as well, still trying to figure out who this extraordinary guy really was. He began gently kissing my face, starting at my right cheek. Each time he would lift his moist lips from my skin, he would whisper one word, until he reached the other side. "You-are-so-beautiful-my-love." He finally completed the sentence upon his last gentle peck. I had never thought of myself as beautiful before, but he certainly made me feel that way now.

I found it was getting easier to share such intimate moments like this with him. Yes, my heart still pounded profusely each time we were alone, but today it gave me an excitement unlike any feeling I've ever had before. "You're not so bad yourself," I finally whispered back.

He only chuckled a bit before pulling me from my chair onto his lap, wrapping my arms around his shoulders. He started kissing my neck ever so gently. My heavy breathing broke the silence that had filled the air once again. In his excitement, his kisses started getting a little stronger until he finally reached my lips, which happily awaited his touch. Passion overcame my senses, and it relieved the pain I had felt only moments before. My thoughts were no longer consumed by the tribulations I was facing. I wanted only to live in the here and now. In this moment of feeling weightless in the arms of someone who seemed to care for me and want to take care of my every need, I allowed myself to break free from the controlled restrictions I had always known. I rubbed my fingers through his glossy, dark hair, gripping it as we pressed our lips together in a fiery passion. He stood up from his chair with ease, wrapping my long legs around his waist, holding onto me with his strong arms. He began walking closer to my bed, still brushing his lips against mine until he breathed the words "I love you" into my mouth, further distracting me from my senses. But these were not words I took lightly. I knew I had to come to my senses quickly.

I forced myself to stop kissing him, fixing my eyes upon his to see the sincerity behind the words spoken. He stared back at me, barely blinking an eye.

"Why did you say that?" I asked.

"I have not felt like this in a very long time. You've made me feel so alive again. I want to be with you, Renee. I want to be with you forever."

"Kyran, we're still so young. How can you say something like that?"

"Do you not have the same feelings?" He answered my question with his own.

"I don't know if I really know what love for a man is supposed to feel like. I've only ever loved my family."

"I can be your family now. I can take care of you."

He was so sincere in what he was saying. As I looked at him more closely, I noticed his eyes were wet. Tears filled them, ready to spill over. I had only ever seen him like this once before—when we were on his balcony watching the sunset behind the mountains at the infamous party that landed me in this place to begin with. I remembered that he was so lost in that moment, so vulnerable.

He gently laid me on the bed, placing himself next to me, but only gazing at me with his penetrating eyes. "You may not feel the same way right now, but I will wait for you. In time, you will love me, too."

Our bodies were parallel as we both lay on our sides, just staring at each other, with our heads resting upon the puffy pillow. In our silence, we each were trying to figure out the mystery of the other. I knew Kyran had many girlfriends before me, so what made me so different . . . so special?

He began stroking my hair with the tips of his fingers. Just as he reached over to kiss me once again, there was a faint knock at the door. I jumped out of bed as quickly as my recovering body would allow me to and clumsily rushed to the door.

"Hi, Renee!"

"Ellie, what are you doing here?" I asked, surprised by her visit.

"Oh, are you not happy I'm here?"

Dang it! That's twice, now, that I gave the wrong impression while opening the door this morning. "No, sweetie, I'm happy you're here. You just surprised me; that's all. Please come in."

She slowly walked in the door with a bag in hand, slightly out of breath. It must have taken a lot of her energy to walk here. Even so, she gave me that sweet smile of hers when I asked her to come in. Kyran quickly hopped out of bed.

"Ellie, I'd like for you to meet my, my . . . ."

"Her boyfriend." He finished my sentence, stretching out his hand to meet my newfound friend. "It's a pleasure to make your acquaintance," he said, so gentlemanly.

"Oh," she said. She looked a bit surprised, but placed her hand in his anyway. "Nice to meet you, too."

"Ellie is my new friend. She's been staying here in the hospital, too," I explained.

"Yes, I see. The robe and pajamas gave it away," he said as he winked at her. She only gave him a halfhearted smile back.

"So, what's up with you this morning, Ellie?" I asked curiously.

"This," she said as she barely lifted the bag she had in her hand.

"May I take a look?" I asked.

She held it out for me to grab and said, "Can you help me with this? It looks like I'm wearing a bird's nest on my head."

I pulled out a brown, so-called wig from the bag. I hated to tell her, but it looked awful.

"You don't even have to say it. It looks awful; I know," she said, gauging the expression on my face.

"Where did you get this, sweetie?"

"My mom bought it for me. I didn't want to hurt her feelings because I know she did the best she could with what little money she has, but no matter how hard I tried to make it look good, it just kept looking worse. Can you help me, Renee?" she said so desperately.

"Let's see what we can do," I replied, hoping I could make it look decent.

"I believe this is my cue to exit," Kyran announced politely.

"Ellie, take care, and I'll see you tomorrow night!" he said as he gave me a peck on the cheek before walking out of the room.

Ellie and I went into the bathroom where I was able to brush out the matted wig. She just sat on the tub, watching me try to work some magic. "So," she said casually, "I thought you and Alek were boyfriend and girlfriend."

"No, we're just friends," I said as I continued to brush.

"Oh, well, I thought by the way you two looked at each other when you came to visit me, you really liked each other."

"Alek is a special guy, but Kyran has been my boyfriend since before I even met Alek."

"Oh," she said again. "Well, that's too bad."

"Why do you say that, Ellie?"

"Because if I had to pick someone, that *perfect* someone for you, it would be Alek. He's such a great guy and pretty cute, too!" she admitted. She had an angelic, yet, devious smile on her face, in hopes of convincing me that I needed to consider Alek as a better suitor for me.

"Well, Kyran's a great guy, too, don't you think?"

"He's different."

Sadly, that wasn't the response I was looking to get from her. I had hoped she was as equally as impressed with Kyran as she was with Alek. Why I cared so much what this nine-year-old girl thought was beyond me, but I did, and it bothered me a bit that she only saw him as different.

"What do you mean by different, sweetie? Different how?" I said in my nicest voice. I didn't want her to think that she had upset me in anyway. To be honest, I had an appreciation for her honesty—I just needed to know more.

"I don't know, like a puppet or something."

"What on earth are you talking about, Ellie?" I had to say with a slight laugh.

"I once saw this show where there was a guy who held a little stuffed man in his lap, and he would make his mouth and body move like he was real. Only it was the real guy doing all the talking through his throat or something."

"Do you mean a ventriloquist?"

"Yes, that's the word. That's what he reminds me of."

"You have a vivid imagination, young lady. That's about the silliest thing I've heard. How did you get that impression?"

"I don't know," she said, shrugging her shoulders and looking down. "He just didn't seem to be the person he's trying to be. That was the feeling I got when I shook his hand."

I could tell I hurt her feelings. I honestly didn't mean to, but I couldn't believe she got that impression from the two minutes she was around Kyran. "I'm sorry, Ellie. I didn't mean to offend you." I bent down in front of her and lifted her head so I could look at her pretty brown eyes. "Hey, I'm glad you were honest with me. I never want you to feel like you have to hide your thoughts or feelings from me. Okay?"

"Okay."

"Now, let's try this wig on and see if we can't put a nice pink ribbon in it to keep it out of your beautiful face. What do you say?"

"At this point, I'll try anything. I want my mom to see me with it on. I hope it makes her feel good."

I instantly felt like crying when she said that. After all she had been through, after all her mother had put her through, she still wanted so desperately to please her. What an amazing girl. I knew this was her way of not only seeking her mother's love, but giving her mother love as well.

"There, what do you think?" I asked as I stepped behind her so she could get a good view in the mirror.

"It's definitely an improvement from this morning. Thanks for helping me, Renee!" she said as she turned and gave me a big hug around my waist.

"Any time."

"Really, do you mean it?" she asked.

"Of course, that's what friends are for; we're there for each other in the good times and the not so good, right?"

"Right!" she said back. "Will you come visit me after you get out of the hospital tomorrow?"

"Only a blizzard could keep me away," I promised.

She gave me one last hug while saying good-bye. She was anxious to go and show her mother how pretty she looked with her new hair. I was sad to see her leave. She made me forget all of my own problems in a different way than Kyran had. A big part of me was happy for her interruption.

TWENTY EIGHT

A Love-Filled Stall

It was February 17, 2010, and the morning was filled with excitement. Not only did I turn seventeen, but most importantly, I finally got to go home. Although my therapy still had to continue on a daily basis, being home gave me a better chance to rebuild my life. There was so much I was going to have to catch up on at school, but I wasn't going to think about all of that right now. Today my daddy was coming home at last, and tonight the big party Kyran had been preparing for would come to fruition. It was a big day for sure.

As I sat in the rocking chair and glanced around the room one final time, I began to think of what my life would have been like had I gone home with my mom that night.

For one, my birthday would have seemed to take forever to get here; now I couldn't believe it was already here. I didn't feel another year older. I suppose missing out on lost experiences or memories never created made me feel that I didn't have the chance to grow, even though physically I had grown another inch. It was a very strange feeling, realizing that these four walls contained within them a year of my life. Even so, I knew there were lessons learned here, even if I wasn't sure what they were yet. I still believed everything happened for a reason, and that soon enough, I would understand.

Alek was coming by to help us with all of the year's accumulations. A big part of me was eager to see him as well.

"I've got everything in the bathroom packed up," my mom said as she was walking out of it. "Did you get the things out of the nightstand?"

"Check."

"What about from under the bed? You know how things seem to grow legs and crawl under there," she said with edginess; the Texas twang was a little thick, too.

"Check."

"And your clothes from the closet, did you get those already?"

"Yes, check! Mom . . . I've got it all, so stop your worrying."

I wasn't sure why her mood was somber. She seemed nervous about my getting out of here for some reason. She looked at her watch and said, "Alek should be here any minute to pick you up. I'm going to stay behind for a doctor's appointment. He'll help you get everything unpacked when you get home."

"Mom! Why didn't you tell me you weren't coming? Let me go with you."

"This is the day we've been waiting on and working so hard for. It would make me happier for you to go home and get settled in. I'll be right behind you. Okay?"

I sighed, "I guess."

"Sit down for a minute, please," she said patting the mattress next to her. *Uh-oh . . . what now?* I thought. *If she wants me to sit down, it must be serious.*

She pulled a small, wrapped box from her pocket and handed it to me. "Happy birthday, sweetheart," she said with a slight smile.

I got excited to open my first birthday present and immediately ripped the wrapping off. I opened the small box, and out fell my silver Ichthus ring.

"After the wreck your hands had swelled so badly, they had to cut your ring off. I wasn't quite sure what to get you, but I know how much that ring has always meant to you," she said, hopeful that I would like the gesture.

"I love it! It's the perfect gift." I quickly put it on my finger. "Thank you, Mom, this really means a lot to me." I gave her a hug. Just as I was about to hop off the bed, my mother grabbed ahold of my arm. I saw concern in her eyes and immediately asked, "What is it, Mom? Is something wrong?"

"I just wanted you to know that things in Westcliffe are going to be a little different when you get there."

"Different, how?" I asked curiously.

"Well, it's not going to look like the same quaint town that you remember. A lot has happened in such a short amount of time. It appears the Dellamorte family has bought out, or forced out, some of the local businesses and ranch owners and put up other establishments in their place."

"Like what?"

"Well, like a new bar, a liquor super store, a couple of restaurants, a church of the Conscious Rebellion of Christ—also known as CROC—and an adult video store. Word has it that they are trying to take over the Livingood's ranch and build some sort of legal gambling operation. I just wanted you to know so that you weren't completely shocked when you saw it."

Before I could really absorb all of this, there was a knock at the door. "Come in," my mom yelled out.

"Good morning, Mrs. Lewis . . . Renee," Alek said as he tipped his cowboy hat.

"Good morning, Alek. Thanks for helping us out," my mom greeted him.

"It's my pleasure, ma'am."

"Can you take down those boxes over there?" she asked, and pointed.

"No problem," he said, happy to help.

He was able to lift both of them with ease and carried them out the door. A few minutes later, Ellie was at the door with an excitement I had never seen before. She looked different, and it seemed to give her a rush of energy.

"Renee, look at what was at my door, wrapped in a pretty box this morning! Can you believe it?" she said as she showed off her new look.

I could hardly tell she had a wig on. I felt of the shiny, long cinnamon-colored locks, which were actually made from real hair. It had to have cost a small fortune. "Wow, Ellie! You look amazing!"

"I know!" she said so innocently and excitedly. "I looked for a note both inside and outside of the box to see who it was from, but they didn't leave one. I think I have an idea who it is, though, and I can't wait to thank him in person."

I had my own idea of who it was from. *Note to self: give Kyran a big thank you kiss!*

"What do you think, Mrs. Lewis?" she asked with anticipation of yet another compliment, something she wasn't used to getting.

"I think you're beautiful with or without your hair!" my mom replied, giving Ellie a wink.

She smiled back before looking around the room. "Looks like you're just about ready to leave."

"Yeah, we're just waiting for Alek to come and get this last load, and we're out of here," I replied.

"Remember your promise," Ellie quickly inserted, finger pointing at me.

"Only a blizzard," I said softly in her ear as I bent over to give her a hug.

Alek walked through the door, and two seconds later Ellie dashed into his arms, giving him a great big hug. She whispered something in his ear that was too faint for anyone else to hear. *I wish I had superhuman powers,* I thought in that very moment. It was so obvious there was a connection between them that only they could understand. It was quite endearing to see the unique gentleness he had with her. He only gave her a tight squeeze back without any reply, and that was all she needed.

"I better get back to my room. The nurse is probably there, waiting to give me my next chemo dose."

"See ya, Ellie," I shouted out to her as she walked out of the room.

Alek grabbed the two larger suitcases, and I grabbed the small bag. I gave my mom one last hug before Alek and I walked out of room 207 for the last time. I was a bit nervous of what lay ahead.

The ride to Westcliffe was unexpectedly quiet. I guess I had too much on my mind, trying to envision the "new" Westcliffe. At least the day turned out beautifully, with a nice crisp chill in the air and a brilliant blue sky with scattered puffy clouds. We had just passed the city limit sign, and it didn't take long for me to witness what my mom had warned me about. Construction crews were everywhere, either tearing down or building up. What on earth was happening to our little peaceful town? Sadness draped over my heart like a cloak. It gave me chills up and down my spine, and all I could do was cross my arms, sit back, and close my eyes. I didn't want to see any more. It was all too much. *The next time I open my eyes will be when we get to the ranch. Home sweet home.* I needed that familiarity, that place of comfort, and I knew all would be well there.

"Here we are," Alek said a few minutes later. "There's a stud that's dying to see you!"

I opened my eyes, and I was not disappointed. I quickly got out of the truck, excited to finally be back. I had never considered our ranch to be breathtaking before, but today, it took my breath away. I inhaled deeply, filling my lungs with the calming air surrounding our peaceful home. I looked out to the pasture and saw Tex coming our way. I trotted over to the fence myself, eager to pet my beautiful white horse. I impatiently opened the gate and ran up to Tex, clasping my arms around his large, sturdy neck. I knew he was just as excited to see me by all of the noises he was making. He even kicked his front legs up, neighing loudly, as if to say, "I've missed you! Where in the heck have you been?"

Shortly into our reunion and to my dismay, he began to walk back toward the barn. I wasn't ready for our visit to be over with. But then he stopped, looked back at me, and moved forward again. Then he stopped, looked back at me, and waited. Alek came up from behind and said, "I think he wants to show you something."

"What is it, boy? What's going on?" I said as we followed him inside. He stopped right in front of the third stall. My eyes widened as I saw our other horse, Blaze, lying next to a newly born filly.

"She arrived yesterday," Alek announced. "She's waiting for you to give her a name."

I was in awe of the innocent beauty that lay before me. I began to gently stroke her soft, yellow-brown coat. She looked at me, unafraid and so trusting. I looked up at Big Tex as he stood there like the proud Papa. "You've been busy, haven't ya boy?" I said to him with a smile. He grunted back at me as if he understood what I had said.

"And look at you, Mama! She looks just like you," I said, stroking Blaze's thick, black mane. "What shall we name her, huh?" I asked this as if she could really give me that perfect name.

"What about Cinnamon, to match her pretty coat? Nah, too ordinary . . . let me think. It needs to be special, something that means to live life to the fullest, and to never give up hope, no matter what battles you face." As I bent back over to pet the filly once again, she looked right at me with her big, brown eyes, and I knew. "I think I'll name you Ellie," I said softly as my eyes began to tear up.

Alek bent down next to me. "I think you've found the perfect name for her."

I wiped away the few tears that managed to escape and said, "This was the best birthday present I could have ever asked for."

Alek and I sat in the hay, stroking both Blaze and Ellie over and over. There were no words spoken between us, but I felt connected with him in a way that I didn't understand. Admittedly, I felt a bit of jealousy at Ellie; she was way more confident in her relationship with Alek than I was. Of course, she looked at him with different eyes—those of a young child. I saw how his radiant, bright blue eyes glinted like still water touched by the sun on a hot summer's day. They were undeniably extraordinary, and each time he would look at me, I could feel them break through the barriers of my soul. Every time he was anywhere near me, I was so uncontrollably drawn to him, like metal to magnet. Even sitting in this stall with these magnificent horses, I had to fiddle around with the hay and look down each time I felt him looking at me to keep from blushing. I would faintly smile, embarrassed from the attention.

I rested my head on the new mama as she adoringly cuddled her newborn baby. It was so amazing. Love and trust filled the barn on that glorious morning. I never wanted the happiness I felt to go away. I looked up at Tex as he stood just outside the stall, protecting all he loved, and thought of my dad. I couldn't wait for him to come home. We needed him so much. Together, with our family united once again, I knew we could get through these tough times.

TWENTY NINE

Confused Emotions

It wasn't long before I heard the honking of a horn back at the house. "It must be my dad!" I exclaimed.

Alek quickly helped me up, and I rushed toward the house. As I got closer, I didn't see his car. As a matter of fact, I saw a big truck with something wrapped in silver on top of it. As we approached the driver, he got down from his cab with a clipboard in hand and said, "You Miss Lewis?" His breath, heavy with the smell of cigarettes, nearly choked me when he spoke.

"Yes . . . yes, I am. Who are you?"

"I have a delivery for you, ma'am. Could you please sign right here?" he asked, pointing to a line on his clipboard. I did as he asked without question, curious as to what was going on.

He then lowered the back end of the truck and started to release a clanking chain. I looked over at Alek with an expression of question on my face, and he only shrugged his shoulders, equally perplexed. Once the driver completed his task at hand, he walked up to me again. "Here, I'm supposed to give you this, too. Have a nice day," he said impassively before getting back into his truck and driving off.

I unfolded the yellow piece of paper, which said "MEMO" at the top of it.

Hi, Princess! Happy Birthday.

Some very urgent matters arose at the last minute that I couldn't get away from, so I won't be able to make it back in time for your birthday. I sent you something very special, though, to let you know how much I love you. Hope to see you soon. Love, Daddy

I couldn't believe this. He promised he would be home for my birthday. I read the memo over and over until Alek had to finally pry it out of my fingers. The happiness I had felt only moments earlier was quickly taken, carried away by the breeze that blew through my body, giving me chills from head to toe. How could he do this? And what in the world did he send in his place?

I walked over to the delivered "package" that was obviously some sort of car covered in a silver protector—his idea of wrapping paper, I guess. I yanked that shiny material off as hard as I could to unveil a black sports car.

"What kind of car is this?" I asked, dumbfounded.

Alek only laughed at me for not having a clue. "Seriously, Renee? You have no idea what is sitting in your driveway right now?"

"Don't know and don't care," I said with arms crossed, mad as heck. "What is it anyway?" I asked while sulking, now madder that I had given in.

"Renee, your dad just sent you a brand new BMW M3 Coupe."

"What's a coupe?"

There was a hint of a smile as he explained. "A coupe just means it's a two-door, giving it that sporty look. Yeah," he said rubbing his hand on the slick machine as he walked around the hood. "I'd say your dad spent a small fortune on this beauty."

"Oh."

I stood back from the metallic black vehicle to get a better look. He was right; it was a beauty, which I hated to admit. Curiosity got the best of me, so I peeked inside the tinted window. I must say it was impressive, but before I got too carried away, I shook my head and took a deep breath to come back to my senses.

"So he thinks this hunk of metal is going to buy my forgiveness? Well, he's got another thing coming. I don't give a flip about driving around in some fancy sports car. I like my Explorer just fine! *Augh!*" I cried out as I turned and walked inside the house, slamming the door behind me. I quickly dialed his cell number and waited for an answer. "You've reached the voicemail of . . ." Click. I hung up the phone and dialed again. I waited for five rings again, and the same familiar recording came back on. Click. "Augh!" I was so angry with him.

Alek came walking in, carrying all of the suitcases. I plopped myself on the couch and pouted, thinking of a few choice words I wanted to scream out loud. I never saw this coming. The dad I knew one year ago wouldn't have missed my birthday for the world.

"You okay?" Alek asked.

"I'm fine," I lied.

"You know, when I get upset or hurt, I pray and give it to God," he suggested.

"Well . . . I'm not in the praying mood right now, okay?" I snapped back.

"I understand. That's when it's good to have praying friends. It's a good thing I'm your friend," he said as he carried the luggage up the stairs.

He couldn't possibly understand what I was feeling or going through right now. Nothing about my life is what it's supposed to be or once was. At least I knew I had Kyran, who showed me the love and attention I needed. He was right all along; I *can* trust him. He's been there for me every time I have needed him since coming out of my coma. I was anxious to hear his voice, so I quickly dialed his number.

"Hello," his soothing voice said, sending a wave of yearning through me.

"Hey, it's Renee. I'm so glad you answered. It's good to hear your voice," I said with a lump in my throat.

"Are you okay, Renee? You sound upset."

"I'm better now. I can't wait to see you tonight. What time will you be picking me up?"

"I'll be there at eight o'clock sharp. I have a surprise coming at six for you, though, to help you get ready."

"Really? But you've already done so much."

"It's only the beginning, love. You deserve to be spoiled, so enjoy it!"

"Kyran." I paused for a second. "I . . . I . . . ," I stuttered.

"Yes, love, what is it?"

"I . . . I think . . . I love you," I admitted to him, still unsure of my own feelings but needing to feel it reciprocated. He sat quietly on the phone. It wasn't quite the response I had hoped for. I started to feel embarrassed for opening myself up to him like that. *I'm so stupid!*

"Renee, do you believe in second chances?" he asked. I didn't understand where he was coming from, but I answered anyway.

"Yes, of course. Why do you ask?"

"*Sei la mia, amore.* I'll see you tonight."

"Oh . . . okay, see ya," I replied, and hung up. Hmmm . . . *sei la mia. What did he say now?* I wondered. I kept saying it out loud over and over, as if it would miraculously make sense to me. *"Sei la mia . . . Sei la mia."* I was even starting to say it with an accent each time I said it. Of course, it still didn't sound as good as when Kyran said it.

"You are mine," Alek said from behind.

"What?"

"You are mine. You keep saying that in Italian."

"Oh . . . you speak Italian?" I was quite shocked that this country boy knew how to speak another language.

"I know a lot of things, Renee!" he responded.

At that point, though, all I could focus on were Kyran's last words.

"I put your things in your room. Is there anything else you need me to do?"

"Huh?" I said, still lost in thought.

"Anything else you need?" he repeated.

"Oh, no, thanks though."

Alek started toward the front door when I foolishly asked, "Hey, are you gonna come to my party tonight?"

"Let's just say my name wasn't on Kyran's guest list."

"Oh, right. I forgot how you two can't be in the same room together. If it's worth anything to you, I wish you were gonna be there."

Alek stepped up to the couch where I was still planted in my pouting position, and he seemed to get serious on me all of a sudden. "Renee, if things start to get a little crazy for you tonight or you start to feel uncomfortable, you need only to call on me, and I will be there. If you invite me in, they can't stop me from coming. Do you understand?"

"Yeah, I guess so," I said, unsure of exactly what he was saying.

"Good. Now, I left a little birthday gift for you on your dresser. Promise me you'll put it in your purse and save it for the party."

"Can't I just open it now so I can give you a proper thank you?"

"I would prefer you just wait. Please, do this for me. I hope you'll understand once you open it," he implored.

"Okay, sure. If that's what you want."

"Thanks, Renee," he said, then reached out and gave me a sweet peck on my cheek. "Happy birthday." And with that, he walked out of the door.

I felt my cheek where his lips had pressed upon it. In the half a second that they had connected with my skin, a jolt of energy shot through my body to the tips of my toes as if lightning had struck. It was so strange and so magical all at the same time. But, the fact of the matter was that I was Kyran's girl, and it was not right for me to even think about having any sort of feelings for someone else. I had to force Alek out of my mind.

I killed time the next few hours watching TV, listening to music, and soaking in a hot bath. Six o'clock couldn't get here quickly enough. I was anxious to see what my next surprise from Kyran was. I looked at my watch and realized I hadn't heard from my mom. She said she wouldn't be too far behind. I'd better call and check on her.

"Hello?" a tired voice answered.

"Mom?"

"Hey sweetheart, how are you?"

"Mom, you sound awful. Are you okay?"

"I'm fine. The doctor just wanted me to stay and rest a little longer. Nothing to worry about."

"Are you sure? I'll come up there right now if you need me to."

"I'm sure. Is Daddy home yet?"

I let out a deep sigh before answering. "No. He sent a present and a note saying something urgent came up, and that he wasn't going to make it home today."

"Oh, sweetie, I'm so sorry. I'm sure he'll make it up to you."

"He already tried, but it didn't work."

"What do you mean?"

"Mom, he sent a really expensive sports car in his place. Can you believe that?"

There was silence on the phone. I could have kicked myself for bringing it up while she was feeling so bad.

"Well, I'm sure he meant well by it."

I could have argued the point, but for her sake, I just dropped it. "Yeah, I'm sure he did. Will I get to see you before I leave for the party?"

"The doctor said I could come home in about an hour, so I should get to see you before you leave."

"Awesome. Just be careful driving. You call me if you start feeling sick or anything."

"Alek is coming back by to pick me up, so don't worry."

"That's good. That makes me feel a lot better. Well, I guess I'll let you go so you can get some more rest. Love you, Mom."

"Love you, too."

Boy, that Alek is a Godsend, isn't he? He would probably drive to the moon and back if we asked him to. "Don't start thinking about him again," I had to tell myself. But really, what a great guy! *He's so thoughtful and considerate. And my mom just loves . . . .*

The doorbell rang and interrupted my train of thought. I looked at my watch, and "it" was right on time. I wondered what Kyran had up his little sleeve now?

THIRTY

Like Old Times with a New Me

I walked down the stairs as quickly as I could, excited for my surprise. I opened the door, and there was Jamie with several bags in her hands. "Jamie!" I shouted as I wrapped my arms around her neck.

"A little help here," she replied.

"Oh, sorry," I said as I freed one of her arms.

"Thanks!" she smiled, and then hugged me back with her open arm.

"What are you doing here?" I asked excitedly.

"Kyran gave me his credit card to go shopping for you and asked that I come help you get dolled up for the night." I could tell it thrilled her tremendously to go shopping on someone else's dime. I could just envision her tearing through every store, searching for the coolest clothes and sparing no expense.

"Oh, my gosh! I'm so happy you're here! Come on; let's go up to my room."

As we walked into the room, Jamie immediately announced, "Okay, before we start making you look fabulous, I want to give you *my* birthday present first."

My eyes and mouth opened wide with delight. I was so happy she was here and thought to get me a present. I couldn't help but stare at her as she dug into her oversized purse and pulled out a wrapped thin, square object. I had missed her even more than I realized, even if she did look different from *my* old Jamie. The times that we had shared over the years, and the memories we had created, made her just the same to me. I cherished our friendship dearly.

"Here you go!" she said excitedly as she handed it to me.

"Hmmm . . . let me guess," I said sarcastically.

"I know, it's not rocket science, but you don't know *who* it is yet. Ha-ha," she said, sticking her tongue out at me playfully.

I ripped it open as fast as I could. *"Ahhh!"* I screamed as I read the label. *"Awake* by Skillet!"

"Like it?"

"No . . . I love it! I didn't know they had released a new CD."

"It came out while you were in your coma."

"How appropriate is that title," I said. We both laughed together.

"Go on, put it in! You're gonna love the first track."

I ran over to my stereo and put it in.

"It's my favorite song. It's called *Hero,"* Jamie said. "Crank that baby up!"

I blasted the stereo so loud I thought my speakers were going to blow. But I didn't care. Jamie and I started doing a little head bangin'; then she started playing the air guitar, and I played the air drums, just like old times. Before I knew it, we jumped onto the bed and kicked everything off as we rocked out. We were laughing so hard while screaming the lyrics into our hairbrushes/microphones along with the band. I had to cheat and read them from the CD cover, but Jamie already had every word memorized.

The lyrics spoke of families torn, faith lost, and falling off the edge of this world. There would be a time in all of our lives that we would have to stand up and fight, but sometimes we needed a hero to help us. As we were belting out the song, I couldn't help but wonder, *Who is my hero now?* I always thought I knew that answer, but these days, I was not so sure anymore. I looked at Jamie, still singing her little heart out, and thought, *Right now* she *is my hero for even being here.* For taking me back to the past, where we danced and jumped around like silly schoolgirls loving life.

After just one song, I was wiped out. My stamina was still lacking. But singing and head banging felt so rejuvenating to my spirits; it was like going back in time by one year when nothing bad had ever happened.

"That song is amazing," I said as I turned the music back down to a respectable level, barely able to catch my breath.

"I know. They really know how to get us fired up, don't they?"

"Thanks, Jamie. That really meant a lot to me."

"No problem. That's what friends are for. Now, we've got work to do to get you ready for your big night," she said as she pushed me into my bathroom. I had hoped this meant I was finally forgiven.

She sat me in my chair and went to get all the supplies needed to make me look "hot" and "worthy" of this big bash we were going to in my honor. She sure had a lot of stuff!

"Okay . . . let's start with the hair," she said as she pulled her Chi iron out of her oversized makeup bag. She worked fervently on my hair, not allowing me to look in the mirror until she said so. I got a little nervous when she pulled out a pair of scissors and started cutting away on my bangs. "Don't worry, I know what I'm doing," she assured me. It didn't help much.

As she began putting on my makeup, I noticed she still had her Ichthus fish ring that she had bought after taking the Pure Love Pledge. We vowed to wear the silver rings until the day our wedding rings replaced them. I glanced back at mine, thankful my mother was able to save it after they cut it off my finger. After seeing Jamie with Aden at the pool party, I had wondered if she had kept her vow. My curiosity got the best of me, so I had to ask. "I see you still have the ring on. Does that mean . . . ."

She shrugged her shoulders a bit, but didn't say anything.

"I was afraid with all that had happened, maybe you and Aden might have . . . ."

"Just stop," she interrupted. I could tell it was a very touchy subject for her.

"Listen, I didn't mean to pry. I guess I was just curious. Sorry."

Great, Renee! Just when we're making amends, you go and bring up something that makes her uncomfortable. You need to work on the timing thing, I scolded myself.

But to my surprise, she thought about it for a minute and said, "No, I'm sorry for snapping at you." She continued putting some blush onto my cheeks. "You're right, a lot has happened in my life since you had your accident. This has been the one thing that I've hung on to, though. But Aden has really been pressuring me a lot lately. He tells me how much he loves me and that he wants to take care of me forever. It's been really hard keeping him under control, if you know what I mean."

"For what it's worth, I'm proud you've stayed strong and kept your pledge."

"Well, don't be too proud just yet. I think tonight's the night. I'm afraid if I don't, Ren, I'm gonna lose him, and I really need him in my life right now."

"No, don't do it, Jamie. If he really loves you, then he'll wait. Please, think about what you just said. Maybe Aden is the one you'll marry some day, but maybe he's not. If you lose him because of that, then he's not the kind of guy you'd want to spend the rest of your life with anyway, and you will have wasted your most precious gift for your husband on someone who doesn't deserve it."

I could see tears welling up in her eyes as she lined my lips in hot pink. She didn't respond to what I had said. I knew she was still unsure of what she should do. "Look, if he pressures you too much tonight, and you aren't ready, just find me. I'll get you out of it one way or another. Okay?"

"Let's talk about something else, okay? The air seems to have suddenly gotten too thick in here," she retorted.

"Okay." I sat silently, not really sure what to say after that, so I went for a time killer question. "So, how's school these days?"

"School is school . . . you know."

That didn't work too well. I glanced at my watch, feeling like I had been sitting here forever. "Are you done yet?" I asked impatiently. Surely I couldn't have looked *that* bad.

"Almost. Wait right there while I get a missing piece to your outfit. And *don't* peek," she threatened, pointing her finger.

First, she walked in my closet and pulled out the black leather jacket that Kyran had bought me, but I never got to wear. "His only request for me was that you wear the jacket he bought you," she informed me.

I thought that was very clever of him. He must have remembered me saying I wouldn't ever have anywhere to wear it; I guess I was wrong.

Then she rummaged through the array of bags thrown on the floor until she found the one she was looking for. "Okay, my friend, strip down."

"What?" I said, already embarrassed at the thought.

"Oh come on, Ren, it's time to get over your prudishness," she said seriously. I took almost everything off. "You're forgetting something, aren't you? Here, I'll turn around, and you put these on," she said as she handed me a cute, tiny pink bag that didn't weigh an ounce. Jamie turned around as promised, and I pulled out a skimpy, lacey bra with matching panties.

"Uh-uh," I argued. "I'm not wearing this. What's wrong with the ones I have on?"

"Besides the fact that my grandmother quit wearing those in 1999? You're seventeen now; it's time to come out of the shell you've been hiding in all of these years." She took the lingerie from my hand to demonstrate how to wear it. "These will make you feel sexy, like a supermodel. Just try them on. What's it gonna hurt?" she pleaded.

"Fine . . . turn back around," I said as I grabbed them back out of her hand. I quickly put them on, trying not to think about it much or I would change my mind for sure. "Now what?" I asked, wrapping my arms around myself for a little added coverage. She only laughed at me while she grabbed the next bag.

"You're gonna love these," she said, convinced.

I opened the bag and pulled out some black denim jeans embellished with metal and crystal studs. There was some sort of tiger hand painted on the right leg, and hand threading throughout. These were the fanciest, flashiest jeans I had ever seen, but I wouldn't say that I *loved* them.

"Hurry up! I'm dying to see what they look like on you," Jamie said impatiently.

I put them on and thought they felt way too tight.

"Perfect fit!" Jamie exclaimed, then handed me a white t-shirt with many of the same designs on it, too.

It was a bit clingy, much tighter than what I was used to wearing.

"Another perfect fit! One more bag to open," she said so excitedly. I could tell she put a lot of thought into this outfit.

Inside the bag was a large shoe box. As I opened the box, the first thing that caught my eye was the four-inch pointed heels affixed to the bottom of the black leather boots. "You must want me to kill myself in these things!"

"No, but you'll look fabulous if you do," she joked. "Time is running out. Put them on!"

"Pushy, pushy," I said in return. I sat back down on my chair and put them on. So far the only thing she got right during her little shopping spree was my new CD.

"Now, stand up so I can help you put your jacket on."

I think the boots made me six feet tall. Jamie had to really stretch to get the jacket around me.

She stood back and put her hands over her mouth. She was

beaming with pride. I could tell she was quite pleased with her ensemble. "Close your eyes," she said and guided me out to my room, standing me in front of my full-length mirror. "Okay, open them."

I gazed into the mirror, perplexed with the stranger staring back. I had to feel my hair and my clothes to make sure I was really looking at Renee Lewis. How in the world did she do this? I looked like a supermodel straight off the cover of *Cosmo*. Of course, I had more makeup on my face than what was left at the Clinique counter at the department store.

"So? What do you think?" Jamie asked eagerly.

"I'm stumped for words. I barely even recognize myself."

"Oh, my gosh, Ren, you look stunning!" she said and gave me a tight squeeze around my waist, as I was now a half foot taller than she was.

I knew it made her happy to do this for me. How could I not appreciate her effort? "Thanks, Jamie."

"Oooh, look at the time, I need to go get dressed myself. I'll see you at the party," she said, hurriedly stepping through the door. She peeked back around to say, "Oh, and there's a little black purse on your dresser that I left for you. The straps are thin and long so you can drape it over your shoulder for the ride there." And she was gone.

"Okay, thanks," I yelled out.

I looked at my watch, and it was seven thirty. I grabbed my purse to head downstairs and noticed Alek's present sitting next to it. The thought of opening it did cross my mind, but I resisted the temptation out of respect for him. It was wrapped in red paper and tied with a white ribbon. The box was long and thin, not very heavy. *I wonder if it's a necklace*, I thought to myself. Nah, why would he give me jewelry? I guess my curiosity would have to wait. I put it inside my purse along with my phone, lipstick, and gum and headed downstairs.

Mom walked through the door just as I reached the last step, almost tripping on the dang heels. I stopped in front of her and gave a quick twirl. She didn't say anything; she only stared in silence.

"What do you think, Mom? Jamie came and helped me get ready."

"Honestly, baby girl, I don't know what to think. You look so, so . . . grown up. Certainly much older than a seventeen-year-old girl."

"I know, but Jamie worked so hard putting this all together, and it's only for this one special night. Don't worry, Mom, I'm still me on the inside."

She slowly walked over to the couch. I followed her and helped her sit down. I could tell she was still feeling a bit weak. "Sweetie, I have to be honest. I'm tempted not to let you go to the party at all. I just don't feel good about it."

"No, Mom, you can't do that. This party is for me, and Kyran has worked so hard putting it together."

"I know, but sometimes it's harder to make the right choice. I don't trust this family. They aren't good people."

"But Kyran is different. He really cares about me, and I know he wouldn't hurt me. I know you don't trust them, but you at least trust me, don't you?" Boy, I was beginning to sound like Kyran.

"Of course, I do. You've never given me any reason not to."

"I'll be fine, I promise."

I could hear her doubt by the heaviness of her breath as she exhaled. As she sat in silence, I knew she was struggling to decide what to do or say next. I could see the moisture building in her eyes. I knew letting me go was hard on her.

"Okay, Renee. But promise me you will remember who you are and where you came from. And if at any point you feel uncomfortable, go to a quiet place, pray to the Lord for guidance and protection, then call someone to come and get you. Do you understand?"

"Yes, Mom, I will. I promise. Thank you so much!"

"Oh, Renee. I love you more than words can say. You were my little miracle baby," she said as we sat on the couch, embracing one another. "May angels watch you through this night."

THIRTY ONE

An Exhilarating Ride...
for the Most Part

Kyran was right on time. I answered the door, ready for the night to begin.

"You look amazing," he said, stunned by my transformation.

"I can't take the credit for this. It was all Jamie's doing."

"Remind me to thank her later," he replied, putting his arms around my waist and giving me an affectionate hug. "Ready?"

"More than you know."

"Your chariot awaits you then, mademoiselle," he said, grabbing my hand to lead the way. But I didn't see any limo, sports car, or helicopter for that matter. No, to my shock and disbelief, the only motor transportation I saw waiting for me was his swanky crotch rocket.

"Are we seriously driving that to your house?"

"You're going to love it, I promise."

"But we're going to freeze to death," I said, separating each word with a slight pause so he would get the full concept of my concern.

"Trust me. I have that all taken care of."

We walked up to his ride where two fancy helmets and some thick black gloves were situated on the leather seats. Kyran began to explain how I would not arrive to the party half-frozen. "Put these gloves on. They are electrically heated to keep your hands nice and warm when I insert the plug into my motorcycle."

I did as he asked, but not without rolling my eyes like a child—still in disbelief that my "grand chariot" was his dream cycle.

"Now, this custom-made seat gives off just the right amount of heat to also help keep you warm." He helped me up onto the back seat and continued with his speech. "This helmet will keep your head warm. Do you see this?" he said as he pointed to a small microphone. It almost felt like show-and-tell in kindergarten. I patiently sat there and listened as he explained. "We can talk to each other while we are driving." He helped me put that on, too, and then got himself situated.

Now speaking through his helmet, he said, "And if none of those things keep you warm, just hold on to me as tightly as you can. I'll keep you warm!" I could hear the smile through the microphone as he spoke so confidently.

Kyran started the engine, and we sat idly, listening to its roar as he revved it up over and over. The exhaust rumbled like music, crisp and smooth, filling the air with its sound of power. Kyran gave it one final thrust, and off we went into the mountains.

I had never been on a motorcycle before. It was a little scary at first, but I got used to it rather quickly. As we sped past the various trees and rocks lining the roads, I looked up into the faraway sky at the clusters of bright, yellow stars, which were tantalizing us with their mysterious marvels. I probably would have never noticed how beautiful the night sky was with the full moon on the rise, beaming light into the darkness, had we been cooped up in a car. The ride was so smooth, and Kyran was able to get up the mountain with such ease on this beast of a machine. My arms were stretched around his waist, and I never wanted to release this enchanting boy who always kept me wondering and wanting more.

"How are you doing back there?" he asked.

"Amazing."

He would round the corners and all of the twists and turns gracefully, as if he'd driven this mountain a million times on this motorcycle. I surprised myself when his fast speeds didn't bother me in the least. Rather, there was a rush that came with this sensation of danger, a rush like I had never felt before; I felt weightless, like we were flying through the air.

Perhaps I didn't worry because I had come to really trust Kyran. I felt safe with him and so alive, able to take my guard down. It was a bit gut wrenching to think how my mom had such different feelings for him, because I cared for and respected her opinion. But she had never seen how gentle, considerate, and loving Kyran was with me. I knew if she would just get to know him better, she would have a change of heart, just like I had.

As we approached Kyran's house, he stopped at the end of the drive and got his cell phone out of his pocket.

"Excuse me, *amore*, as I make a call." He took off his helmet—his hair was still perfect, of course—and dialed a number. He was speaking so fast in Italian to whomever was on the other end of the phone that I couldn't understand a single word.

"Okay, they're ready for us. Are you ready?" he asked.

"Ready as I'll ever be."

"Good. Now, I need you to hold me as tightly as you possibly can. Do you trust me?"

"Yes," I replied.

"Just remember that because this will be a little dangerous, but so exhilarating!" His voice was filled with enthusiasm, and he gave me a big smile. "Remember, hold on tight, alright?"

I gave him two thumbs up.

He put his helmet back on and said, "Here we go!"

And off we went, building up just enough speed to go up the massive set of stairs that led to the front door. Just as we reached the top, the two front doors magically opened, ready for our entry. Kyran turned to the right, the bike gliding across the marble floor but still in his control, to where the grand ballroom was. We drove to the middle of the room, where we finally stopped. I thought my heart was going to pound right out of my chest, and all I could do was to sit there, completely frozen. Exhilarating? *Maybe . . . once I get over the shock and start to breathe again . . . I'll think so.*

THIRTY TWO

All for "Me"

As everyone around us began to clap and cheer, Kyran had to force my stiff arms from around him so that we could get down. He went first, removing his helmet, and then graciously put his hand out for me to follow. As I took my own helmet off, the crowd got even louder. It was unbelievable. I felt like a superstar as camera bulbs flashed and people were cheering my name. I didn't even know most of them, yet they treated me like royalty, holding their hands out for me to shake. I actually found it quite odd as I couldn't figure out what I had done to deserve such a welcome.

"This is all for you," Kyran whispered in my ear.

All I could do was smile and wave to everyone.

The DJ walked up to us with a microphone and handed it to Kyran while someone else handed him a drink. "Thank you, everyone! Thank you for coming to this very special celebration. As many of you know, not only is it Renee's seventeenth birthday today . . ." And with that, everyone began to hoot and holler again.

" . . . but today marks the first day of Renee's new beginning. You see, for those of you who don't know, Renee was in a terrible accident almost one year ago. Everyone thought she might die, but luckily for us, she was spared. After being in a coma for eleven months, Renee came back to us. So, please join me in raising a glass to Renee, and let the party begin!"

Everyone started going wild again, cheering my name, and patting my back, as Kyran escorted me to another room. I had never seen so many people in one place before. It was totally surreal.

We finally made it to a quieter room so that I could at least catch my breath. "Wow! That was unbelievable," I said. I took off the gloves that kept my hands nice and toasty, just as Kyran had said.

"And that's only the beginning. But first, there's something I've been dying to do since I first laid eyes on you this evening," he said as he pulled me up to him. He began kissing me with such passion and emotion that the room began to spin as I became lost in him.

He stopped momentarily, looked strangely into my eyes, and with a whisper in his voice said, "Tell me now what you said on the phone. I want to hear it in person."

I thought I knew what he was talking about, so with caution I said what I thought he wanted to hear.

"I love you." And with that, his lips connected with mine once again, until there was a knock at the door.

Some young guy I had never met before walked in. No doubt he had to be another member of the family by his looks. "Hey, bro, everyone's waiting for the guest of honor so the show can begin. Come on, man," he urged us.

"We'll be right there," Kyran replied and then looked straight at me.

"It's a little wild out there, so make sure you stay right by my side. Okay? Don't leave me without telling me where you're going."

I was surprised by his worried tone. It caught me off guard. "Sure, okay."

"Let's go," he said as he reached for my hand, and we left the only quiet room.

As we walked down the hall, I could see various gatherings in other rooms of the house. There appeared to be blackjack, poker, and craps tables set up everywhere like a mini-casino. In another room, there was a man and a woman with tattoos all over their bodies breathing fire from their mouths. It seemed to be a real crowd pleaser.

As we stepped into the main ballroom, I immediately noticed that there were cocktail waitresses walking around, dressed like Las Vegas showgirls. They were handing out drinks to everyone, wearing flashing buttons that said, "I won't tell if you won't." A scantily dressed woman with bushy hair walked by us yelling, "Cigarettes, cigars, giggle sticks," over and over. If I didn't know better, I would have thought we *had* arrived in Vegas.

"What are giggle sticks?" I had to ask. I'd never heard of such a thing.

Kyran only shook his head and gave a slight laugh. He appeared amused by my question, but never gave me an answer. Instead of getting irritated with him for ignoring my question, I took it as something I was better off not knowing. He walked me over to a booth-like table with a U-shaped seat covered with black leather that sat to the side of the stage. The sign sitting on the black linen cloth said, "Reserved." We sat down, and he called a waitress over to us. He said something into her ear and showed two fingers on his hand as she walked away. He put his arm around me and said, "This should be good."

The waitress came back within minutes with two cocktails in her hand. She wished me a happy birthday as she set them on the table.

Kyran handed me my drink and said, "Here's to a magical night." He tapped his glass against mine. I took a sip and started to cough. It was so strong I was afraid to breathe on the lit candle sitting in the center of the table. It didn't seem to bother Kyran one bit.

The DJ tapped the microphone and started talking. "We've got a great lineup for all you ladies and gents in the house. Give it up for the hottest rap group in America, who just went platinum with their latest CD. Put yo' hands together for Holla'."

The crowd went completely mad as an entourage of singers, dressed in baggy clothes, and dancers, who barely wore any, took the stage. I had never heard of Holla' before, but everyone else sure seemed to like them. After his first song, "Don't Let Yo Mama Know," the overly large, bald guy with dark shades yelled into the microphone with his husky voice, "E'ryone give it up for da' birthday girl!" Everybody screamed.

"So check it . . . this next song is fo' my man o'er there, Kyran," he said, pointing to our table. "This song just went to numba one on the charts, and it goes a lil' sumpin' like this."

I could hardly understand any of the words they were yelling into the microphones, but I did catch the title of the song in the chorus, "Gettin' Low 'n Dirty." By the time the song was over, I felt like I needed to wash my ears out with soap. This was definitely not my thing.

Kyran must have seen the distaste in my expression and said, "I think you'll like the next act a little better." I just smiled back at him.

As the rap group continued their show, I scanned the audience, trying to find Jamie. I was hoping she would come and join us at the table. All I could see were people dancing provocatively, which suited the songs that they were dancing to. I admittedly felt uncomfortable and awkward being in the same room. I recognized a few people: Brandon Grinn, Greg Saddler, who was now the shoe-in for valedictorian, and even Beth, who was dancing with the guy who had come and got Kyran and me from the room. She was on him like "stink on a skunk," as my mother would say. She noticed I was looking at her and threw me a sneering look. I smiled and gave her what I thought to be a friendly wave in an effort to let her know that I didn't hate her for stealing my best friend, but she didn't take it that way and yanked her dance partner away from view. I continued to look around, but was disappointed that I didn't find Jamie. I hoped she was okay.

Meanwhile, Nate was putting whispers of prayers into Evelyn's ears. She began to pray:

"Dearest Lord Jesus, thank you for this day. I come to You humbly with a heavy burden on my heart. I fear for the safety of my daughter as she celebrates her birthday this evening. I ask that You protect her and guide her as she makes her choices. I trust in You and know Your Will will be done. Show me what to do so that I can help in some way to bring her home safely. Give me the strength I need. I pray this in your name. Amen."

As soon as she was done praying, Evelyn felt the urge to start making some phone calls. She began with Willard Tyler, the Pastor at Hope Church.

"Hello," said Pastor Tyler.

"Pastor Tyler, this is Mrs. Lewis."

"Good evening, Evelyn, how are you doing?"

"I'm fine, thank you. Listen, I feel the Lord is calling us to get a prayer chain going. There are souls at stake, pastor, and we need to all be praying for their protection."

"I'm listening."

"There is a big party going on at the Dellamorte house for Renee's birthday. I think every kid in town is there, but I am not getting good feelings about what they may be doing. Can you pray for them, pastor?"

"Yes, of course. Let me make a few calls to some of the staff as well. I get the feeling they will be needing a lot of prayer tonight."

"Yes, I agree. I'm going to call Miss Adamma and a few others that I know are still strong in their faith. As a matter of fact, I'm going to ask them to join me here so we can all pray together. Please, feel free to stop by as well."

"Will do."

And with that, they both got to work.

THIRTY THREE

A Final Hint Attempted

"E'rybody make some noise for Holla' as they exit the stage," the DJ screamed into the microphone. The buoyant crowd obliged his request. "As the crew gets ready for the next act, I'm gonna play a few jams for you to get down with. I'll check you in a few."

The next song the DJ played sparked Kyran's interest. "Come on, let's dance."

"I don't know, Kyran. I don't dance like they do," I said as I looked around at the other guests.

"Here, gulp this down. It will loosen you up some." I just looked at him, unsure of what to do. "You trust me, don't you?" Without putting any more thought into it, I gulped down the strong drink.

"Good, now let's dance!" As he pulled me out to the dance floor, everyone started cheering for me once again. "Go, Renee, it's your birthday, and we're gonna party like it's your birthday," they all chanted.

I was still feeling nervous. Kyran started moving first. He grabbed my hands and started to twist my body in an effort to get me going. It worked. It made me think of the last time he was able to get me out on this dance floor, and I started to loosen up some.

Then I heard a long, drawn-out "Hey!" Dancing up to us were Jamie and Aden.

"Ahhh!" I screamed, and hugged her. I was so happy to finally see her.

"Look at you move!" she said playfully and started dancing herself.

It was obvious by her red eyes and the smell of her breath that she had already tried a few drinks herself. We ended up dancing two more songs before I told Kyran I needed to rest. The four of us walked back over to our table, where Aden ordered a round of drinks for us.

"None for me, thanks," I said. But he didn't pay any attention to my request. The waitress brought over four more drinks.

Kyran, Jamie, and Aden all held up their glasses as Aden announced his toast. "Here's to the two most beautiful women here, and to a night we'll never forget!" And with that, they all clanked their glasses together. I found it funny that he called Jamie and me women. I still felt like a young girl on the inside. Or maybe it was that I had never been referred as such by anyone before.

"Come on, Renee, you have to toast, too," Aden demanded as he handed me my glass. I looked over at Kyran for guidance, or maybe a little help, and he just nodded his head toward the glass. They each took a turn tapping on it before taking a big swig.

"Here goes nothing," I said, and chugged the whole drink down. It was the only way I could get past the terrible taste.

"That a girl! You've got a real partier there, Kyran," Aden said obnoxiously. "Let me see *you* down one like that." He said this contemptuously to Jamie while putting a cigarette in her mouth, then lighting it. I was shocked to see her smoking, another unexpected change. It was painful just watching her puff away on that stupid thing knowing how hard it was on her to watch her grandfather pass away from lung cancer, the result of his smoking for many years. He suffered a slow and excruciating death, and we had both sworn that we would never touch a cigarette.

Aden whistled to the waitress to come over and ordered four more drinks. I was beginning not to care for him. Besides the fact that he was a handsome guy, I didn't quite see what Jamie saw in him. He was obviously a bad influence on her—couldn't she see that? But then again, my mom couldn't see what I saw in Kyran either, so who was I to judge?

The DJ came back on to make his next introduction. "Is e'rybody havin' a good time?" he yelled. He always knew how to get the crowd roaring. "So check this. My man Kyran o'er there was able to bring in the hottest act on the planet. He pulled enough strings to get this award-winning, multi-platinum singer off her Zoo tour and here for you tonight! All I can say is, Renee . . . you must be one special girl. Now without further ado, singing 'Oops, I'm in It Again'—show some love for the phattest chick in da biz—Brandi Sparks."

The crowd went completely berserk as a beautiful blonde girl took the stage and started singing. Jamie seemed equally as impressed by this starlet and pulled Aden back out to the dance floor.

"How do you like your big surprise?" Kyran asked genuinely.

I thought to myself, *At least I've heard of her. I mean, who hasn't? She's been on countless magazine covers and seems to make headline news all of the time.* I was more impressed at the fact that Kyran was able to bring in such a huge star to a relatively unknown town for a seventeen-year-old girl's birthday. I had to show him some excitement for all of his hard work.

"I'm completely shocked! I can't believe you did this for me. Thank you so much," I said with a huge smile and gave him a peck on his cheek. That seemed to satisfy him.

"For this next song, I'm gonna ask the birthday girl to come up on stage with me," Brandi announced for all to hear, but there was no way I was going up there with her. "Come on, Renee, we're all waiting for you!" the persistent singer said, urging the crowd to try and persuade me with her.

Kyran had to do more convincing to get me up there, so he grabbed my hand and led the way.

"Please don't do this," I begged.

"You must be the only girl I know who doesn't love getting all this attention," he said with a chuckle.

Before I knew it, he had lifted me up onto the stage. Everyone started clapping and cheering once again, feeling they had won the battle. Brandi put her mic down, shook my now sweaty hand, and said it was nice to meet me.

She seated me on a chair right next to her and said, "This next song is called 'I'll Make You Love Me,' and it goes like this." The music started to blare once again, and as she sang the words to her hit song, a group of dancers started prancing all around me. One of them put a black feather boa around my neck while another put a tiara on my head. All I could think about was getting off that stage and killing Kyran.

As soon as Brandi finished her song, I started to get up from my chair. "Whoa, there," she said. "You're not done yet! Bartender, bring me and my friend here a drink!"

I sat in the chair, paralyzed. I didn't want another drink. The two I had were already making me feel a little weird. What was I going to do now? Everyone was watching me, waiting to see me have a drink with the biggest star on the planet.

"I can tell this girl needs another one," Brandi said as she handed me a small glass with a clear liquid. I took a sniff of it and was thankful it didn't really have much of a smell. *This one must not be too strong*, I thought to myself, grateful it was much smaller than the other cocktails.

"Okay, when I say three, take your shot," she explained. "One, two, three." And down it went.

"Everyone give it up for Renee!" she yelled as Kyran helped me off the stage.

As I walked back to the table, I started feeling woozy. It was all becoming too overwhelming. The last thing I could hear clearly was Brandi saying her next song was "Baby, One Last Time," and after that, it all sounded muffled. "I think I need to go to the bathroom," I told Kyran. "I'm not feeling too well."

I grabbed my purse from the table, and we walked down the hall toward the pretty powder room that I had been in once before. It was a relief to get away from all of the noise.

As we walked, I noticed Aden pulling Jamie's hand, urging her to go up the stairs. "Jamie," I cried out, but my raspy voice was not loud enough for her to hear.

"Don't worry about her. She's fine," Kyran assured me.

When we approached the restroom, I really started to feel sick. My stomach ached like I needed to put something of substance in it. "Can you get me something to eat? I haven't eaten anything all day."

"Renee, sweetheart, you should have told me. It's not good to drink so much on an empty stomach."

"I didn't know. I've never drunk before. Please, give me a few minutes, will you?" I said holding my stomach.

"I'll go get you something to eat. Lock the door and don't leave this bathroom until I get back," he implored.

"'Kay" was all I could say before running in and puking what little I had into the toilet; then I locked the door as he had wished. The taste in my mouth was horrific, so I rinsed it out with the mouthwash that conveniently sat on the counter with an array of other products to freshen up with. I looked at myself in the mirror and was surprised to see the tiara, now tilted on the side of my head, still hanging on. My black eyeliner was beginning to smear under my eyes; I was definitely a poor sight to see. I felt disgusted with myself for allowing this to happen.

I leaned back against the wall and slid down to the floor. I could barely think straight, much less stand straight. If my mother saw me right now, she would be so disappointed. I could hear her saying as if she were right next to me, "Renee Brianne Lewis . . . what were you thinking? If you're going to lie down with dogs, you're going to get up with fleas!" She always had those silly little idioms to teach me another life lesson.

As I sat on the floor, room slightly spinning, I thought I saw dark shadows moving on the wall. It began to really freak me out. I looked around again, still seeing them crawl about, and I began hearing hushed whispers all around. They were starting to make me feel a little crazy, and I knew I needed to get out of here. But I couldn't leave without Jamie; I had to find her before she did something that would forever change her life. How was I going to get home, though? I knew Kyran would never agree to take us.

I opened up my purse to find my phone. I didn't want to call my mom; she didn't need this right now. The only other person I could count on was Alek. As I dug through the purse, I saw the present he had left for me. "Well, he said I could open it at the party." So, I took off the ribbon and ripped the wrapping paper off.

It was a silver box with a lid. I opened it up, and inside was a candy bar. "That's weird. Why would he give me this?" Oddly, I was grateful for the present and tore it open. "Ummm!" It tasted amazingly delicious as it began to soothe my aching stomach. What was this deliciousness that consumed my mouth? I had to squint my eyes to read the words "Baby Ruth" on the wrapper. Something was so familiar about this, but I couldn't quite put my finger on it.

As I sat there eating the last bite, pondering the idea behind Alek's gift, I looked down and noticed a small note inside the silver box. I had to squint really hard again just to read it.

Remember, L.

Without further hesitation, memories that had once vanished now reappeared in my head, finally breaking through the built-up walls as if the Hoover Dam itself shattered. All I could scream out was "Liam!"

THIRTY FOUR

The Truth Revealed

I was dizzy from the tunnel vision that consumed my sight. I felt like I was going through a black passageway when suddenly, scenes from the crash flooded my mind. I could see it all happening right before my very eyes, now as a witness to this horrible event. As the fiery sparks burst into the air, I saw Liam bravely placing himself between the two colliding vehicles before flying away. He was seemingly hurt as he struggled to fly deep into the sky with unsteady wings. I saw two other angels appear, helping him on each side, and then they were all gone before I could blink an eye.

The next vision I encountered was Grandma and Grandpa J walking with me through the beautiful garden, arm and arm. I was smiling and laughing as we strolled down the jeweled pathway. But this time, I could see Liam in the midst of all the trees and bushes that helped fill the flowery garden just standing there watching over us. I noticed a smile on his face. He looked content.

And last, it was as clear as if the experience were taking place at this very moment, was Liam saying good-bye just before I left the magical place that had brought us face to face, or should I say, soul to angel. "I'll never leave you . . . remember," he had promised me.

Yes, it was all becoming so clear: the dreams, the flashes in my eyes, Alek being such a godsend. A battle for my very soul had been occurring all this time. But something still puzzled me. Something that was so obvious now, but still didn't make sense—Kyran.

There was a knock on the door. "Renee, let me in," he said softly.

I didn't budge. Fear suddenly struck my heart as I realized that I was alone in a place filled with evil spirits all around. I looked for my cell phone once again and started to call Alek's number. My hands were shaking so badly, and my vision was so blurred from the cascade of tears that were rolling down my face that I couldn't complete the call. "Dang it!" I said, frustrated. "Liam, can you hear me?"

The knock became harder, and the voice louder as Kyran demanded I let him in.

"Go away," I shouted, still trying to dial the number to reach Alek . . . or Liam. I wasn't quite sure anymore. I felt so confused.

Kyran burst through the door with amazing force. I looked at him with fear in my eyes, unsure of who he really was or what his plans for me were.

Lord, help me! It was all I could think.

"What is going on?" Kyran asked sternly as he looked around the restroom.

I stood up with confidence and said, "I know, Kyran. I know everything."

"What are you talking about, love?"

"Don't give me that! You never loved me. It was all part of some evil scheme, wasn't it? You're nothing but a liar who has manipulated me to get me to this place. Now get out of my way so I can get Jamie and we can get out of here," I demanded.

"Wait . . . let me explain," Kyran replied.

"No! There's nothing to explain. You were my temptation, weren't you? Satan used you to get to me with your glorious looks and over-the-top charm. None of it was real. My mother was right about you all along. I guess I am a bigger fool than I ever could have imagined!"

"Listen to me; I'm not going to lie to you, Renee. You are right in some respects, but there's more to it than just that. Please, come to my room and let me explain. Please," he begged sincerely.

"I'm not buying that one bit; now get out of my way," I said as I shoved him enough to get through the door. I quickly ran up the stairs to try and find Jamie. I needed to save her from falling into their trap any more than she already had.

I could hear Kyran quickly running up from behind. It didn't take him long to catch up and grab me, dragging me into a room. He had ahold of both my arms and started to shake me as he said, "Now you've really done it. They know that you know, Renee. We've got to get out of here! They will be coming for you any minute."

"I'm not going anywhere without Jamie or with you!" I yelled.

"Listen to me," he said harshly. "*They* are coming!" He threw me onto the bed. His face was red with anger, and the veins on his forehead were protruding as the hot blood rushed through his face. He started pacing the floor as he planned his next move. He looked out the window and grabbed me from the bed. Then he extended his right arm out where a wave of incredible power rippled from his hand and shattered the window. "Let's go!"

But before he could take me even one step further, the bedroom door flew open. To my relief, there was Alek, standing at the door. "Let her go!" he demanded of Kyran.

"Never!" Kyran said and sent another wave of power through the air, forcing Alek against the wall on the other side of the hallway.

Alek quickly got up, seemingly untouched, and charged at us with incredible speed and strength.

Kyran threw me back on to the bed and charged back at him. As they collided with one another, they both began to fight, moving their arms and legs as they pounded on each other at such quick speeds that my eyes couldn't keep up. I had never seen anything like it.

I noticed a glow coming from Kyran's eyes. I had seen that familiar glow once before. This was the angry side of him that I had hoped to never see again. But no one can contain his or her true colors forever. *This must be who he really was . . . right?* I recalled the picture in my mind that I had taken of him after the sunset at the dinner party, and had a hard time really believing this was the same person—the same creation—that was in that memory picture.

The room was being completely destroyed as they tumbled around, attacking one another. Neither of them seemed to have the upper hand, and suddenly a force between them separated their bodies, sending each to the opposite side of the room.

"You know how this will end," Alek said to Kyran. "Leave her with me, and I will spare you from the fiery furnace."

"I won't lose her again," Kyran replied.

"She is not Faith!" Liam argued.

"I know she's not! I lost Faith a long time ago. But Renee is my second chance, and you will not take her from me." And with that, Kyran crouched down, placing his head between his uneven knees. When Alek saw Kyran's transforming position, he placed his hands together, palms flat against each other, and a bright light began bursting through every pore of his body. Liam began releasing himself from the human vessel. The light got so bright I had to cover my eyes until I heard swords clashing against each other.

What I witnessed next was completely unbelievable.

While the fight was taking place upstairs, there was another battle occurring in the ballroom. The party had been raided by the faith keepers who had all gathered to pray, their angelic guardians, and by Liam's troop, who had been standing by ready for their time to enter into the evil domain.

The prayer warriors had felt the urge to invade the party in an effort to bring back the innocent and hopefully reclaim those who had turned their backs on God.

The raiders consisted of Jamie's dad, Paul, who had hopes of bringing his daughter home; Pastor Tyler, along with several members from his church; Jane Middleton, who was Beth's mother and had recently turned over her life to Christ in spite of all the attacks on her family; Miss Adamma; Mo and her husband, John; Sheriff Hunt and a couple of his deputies; Miss Wright, the assistant principal at the high school; Barry Smith, who was lead minister of the Wild West Cowboy Church; and Chad Barrett, the youth pastor at First Baptist Church.

As Sheriff Hunt announced into a bullhorn that the party was over, and anyone drinking under the age of twenty-one would be arrested, the partygoers began to scatter. They ran in all directions, trying to leave the house.

The praying saints quickly began dispersing, looking for loved ones or for those who seemed to be in trouble and needing some help, hoping they weren't too late.

Paul ran upstairs, guided by his protector, who knew where Jamie was. He flung open the bedroom door where Jamie was lying, stripped down to her lacey underclothes and held down by Aden. Without a moment's thought and without any self-control, Paul tackled Aden, and the two fell to the floor wrestling. Jamie covered herself with the sheet from the bed and screamed for them to stop. She could see the hatred in Aden's expression. The skin on his forehead became wrinkled and deformed; two thumb-shaped knots were trying to break through his brow as he pounded his powerful fists into Paul's bleeding face over and over.

"Somebody help him . . . please!" Jamie screamed out.

Just then, Chad Barrett came running up behind Aden and tackled him, much like Paul had done. When Chad saw the evil in Aden's eyes, now glowing, he immediately began to pray and rebuke the evil demon in the name of Jesus.

"No . . . stop that," Aden said in a guttural, evil-sounding voice while covering his ears. When Paul saw what Chad's praying was doing to Aden, he quickly joined in. The demon quickly fled from the room, releasing Jamie from any spells he had her under.

The angels, with their various weapons of choice, were also fighting off the countless evil spirits that filled each room. The demons disintegrated into the abyss at the piercing of the angelic warriors' sharp blades and other slaughtering devices. As the wicked ones perished, the chains that bound the humans, slaves of the tempting spirits that were consuming their bodies, began breaking and returned the possessed ones to their own senses. While the demons far outnumbered the white knights, their skill was no match for the angelic band. This troop under Liam's command had fought and won numerous battles before. "The Mighty Twelve" they were nicknamed, and their reputation itself was a threat to many of the demons. Some of them instantly cowered and tried to flee. But Hakim was too quick with his arrows for their escape.

Benjamin's overly large and muscular body appeared very daunting, so he chose an equally daunting double-bladed medieval axe as his prized weapon. He dexterously fought with this terrifying axe and easily pulverized anything that came his way. It wasn't uncommon to witness frightened demons trying to escape Benjamin's presence upon seeing his deadly weapon. So far, none had succeeded.

Ezekiel, who fought with stiletto daggers in each hand, kept guard of Evelyn, as she was being heavily attacked for her lead in this abrupt interruption. Nate continued to guide her mind, but it was Ezekiel's skilled fighting, much like that of a Japanese samurai, that kept her soul from further attack.

Gideon whirled his war scythe like a propeller in the air, hacking away at the weaker monsters who felt brave enough to oppose him. "Silly little demons, tricks are for kids," he smarted off as they melted into the abyss.

There was a mighty battle being held indeed.

THIRTY FIVE

The Unseen Realm Exposed

Completely dumbfounded, I watched the white angel and the dark angel twirling and fighting in the sky through the shattered window. I had figured out that Liam was using Alek as his human carrier, but Kyran still looked like Kyran—only with darker, grayish-colored feathered wings. *So if he's a demon, why does he still look so beautiful in his true form? Demons are supposed to be ugly and grotesque looking.* My mind was consumed by a thousand thoughts and questions, so much so that I didn't hear anyone enter the room. Suddenly, without any warning, I was grabbed with tremendous force from behind.

Two huge, bulky, dark men were holding each of my arms as they turned me toward the door. There, standing with her expensive full-length gown as to flaunt her importance, was Kyran's so-called mother: Richelle Dellamorte. She met my eyes with a scorching glare filled with hatred and disgust.

"You've caused a lot of trouble for me tonight, and you will pay for it. Bring her," she commanded of the hideous rogues.

I tried to kick and scream, fighting with every ounce of strength I had to try and get loose from their firm grip, but they didn't even flinch at my attempt. "Alek . . . wake up!" I shouted. His limp body was still lying on the floor, but he was passed out cold. They dragged me out of the room and down the hall to what appeared to be the master bedroom. Knowing I was absolutely no match for them, I began to pray in my head, asking the Lord to help me. That's when Exodus 14:14 filled my thoughts: *The Lord will fight for you; you need only be still.*

Richelle reached under her vanity where she pushed a button that magically moved the stone fireplace to one side. Upon its opening, I could hear loud screeches and wailing of warped voices from down below. Hot air blew into the room, bringing with it a foul stench that stung my nose and throat as I inhaled it.

"Where are you taking me?" I demanded to know of the evil witch holding me captive.

"Tonight there will be a great sacrifice to Prince Lucifer. The blood of a virgin saint should be very pleasing to him. After all, it's the least you can do, since you brought the Heavenly Hosts upon us tonight to ruin all of our plans." She began walking down the makeshift stairs, which had been carved from the rocks of the significant mountain the house sat upon.

"If you let me go right now," I said to the two demon-possessed hooligans guarding me, "you'll have a better chance of living another day."

They each cackled, confident they had the upper hand in this warfare.

"Okay, but don't say I didn't warn you," I said with arrogance.

They shoved me through the opening of this demonic tomb, forcing me down several of the stony stairs, knocking the breath out of me when I landed on my back on the steps. I lay there as my eyes wandered aimlessly, lost in the unseen realm of the dark side. My body began shaking, feeling scared, but trying to remain calm. I knew Liam would find me.

Upon entering the dark cave, the burly men transformed themselves into the hideous monsters they really were. One was fat, and the other skinny, both with reptilian skin, bulging eyes, and thin leathery wings that fluttered on their backs. "Get up, you pathetic girl," one of them yelled as he kicked me on my side.

"Augh," I yelped as the blow released what air I had left. I couldn't move as the pain from my now-broken ribs immobilized me.

From further down below Richelle called out to them, "Botis . . . Amon . . . bring her down." One of them then lifted me from the stairs, and began to carry me the rest of the way.

As we reached the end of the stairs, Richelle, now in true form, said, "Tie her to the sacrificial table."

She sat and watched as these goons forced me down. She was clothed in a fine violet-colored silk gown embroidered with golden thread, which was woven into intricate designs suited for a queen. Her contorted fingers were adorned with overly large diamonds, rubies, and emeralds, bringing much attention to her sharp claws. She stared down upon me pompously, filled with pleasure at my seemingly helpless state. It was as though I found myself deep in the bowels of a sunken ship, suffocating and drowning in despair. That was what the darkness did. It robbed a person of his or her own thoughts and beliefs. Panic tried to creep in, but I had enough will still in me to remain calm, not giving Richelle any more satisfaction. I couldn't help but wonder, though, if I would ever get to see my family again.

"Liam, where are you?" I managed to softly cry out through the pain.

More laughs came my way.

THIRTY SIX

The Immense Battle Begins

The two angels continued to fight, each of them equally matched. The dark angel turned his head with sheer panic as he heard whispers from the evil spirits down below, excited about the virgin blood to be shed. It was then that Liam found his opportunity, and stabbed his opponent with his powerful sword in his stomach. A loud, thunderous cry came from the hurt angel's mouth as he began spiraling downward toward the mountaintop.

"She is in trouble," the dark one cried out to Liam.

"No! What have I done? Kristar . . . ," he cried as he built up speed to catch up with the fallen angel.

Just before Kristar hit the surface, Liam swooped down and lifted him, placing him down upon the earth in a gentler fashion. "We must save her," the dark one said.

"Where is she?" asked Liam. "Kristar . . . do you know where they have taken her?"

"Do not call me that!" Kyran said in an angry voice. "I have not been Kristar in a very long time."

"Brother," Liam begged, "where is she?"

"And we are no longer brothers. I will save Renee. She is mine," he retorted as he tried to get up, but quickly fell back down.

"Please, time is wasting away. Tell me where she is," Liam pleaded.

As the fallen angel lay there, deeply wounded, he knew Renee's only chance was to give in to Liam's request. He loved Renee too much to let his own selfish pride get in the way once again.

"Go to the master's bedroom. There you will see a vanity with a button underneath it. It will open the doors to the devil's chamber. Now go, before she is their sacrifice!"

"I will come back for you, brother," Liam promised before speeding toward the house at the speed of light. As Liam entered the battlefield, he called upon several of his soldiers. "Chazz, Boris, Armand, Daemon, Gunner—come with me." Each of them finished off the weak demons that were attacking them, and went to Liam's side.

"Prepare yourselves, warriors. We will be entering into the evil one's chamber, where surely his more powerful demons await their time for battle," Liam warned.

Gunner, who battled with a morning star, was exceptionally excited for a new challenge. "Good. I was beginning to get a bit bored, pulverizing these weaklings," he stated with his deep powerful voice. He placed his daunting weapon into its carrier, which was affixed to his tunic.

And with that, they were off, racing to the master's room. Liam found the button, just as Kristar had said, and in went the protectors with much caution. They could feel the darkness press upon them as they took each step with care. Dark shadows with green and yellow eyes penetrated the rocky walls and crept up and down, anxious for what was to come. As the screeching became louder and the hideous laughter rang in the angels' ears, they each drew their preferred arms, shields steady by their chests. They were ready for anything that flew or crawled their way.

As they neared the bottom of the stairway, an evil voice muttered, "Ahhh! Our friends have come to watch. Please, join us!"

The cave was consumed by darkness, but the light reflecting from the angels and their gleaming weapons gave way and enabled Renee to see Liam with his small troop. "Liam!" she shouted out, and was quickly hit across the face by Botis. "Shut up, you stupid girl."

"That will be the last time you will ever use that hand," Liam stated brazenly. Botis only laughed in confidence.

"Come," Richelle urged. "You are just in time to see a great sacrifice."

"Naphula." Liam called her by her real name. "I strongly beseech you to let her go immediately, or I will send you to the fire for eternity."

"Ha, ha, ha, ha . . . with what army? Surely you don't think the five of you will ever leave this chamber, do you? Need I remind you what happened to your heavenly brother only half a century ago? I must say, he has been an excellent slave," she said smugly.

"I assure you, history will not repeat itself. Now, draw your sword and fight for your sacrifice. Or are you too much of a coward?" Liam taunted.

"Oh, a little challenge, I see. And you're willing to give her as the prize?"

Liam hesitated, now questioning himself, and said with less confidence, "Yes."

"Demons . . . attack!" she yelled, hoping to gain an unfair advantage. And just as quickly, all the demons still in human appearance instantly turned into their true demonic forms. Some had scales all over their green bodies, some had rows of spikes down their humped backs, and others had bat-like wings that could drape over their bodies. Their hands turned into sharp claws, and fangs hung from their drooling mouths. Some of them were hissing as they slithered toward their enemies, flashing their snake-like tongues.

Immediately, both demons and dark shadows began viciously attacking the angelic warriors, who all stood in a circle protecting each others' backs. Liam with his saber sword, and Chazz armed with his sword, swung their blades in fiery arcs, killing off dozens of the flying dark spirits at a time. The incarnate demon warriors were more of a challenge as they attacked with scorching swords of their own. The angels fought quicker and harder than they had ever fought in any battle before. Sparks showered the cave like fireworks on the fourth of July.

Armand was quite skillful with his long whip. He would lash out the twelve-foot-long plaited leather whip to carefully strike his victims. They would immediately become paralyzed as the lethal iridescent tip would cut right through their demonic bodies, sending an electric shock through every inch. Then, "poof" . . . they disintegrated into smoke. As he waved his unusual weapon through the air it wasn't uncommon to hear thunderous cracks as several demons fell prey to Armand's lashing all at once.

Gunner kept a boastful smile upon his face while killing his opponents. "Take *that*, you ugly slime-balls." Yes . . . this was the kind of fight he had been waiting for!

The herds of shadows and demons seemed never ending. Naphula sat at her makeshift throne, carved from the rocky wall within arm's reach of the sacrificial table, witnessing the grueling fight. Within minutes, the air was filled with black, yellow, and red smoke—remnants of the dead, disintegrated demons. The angels were much more powerful than Naphula had expected.

As the count of the evil opponents began to dwindle, the angels began to slow their pace, knowing they had won the battle. Naphula called out to the demon who had once looked like the stuffy butler at the front door, who was now standing guard by a cave door. "Saiko, release the other beasts."

Upon word, Saiko pulled down a lever that opened the stone door. Just as Chazz stabbed the last demon around the encircled force, their attention was quickly drawn toward the legion of demons that was headed their way. They slithered, crawled, jumped, and dragged their grotesque bodies toward their enemies, with loathing in their bulging, wild eyes. Smoke billowed from their deformed nostrils, releasing disgusting sulfuric fumes into the air.

"Hakim, Ezekiel, Herick, Gideon, Cavan, Benjamin, come to my voice and fight with your brothers!" Liam stated authoritatively. And just before the hundreds upon hundreds of the devil's warriors got to the circle of angels, the other warriors fell from the top of the cave and joined their heavenly brothers, weaponry in hand.

The massive fight resumed as Renee lay helpless on the hot stone table, waiting for the outcome. She was filled with agony and shame, as she blamed herself for getting into this situation in the first place.

The battle raged on with the angels keeping the upper hand. But six demons teamed up and attacked Herick at once. He was able to kill off five, but the sixth was able to get past his protective shield, and pierced his sword through Herick's left side. The wounded angel fell to the ground, no longer able to fight, but not before he took his revenge on the slimy demon that was lucky enough to stab him. The other angels surrounded him, shielding him from any further injury to allow him time to heal, although it would take much longer in this place of darkness.

The warriors continued to thrust their weapons in countless directions as demon after demon was slaughtered. Then, unexpectedly, some crawlers managed to attack them from above as they fell upon the angels from the top of the cave. The diversion enabled some demons fighting on the ground to stab Daemon and Cavan, sending them falling to the corpse-covered ground.

The evil soldiers continued to spill out of the opened cave door, some so eager to fight they would fight amongst themselves like rabid dogs, and Liam began to wonder if they would ever get out of the darkness.

The nine remaining angels fought with even more of a vengeance. They were none too pleased that their brothers had been wounded and taken out of the battle. Boris threw his shield down, grabbed Cavan's sword, and began doubling his killings as he skillfully fought with two swords in hand.

Hakim flew to a corner of the cave where he had a wider angle, in order to shoot his translucent arrows more effectively. He drew them rapidly from the quiver that lay upon his back, shooting off five arrows before the blink of an eye, never missing a target and never running out of the arrows. Each arrow emulated a bolt of lighting; it struck its victim, and sent waves of shock and fire through their bodies before exploding.

The angels were beginning to regain the ground they had lost.

THIRTY SEVEN

Ultimate Temptation

As Naphula witnessed her troops being destroyed once again, she cut the ties to Renee's wrists and feet. Then she forcefully grabbed her, placing a sharp blade to her neck. "Enough!" she cried out. All of her slaves stopped their attack.

The nine angels, breathing hard and thankful for the rest, turned their attention toward Lucifer's right-hand pawn. She now held one of their Father's saints in her gnarled hands.

"Let her go," Liam demanded once again.

The knife began to cut into Renee's throat, and blood slowly trickled from the small wound. "I will let her go if you agree to come over to the dark side and work for me."

"Don't do it," Renee cried out bravely with tears flowing down her face. "I would rather die."

"Ha-ha-ha-ha—how easy this was! You heard her words . . . she wishes to die. That gives me the authority to kill her! But *you*, my dear Liam, you can save her. Think of her poor suffering mom, who needs her," she said, with extreme sarcasm, pursing her black lips and pretending to feel bad. "Not to mention, there is much good Renee could do on Earth if she were to live." Naphula was so conniving; the weak would easily fall into her trap.

"*Do not* try to tempt me. My faith in the Lord will not waver," Liam responded sternly.

"But you can rejoin your brother. You two make such a good team. Think of all of the worldly pleasures that will be at your disposable. I do not ask much of Kyran, only to help me gain a few measly souls is all. But he gets all of the finer things of this world, all the women he could ever want, all the money, and his youth for centuries upon centuries.

"And what about Renee? I know you love her. Don't you want to be able to see her happy? Don't you want to be able to feel her soft, smooth skin and kiss her voluptuous lips?" Naphula continued on, using her most tempting and soothing voice.

As the evil one was talking, keeping the fierce enemy occupied, wicked spirits were filling the room, penetrating the walls, ready for their revenge. More demons began coming from the dungeon door, swords in hand, waiting for their moment to strike.

"Again, I say, *do not* tempt me. My Lord has control over this situation, and my faith will not waver. Now I demand you release her!" he said as he glowered at her evil grin.

Meanwhile, as the negotiations continued in the devil's dungeon, the faith keepers upstairs, along with a few dozen of the rescued partygoers, all began to pray at the urging whispers of their guardians. United together in prayer, they asked for the Lord's mercy and grace. They prayed with all of their hearts and souls for forgiveness, for strength and courage, for protection upon all of the Lord's people and for their guardians.

Then Evelyn, feeling compelled in the moment, began singing a beautiful melody of redemption and praise.

Amazing grace, how sweet the sound, that saved a wretch like me.

The rest of the group began to sing with her.

I once was lost, but now am found; was blind, but now I see.

'Twas Grace that taught my heart to fear, and Grace my fears relieved.

How precious did that Grace appear, the hour I first believed.

The believers continued on, not realizing this very act was helping to heal the wounded angels and giving the other warriors the power and strength they needed to continue their grueling fight.

"You have made your choice, then. Renee will go to hell with me. Demons, attack with all of your strength and all of your might! Give Prince Lucifer the honor of winning this battle!" And then she disappeared into the walls with Renee as her prisoner.

"No!" Liam screamed, but could not run to her, as he was surrounded by evil spirits and demons that were unwilling to surrender their potential kill. The fight was vicious. His full concentration was not on killing his attackers, though, as he could not get Renee out of his mind. He was getting hit, poked, and prodded by the evil spirits, and each blow drained his strength and power. How could he have let her go? How could he have put her life, her soul, at the mercy of the devil? He had to find a way to save her. He had to. He was willing to give his own life for hers.

He began backing up toward the wall in which they had disappeared, fighting off the demons as he slowly stepped backwards. And as Liam reached his destination, Botis was there, waiting for his moment of glory: to kill the leader of the troop.

"At last," Botis stated boldly and drew his sword, "you will be *my* prized kill!"

Liam knew he didn't have much time. He was oddly thankful for the challenge Botis brought him as it caused the other demons attacking him to part, leaving the battle for their superior.

Recalling the abuse Botis bestowed upon Renee gave Liam a surge of energy. The intense fighting began, but to Botis's dismay, ended quickly. His skills were no match for the astute colonel's. Liam fulfilled his promise as he chopped off the arm that slapped Renee just before piercing his sword through Botis's chest, sending him to the abyss with only a puff of red smoke left behind.

Liam then closed his eyes and allowed himself to pass through the thick, concrete wall just as Naphula had done moments before. He found himself surrounded by total darkness and unsure of his next step. It was unusually quiet, but his keen ears were able to barely catch the sound of dripping water as they gently splashed into a puddle, breaking the immense silence. Liam began to walk cautiously forward, sword steady in his hand, ready to take out anything that came his way.

A malicious laughter echoed in the enclosed room, bouncing off the walls, multiplying its sound. The darkness was so thick; Liam could only see his faintly lit sword in the air. He heard the sound of flapping wings. They would get closer, then further away, like a bee teasing a young boy. He began swinging his sword, hoping for a lucky kill. The sound of fluttering wings was growing louder. Soon, unseen creatures began quickly flying by, pricking him with their sharp, pointy claws, taunting him in hopes of making the angel cower and surrender. Several of them struck at the magical shield that protected Liam and were instantly zapped, vaporized on the spot. The brave angel swiftly waved his sword in the air, sweeping it back and forth, eager to kill more of the spirits pestering him.

"Have you changed your mind, or do you think you are here to rescue your little saint?" the sadistic voice asked.

"Do not sacrifice her to the devil." Liam paused, unbelieving of his own actions, feeling ashamed for what he was about to do. "I . . . I . . . ."

"Yes, spit it out. You what?" Naphula asked impatiently.

"No! Don't do . . . ," Renee tried to say, until the knife dug into her throat a little more.

Liam released a heavy breath into the air. Surely this was not what the Lord wanted. But he was Renee's protector. He was responsible for keeping her alive until the Lord called her home. He knew it was not her time to go. The confusion he felt was overwhelming, a place he had never found himself before.

As Liam pondered his final answer, Renee began thinking of 2 Samuel 22:2-4, hoping Liam was still able to hear her thoughts. *Liam,* she called to him in her head, *the Lord is my rock, my fortress, my deliverer. . . .*

And then, so Renee would know he was still connected to her thoughts, Liam finished the scripture aloud. " . . . my God is my rock, in whom I take refuge, my shield and the strength of my salvation. He is my stronghold, my refuge and my savior; from violent men you save me. I call to the Lord, who is worthy of praise, and I am saved from my enemies!" He finished the scripture with astounding stamina and strength.

Upon his conclusion, Liam was once again viciously attacked; only this time he did not have his warriors to help him. Stabs were piercing him left and right, and though he was able to kill many of the demonic predators, he was beginning to lose the battle. He continued persevering, praying that he was acting out God's will. Suddenly, from the heavy rock walls, a powerful force broke through, and began fighting the demons that were slowly draining Liam's heavenly strength.

"Kyran!" Naphula called out. "I demand you to kill the white angel."

Kyran did not obey the command, but instead continued to fight those on the dark side . . . his side.

"You dare go back on our agreement?" Naphula asked threateningly.

"Liam," he said softly, as close to Liam as he could get while still fighting the demons. "Naphula is on the northern wall exactly two feet to your left, standing with her back against it. One false move, and she will have Renee down into the pits of hell with her. When I say 'Forgive me, master, your wish is my command,' you go faster than you ever thought possible and grab Renee. Go straight up through the top and that will take you to the mountain forest."

"I cannot leave you, brother. I cannot do that to you again."

"Go, save yourself and Renee. We have no time to argue." And before Liam could say another word, Kyran did as he had said. "Forgive me, master. Your wish is my command."

With his having said that, Naphula let her guard down a bit, thinking she would no longer be in danger of losing her prisoner. But before she could blink an eye, Liam came at her with superluminal velocity, grabbed Renee from her loose grip, and flew straight up. He tunneled through the heavy rocks, dirt, and minerals that formed the mountain, and out of the devil's dungeon. As the evil temptress began to fly after them, Kyran grabbed at her scaly legs, forcing her back down, where a battle between them commenced.

"You imbecile! You will pay for your betrayal!" Naphula cried out.

"I have already been paying for my betrayal all of these years by being your slave. Now it is my turn to give back for what I have done and hope for a second chance," Kyran stated as he tried to stab the evil demon who had held him captive for too long. But she was quick and strong, and he knew it would be a grueling fight to the end.

THIRTY EIGHT

Healing, Heartache, and Happiness

Liam continued to soar high into the sky, surpassing the floating clouds, as the intense energy he held could not keep him grounded within the natural realm any longer. Renee was unconscious, unable to withstand the quick speeds they were traveling. As Liam held her limp, broken body, he saw the slash across the side of her neck. It was bleeding profusely, and he knew she would die soon if he did not get her mended.

He took her back to the room her soul had once occupied. He remembered so vividly their time together at that special holding place. That was when he had discovered a deeper feeling than what he knew was possible for an assignment. While he had always shared a brotherly love with others he had protected, what he experienced with Renee was so different and bewildering to him.

Now he laid her whole self, body and soul, gently upon the white, satiny bed. She was the first that he knew of to have both presences here.

He tore the bottom of his shimmering white battle-tunic, and carefully wrapped it around her neck to control the bleeding. He began to pray for healing to the Lord as he pressed his palm against the wound. The bleeding completely stopped, and the cut began to heal quickly, leaving only a small scar behind. He closed his eyes and waved his hands just over her body as he checked to see if there was any other damage. He sensed the break in her ribs and laid his right palm upon them. He sought the Lord's permission for healing once again, and the energy flowed from the light of his hand, soon mending the crushed ribs. With her physical body now healed and no longer in danger, he looked down upon her blackened face and gently wiped the streaked mascara from her eyes and cheeks with his tunic. He wanted to see her simple beauty once again.

While she peacefully rested, Liam flew into Heaven to quickly heal from all of his own wounds and gather more forces to help his courageous troops, which were still in combat inside the devil's dungeon. He also asked to meet with the Lord about a certain request, which was granted.

It wasn't long before Liam knelt beside Renee once again and watched the beautiful human girl sleep. He gently rubbed his finger upon her blushing cheek, knowing their time together was nearing an end. She began to stir, and he quickly withdrew his touch from her silky skin. Joy filled his face as Renee opened her eyes.

As I opened my eyes, still a bit groggy and unsure of where I was, I looked upon the most beautiful, glowing face. Instincts controlled the motion of my body, and I immediately threw my arms around his neck. "Liam!" I cried out. I pushed him back to see his face once again to make sure I wasn't dreaming. He looked different though, almost human. His wings were tucked neatly away and he wore clothes that any boy in school would wear, hiding his muscular physique. But as soon as he flashed those pearly whites, I knew it really was him.

"Did I make it to Heaven?" I asked sincerely.

He laughed at my ignorant innocence and said, "Not this time."

I glanced around, senses now fully intact, and said, "Is my body in a coma again?"

"No, you're here in the flesh."

"How . . . why . . . when?" I couldn't gather my thoughts to ask him the right question. *Okay, Renee, get it together.* "I mean, how can I still see you with my eyes and touch you with my skin?" I reached out and stroked the back of his hand where it lay upon my bed, just to be sure one more time.

He put his other hand upon mine, sandwiching it between his, and said, "Do you remember anything from tonight?"

As I concentrated on his question, I started to recall everything that had happened and gasped as panic struck my heart. "Jamie . . . I never found her. We need to go back, Liam," I said as I jumped off the bed.

"Jamie is okay," he assured me. "She is with her father and they are doing a little healing themselves." It didn't take long for my heartbeat to jump back down ten notches with the news.

"What about Kyran? The last thing I remember was him helping you fight off the demons. He helped save me, didn't he?"

"Yes, he did."

"So where is he? Is he okay?" Liam lowered his head. That was all I needed to know. "We need to help him, Liam. He's not all bad. There is still good in him . . . I know there is."

"His fate is not in my hands, Renee. He chose his own destiny."

I began pacing the white room that once housed my resting soul. I couldn't accept what Liam said. If Kyran hadn't shown up when he did, who knows what would have happened to us? *We have to help him,* I thought to myself.

"We can't help him," Liam replied.

"Will you stop that for a moment? I want to think in private," I said, still pacing the floor.

"Renee, I don't have much time. Please, stop for just a moment," he said as he placed his hands upon my shoulders to try and keep me still. "Listen to me . . . please," he begged. I saw concern in his eyes, something I had never seen before. I did as he asked, almost afraid of what he needed to tell me. "You wondered why I am allowing you to still see me if you weren't in Heaven or in a coma. Well, I wanted you to know that I asked the Lord to return me to my commanding post. Renee," he said with much difficulty, "I needed to tell you good-bye."

"No! Don't say that. Why are you saying that?" I asked in disbelief.

Liam paused, and put his head down. I was even more confused by his silence. *What is going through his mind right now?* He relieved me of my torment when he began to speak.

"How do I begin to explain the unexpected feelings I have found for you, Renee? Angels and humans, though we're created by the same Father, are part of two different worlds. My love for you has grown deep, becoming a double-edged sword. On one side, it gives me the great strength and courage I need to protect you. But on the other, it is also my temptation . . . my weakness," he confessed.

What was I to say to his profession of love for me? It was in that moment I realized the intensity of our connection. The butterflies that constantly fluttered in my stomach every time I thought of even his name had become more than just a school-girl crush. It was love. And I was not going to let go of it so easily.

"Please, don't ever leave me. Isn't that what you promised? That you would never leave me," I yelled at him, my eyes stinging as I grew more irritated with the thought of never seeing him again.

"Renee, I almost lost my faith in the Lord's plan because of . . . ."

I looked at him with narrowed eyes filled with accusation. "Because of what? Because of me?" I retorted.

"You wouldn't understand. Please, please don't fight me on this. It's for the best," he said as he gazed upon the floor. "You will be guarded by Gerard. He's one of my most trusted brothers and an outstanding warrior. He will serve you well."

"I don't want Gerard . . . I want you!" I begged dejectedly. I forced my arms around him and began to kiss his chiseled cheeks, then all over his face.

At first, Liam allowed me to show my earthly affection. As he stood sternly and seemingly unable to reject me, his eyes closed. I could see with each loving peck I placed upon his smooth skin that his guard was crumbling. Finally, he completely broke his bold stance. He allowed himself to get lost in the moment. As I neared his red lips with my loving kisses, he quickly opened his eyes and just as suddenly magically disappeared from me.

"Please," he spoke softly through the air, though I still could not see him. "This cannot be."

I stood alone, broken and humiliated, unable to move, unable to think my next thought. I could only stare at the empty space where he once stood with shattered eyes as he kept his appearance from my sight.

After an eternity of silence, with a pathetic voice, I muttered the question: "Will I ever see you again?"

"You will never be far from me, Renee."

That was his way of gently telling me no. No, I would never see his pure beauty before me again. I would never feel the sensation of his touch or the warmth of his captivating eyes. I couldn't accept this. He had been with me my whole life. There had to be a way, there just had to.

I quickly thought of a solution and begged him, "Come to me in my dreams, then. Just think of it as a friendly, harmless visit where nothing could happen between us."

"Renee." He finally came back, but kept a small distance between us. "Be careful of your dreams. You never know what they may bring."

"If they bring you back to me, then I will wish for you every night."

He released a heavy sigh, held out his hand, and waited for me to come to him. I didn't dare budge.

"Come, there's something I want to show you before we part," he said, hoping it was enough to convince me.

It didn't work. I feared it was only to send me back, never to see him again. "Please, I think you will like it," he continued to urge, giving me his irresistible grin.

I slowly began moving forward until finally, I grabbed his welcoming hand, still having complete trust in him. He lifted me into his arms, and unfurled his beautiful, white-feathered wings. He asked that I close my eyes until he said to open them. As the sight of his flawless face disappeared, all I knew was the sensation of flying into the air, traveling to who-knew-where. The wind blew through my hair, and I could smell fresh air like the morning after a heavy rain. I felt the warmth of the sun's rays prickling my face and giving a glow to the lids that still blocked my eyes. Suddenly, the light vanished, and my eyes filled with darkness once again. It was only minutes before he said, "Okay . . . open them."

We were still flying, but now back in the natural realm. He held me close to him as he allowed me to experience his wonderful gift of flying.

"When I was a little girl, I used to wish I could turn into a bird so I could soar in the air and feel the rush of wind massage my face," I admitted.

"I remember," he replied. Of course, he did. He knew everything there was to know about me, and now he was ready to give it all up.

He came to a stop, still hovering high above the highest mountaintop. "I'm going to let go of you, but hold onto my hand. When I do, stretch your arms out as far as they will reach."

I should have been scared for him to release the grip he had on my back and legs, but I wasn't. Instead, I was anxious for the adventure that awaited me. With arms outstretched and our fingers intertwined, Liam began to lead the way, soon forcing my body horizontally so I could fly with him. We soared like eagles miles in the air, spiraling up and then swooping down. The sky was our haven, and I felt so confident, so alive. Flying through the air felt exactly as I had always imagined. Liberating, invigorating, carefree—these were only a few of the words to describe the unforgettable experience.

Lost in our adventure, the sound of a trumpet brought us back to reality. Liam looked north toward the Sangre de Cristo Mountains as dark, hovering clouds appeared to lift and lightning bolts ceased over a very certain house. How selfish I had been, only thinking of my upcoming loss, forgetting about all of the angelic forces still battling the darkness. But the sound of that trumpet seemed to be very pleasing to Liam.

"Did you hear that?" he asked.

"Yes . . . what was it?"

"That was the sound of victory!" And with that he wrapped his arms around me to hold me tight, and gave us a celebratory spiral even higher into the air. We flew around aimlessly like wild birds and laughed; we were utterly and completely consumed with joy in this monumental speck of time.

But eventually, all birds must come down and perch upon a tree to rest their weary wings, and so it wasn't long before we came to my house. How I wished I could turn back the hands of time and relive our last moment together once again.

Liam regained his grip on me, carrying me like a wounded soldier, and then impressively opened the double doors between my balcony and my room with his angelic power. He laid me gently on my bed, still disheveled from the impromptu air-band concert earlier in the night, and said, "It is time for me to leave."

The psychological torment began to creep back into my mind at the disheartening announcement. It was too soon. I didn't have the strength to let him go. "I meant what I said earlier, Liam. As I fall asleep each night, I will dream of you and wish for you to come back to me."

He looked into my saddened eyes with sincerity. "You have a wonderful, earthly life ahead of you. You will marry a magnificent man, have a family of your own, and together you two will change so many lives. God needs you, Renee. There are so many lost souls who need saints like you to give them some hope and to let them know they are loved. Helping them find eternal life with our Creator, that should be what you wish for."

"I do wish for that, you know I do, but does that mean I can't have you in my life, too?"

He quickly became serious. "Please, don't do this again. My time with you is up. It is vital that you remember the things you've learned, the things you've seen firsthand. You are a blessed saint for what God has revealed to you, and the enemy will never give up trying to steal your soul. I need you to be strong, Renee . . . please." And with that, in the blink of an eye, he abruptly disappeared, flying into my ceiling casting a gust of wind behind, without so much as a good-bye for me to hang on to.

"No!" I shouted as I sat upon my bed, sobbing. My heart ached for him. There was a love between us so different than I had ever known. It was a heavenly love, more powerful and more vibrant than any feeling could replicate on earth, and it was gone. Taken from me as two worlds collided that should have never met. I would have been better off had he not ever revealed himself to me. I would have never felt the loss of innocent love that is meant to be between a man and a woman, not a girl and her angel. How could anyone on earth ever compare?

As I wallowed in my sorrow, a gust of wind broke through my walls once again. Just as suddenly, Liam brought me to my feet. Putting my face between his strong, tender hands, he said, "I can't leave without ever feeling this." He began tenderly kissing my lips. A tingling sensation rushed through my body. The power behind the loving kiss was indescribable, and suddenly every care in the world swiftly disappeared. My tears of sadness became tears of happiness. Our embrace got tighter as he began lifting me into the air. My feet rested upon his like a little girl dancing with her dad. He slowly spun us around as we climbed higher into the air; he was careful not to release his lips from mine. Perhaps only seconds ticked by, but to me they equated to a lifetime of love and happiness. As our mouths slowly parted from their embrace, I began to laugh as I touched the ceiling with my hand.

"Wow, you really know how to sweep a girl off her feet," I teased, my eyes alight with joy.

"The horror in your face when I left you stabbed at my soul. I couldn't leave you like that. It would have haunted me forever. This," he said as he gently stroked my smiling lips, "this is the beautiful face I want to always remember."

We began to gradually spiral back down until we reached the beige carpet that covered my floor. I stepped down from his feet, convincing myself to stay excited for his sake. Suddenly his feelings were of greater concern to me than my own, so I decidedly molded the expression to my face that brought him pleasure, knowing he was leaving me once again.

"I will never be far," he promised, slowly walking backwards toward the outer wall, careful not to remove his eyes from mine. "Happy birthday, Renee," he said. These were the last fading words I heard from his magnificent voice, which I knew would stay with me forever. He slowly vanished with each step until he was no longer within my sight. I glanced at the clock and realized it was one minute before midnight, the last sixty seconds of my seventeenth birthday. Sitting next to it was a beautiful snow globe. I walked over to it and looked at the bottom. "There is no fear in love" was engraved on it. It was *my* snow globe.

I wound the key that released the sweet melody and listened to it play while watching the snow gently settle upon the village. The tears continued to flow down my face, and though inside I felt like a part of me was dying, I did not let go of the smile that brought him back to me one last time.

THIRTY NINE

Heroic Mother

I laid on my bed, hugging my last birthday present like a stuffed teddy bear, and continued to bathe myself in tears. Was that *really* the last time I would ever see Liam? I had such a hard time believing it. I began to think about what he said to me before leaving the first time. *You will marry a magnificent man, have a family of your own, and together you two will change so many lives.* Did he really know that? I got goose bumps at the thought of getting married and having my own children. Of course that was part of what I wanted in life, but would it really happen for me? Would I really be able to find a man who compared to Liam and all of his amazing qualities?

And then I began to think of Kyran. He came back to save me, and that had to mean something, right? What in the world ever caused him to fall from grace? I knew he longed to still be in Heaven; it was so obvious when he gazed into the sunset and got completely lost in it. That was his only way of catching just a glimpse of God's wondrous power and beauty. I wondered if I would ever get to see him again as well.

As I continued to recapture the night, I couldn't help but think of Alek. I hoped he was okay. The last I saw of him was when he was completely unconscious on the floor. I concluded that when Liam was fighting Kyran with Alek's body, he must have really gotten beat up, much more than he could have naturally withstood. Although it was obvious to me now that Liam had conjoined with Alek from time to time, I had to wonder about each moment I spent with Alek. How much of his personality or actions were really his, and how much were Liam's? My curiosities about everything were starting to get carried away when I heard the front door slam shut.

"Renee! Renee!" I heard my mother shouting from downstairs in a panicked voice.

"Mom!" I hollered in return to let her know I was there. I quickly ran down, throwing myself into her waiting open arms.

"Oh, my baby, my baby," she said with tremendous relief. "I'm so thankful you're safe. Praise God you're home. We looked all over that monstrous house for you. Alek said he thought he saw you leave with someone, but he wasn't sure."

"I'm safe, Momma, I'm safe."

She looked at me and pushed back the hair that fell upon my eyes, which was damp from the rivers that had coursed down my face earlier. She said, "Are you sure? Are you sure you're okay?" Then she began checking me over.

"Yes, Mom, I'm sure." I was thankful she didn't see the cut on my throat. There would come a day I would have to explain everything to her, but this was not it.

And then it dawned on me that she said she saw Alek, and looked all over the "monstrous" house for me. Did she do what I think she did? Nah . . . surely not!

"Mom, did you go to the party tonight?" I asked dubiously.

"Yes I did, with about twenty others," she admitted with her head held high, proud of her actions and ready to defend them.

"What? Why?" I asked, shocked.

"Something wasn't sitting right with me when you left, so I called a prayer group together, and we felt led to go there and stop the party. We knew something bad would happen if we didn't."

Surprisingly, I wasn't mad that they crashed my birthday party. I still couldn't believe that my sick, weak mother invaded that out-of-control bash, though. What was this woman thinking? Nate must have given her a dose of energy!

"Paul took Jamie home, you know," she inserted, knowing this would please me. Of course, I acted happily surprised since Liam had already filled me in on that little detail. "It was quite heroic what he did." She began to tell the story as we walked over to the couch to talk.

As I sat and listened to all of the details about the people who went with her, the kids they helped rescue, and how they all joined together in prayer, I was quite proud of her and found it all rather inspiring. It took a lot of guts to do what she had done tonight.

I conceded that her little party crashing played a key role in the spiritual war that took place this evening. Though they weren't able to physically see with their own eyes the evil demons that held me captive, they too were my rescuers . . . my heroes. The Lord knew exactly who needed to be in that place at that time, including the one who had fallen all those years ago. One missing contributor may have resulted in a different outcome.

I just watched her excited expressions as she continued on, her soothing voice merely a mumble in the background now as I filled my mind with other thoughts. I gave her a sincere smile through my puffy eyes and red nose, remnants of Liam's departure. I was so thankful for such an amazing woman in my life. She wasn't only my mom or my friend; she was my role model and my personal hero. I was reminded of the song that Jamie and I sang earlier, and I realized that we will all go through life either needing a hero, or needing to be one. Only God knows the difference and will deliver accordingly, as He is the true hero inside all of us.

I recalled the triumphant battle tonight, and though it was promising, there were so many unanswered questions still crowding my head. Like where my dad was, and what was happening to him.

Even though my mom had mentioned earlier that she had talked with him from the hospital, and that he had told her that Mr. Dellamorte had him "tied up with a major deal going on in Sweden," something didn't feel right about it all.

And what was to become of Kyran? Would he ever get his second chance? Would Ellie and my mom win their own personal battles? Would life as I once knew it ever return? Silly question . . . of course it wouldn't. It could never be the same, knowing what I know now. So, I guess the real question would be, "What will I do from this point on?"

Yes, the battle tonight went to the Heavenly Hosts, but I knew the war was far from over. The devil still had his quota to meet, and this town, this once peaceful quaint town, would not be given up so easily. He had invested too much time into stealing souls. If anything, he would be more hell-bent to take control, as his pride was at stake.

But for right now, for this very moment, I'm just going to lay my head on my mother's lap while she brushes my hair with her fingers like she's always done, be happy that I am still a seventeen-year-old girl with my whole life ahead of me, and bask in the love shared between us. This was my time of rest. I knew deep down inside that tonight would not be my last with Liam. I knew because this was only the beginning of what was to come.

ABOUT THE AUTHOR

Even as a young girl, Lynette Theisen knew she liked telling stories. However, it wasn't until her mid-thirties that she realized it was more than a passion, but a purpose. Lynette took a job working part-time for *The Town Charter,* her hometown newspaper. She quickly gained popularity and began a weekly inspirational column. It wasn't until some of her readers urged her to write a book that the idea intrigued her. However, it took trial and error and nine months' time before she got the idea for *Through the Night.*

Lynette currently resides in Denton County, Texas, with her husband, two teenage boys, twin daughters, and three dogs. She enjoys going to church and Bible study, going to the movies with her husband and kids, scoring higher than her sons in laser tag (though they will deny that Mom can beat them), fellowshipping—aka hangin' out with girlfriends—dancing around the house to loud music for some exercise and stress relief (a little head banging and air band to go along with it) and, of course, writing! She is currently working on the sequel to *Through the Night.*